K.C. MCMILLIAN

Is Love Enough?

BOOK TWO
LOVE & REIGN

Kiana (K.C.) McMillian

<u>*NOTE:*</u>

If you or someone you know is enduring any form of abuse, find someone to confide in.

The resources are available: 1-800-799-7233 or text 'BEGIN' to 88788.

Dealing with any form of abuse is unimaginable.
I experienced a loaded gun being aimed at my head by a former boyfriend. Another attempted to control and force himself on me; he didn't hit me, but he grabbed my arm to the point where it left a bruise.
Thank God for the people around me who came to my defense.

For me, writing is a therapeutic practice, and as I create stories, I often find myself drawing upon my own experiences and those of my friends and family. While writing this story, I looked back at memories, some of which I had suppressed, and realized that I was able to escape not one but two abusive relationships.
I was fortunate, but not all women are.
I'm so sorry for the women who couldn't get away.
And for those of you who have survived all forms of abuse, you are strong, and you are loved!
Please be aware that this book contains detailed sex scenes, foul language, mentions of cancer, kidnapping, talks about Black history, racism / slavery, religious mentions, and family trauma.
It is recommended for mature audiences 18+ and older.
Refer to my website for a detailed list of trigger / content warnings for this book.

Your mental health matters.

*Do **not** read this book if any of what I said is triggering for you.*

Please visit my website: https://kcmcmillian.mailchimpsites.com/

To my family members and returning readers who purchased this book to support me, I want to express my heartfelt thanks for your continued support.

To all new readers, welcome! Thank you so much for taking a chance on my book. I hope you enjoy reading about Reign and Dion's journey.

Thank you for joining me on this ride and supporting me as an author.

Dedication

To the person who holds everything in.
I see you and I hear you.
Let that pain go, stop allowing it to weigh you down.

To my husband who believes in me, always.
To Shalinie, who believes in me and my writing.
To Amy, who believes in me and encouraged me to write romance.

I love you all!

Table of Contents

Summary of Loving Reign

Please note: *If you have read* <u>*Loving Reign: A Fake Dating Romance*</u> <u>*Story*</u>*, you can skip this. While both stories are standalone, I felt it was important to summarize the first story for new readers.*
Also, I've made some changes to Chapter 1.

Reign Amara Brown never expected to find herself in a tangled web of deception!

She is a confident and thriving wedding planner who has arranged countless love stories for others.

But just as Reign settles for the possibility of never finding love for herself, her younger sister Skylar, mommy's favorite daughter, announces she's getting married, leaving Reign in search of a plus one. With the help of her best friend Scarlette Rodriguez, who owns a dating app, Reign hires a fake boyfriend, a struggling actor known for his peanut butter commercial named Dion Atom James.

Despite Reign's constant efforts, she has consistently fallen short of her mother's expectations of being married to a rich man by the age of twenty-five. Blinded by the allure of wealth, her mother, Aunt Shirl, and three cousins, Shonda, Raquel, and Robyn, had all happily married rich men, living the high life. However, the thought of this life filled Reign with a sense of dread; her heart ached for something more. For her, independence isn't just a preference—it's a source of pride, a testament to her resilience.

With Reign's sister's wedding fast approaching, it was becoming more difficult to ignore the electric energy between Dion and herself as their mutual attraction grew stronger each day.
From different sides of the economic scale, this is a story about two souls intertwining.
For six months, despite uncertainties about their mutual feelings, a genuine connection blossoms between them, fueled by their shared passion for basketball, the comforting silences they share, the simple pleasure of each other's company, and the effortless laughter that constantly fills the air whenever they are together.

I do hope you enjoy this story.
Happy Reading!

"Total Bliss"

Instant attraction, chemistry, excitement, and mind-blowing sex.

Chapter 1: Reign

January 1st, 2025

As the clock strikes midnight, New Yorkers erupt in cheers on my television screen, filling the room with sounds of fireworks and celebration. This New Year is different from my previous ones with Scarlette, when I was drunk on champagne and living my single life to the fullest. This year we spent it with our men, and I couldn't be happier. Scarlette and Eddie are still going strong, and I love that for them. And, of course, August is spending the New Year with her husband, Calvin. They are a perfect match.

The six of us enjoyed Thanksgiving and Christmas together and had the best time. My sister and her new husband, Peter, are still relishing the honeymoon phase of their marriage, as far as I know.

She hasn't returned any of my calls or texts lately, so I'm guessing they're just caught up in newlywed joy, like Dion and me, although we are not married. Every relationship has those moments where you are in total bliss until shit hits the fan; I'm hoping that Dion and I stay in this phase a little longer.

The last time I saw Skylar and Peter was at the Christmas Eve party my mother insisted on throwing. She forced me and Dion to attend, and being the bitch that she is, she also invited my cheating ex, Max, and his new wife. It was awkward, to say the least, but fortunately, Max kept to himself. The evening was bearable; however, now that Dion and I are together, I haven't spent as much time with my family. *What's the point?* They are hostile, manipulative, and toxic individuals who only bring misery into my life. I used to justify their behavior because we were related, but now I realize I don't have to tolerate their disrespect. I'm just sorry it took me so long to grasp that. *I could have cut ties with them years ago.* My mother made it clear that she was the one who brought me into this world and could take me out. She instilled in me that no one else would *care* for me as much as she and my relatives did. My father, on the other hand said we are all we have and that, no matter what, we are family. He was an only child, and his parents were as well, so looking back, I can understand why he held onto that belief so strongly. However, my therapist has taught me that it is okay to love them from a far, and Dion, too, played a significant role in my decision to distance myself from them. He has nothing to do with the toxic members in his family. He explained that we are taught from a young age to believe that the poisonous traits in our families are normal and that we are simply expected to bend the knee and perpetuate the generational curse. His parents chose to break the cycle, showing that there's no need to keep in touch with a family member who isn't adding positivity to your life. Dion's example has shown me that when it comes to my cousins, fuck those bitches!

"Happy New Year, babe!" Dion says, placing a gentle kiss on my cheek, causing a warm sensation to travel down to my labia.

I am so in love with this man!

Who knew that three months ago, Dion and I would take our fake relationship to the next level? When he tore up the checks and confessed to me that he had wanted me since the first time he laid eyes on me, my heart leapt out of my chest and into my hand. I never expected to fall for Dion Atom James, but here I am, head over heels.

The corners of my lips curl into a smile. "Happy New Year, my love."

He rests his forehead against mine and says, "I love you, Reign," making my heart swell with happiness.

"Show me how much you love me," I whisper, undoing the buttons of his shirt and tossing it aside.

With a mischievous glint in his eyes, he effortlessly scoops me up and throws me over his shoulder. I squeal as the glass of champagne in my hand spills on me, the bubbles trickling down my shirt. He chuckles, carrying me to the bedroom while holding the bottle of champagne in his other hand. As he gently sets me down on the bed, his eyes darken at my wet shirt clinging to my body.

"Let me take care of that for you," he says huskily, lifting the wet fabric over my head and leaning in to lick the champagne from the crevices between my breasts.

Surrendering to the wetness of his tongue, I close my eyes as a wave of goosebumps follows in its wake. Dion continues to trace his tongue along my collarbone and then to the curve of my neck, gently sucking as my breath hitches in my throat. His hungry eyes meet mine, a sly smirk playing on his lips. Dion grabs the bottle of champagne, pouring the rest over my exposed skin. I shiver as the cool liquid trickles down my body, contrasting with the heat of his mouth on me. With each lick, I gasp and squirm beneath him until every droplet of champagne has been licked clean. My breathing becomes shallow as he firmly sits me up, reaching behind me to unclasp my bra. My breasts spill out, my nipples hardening under his gaze. Dion captures one of my nubs between his fingers, pinching and rolling it between his thumb and index finger, sending a jolt of pleasure straight to my core. I bite my lip, trying to stifle a moan as he lowers his head to take my nipple into his mouth, sucking and swirling his tongue around it. The sensation is overwhelming, and my body reacts instantly as fluid pools between my thighs.

My hands grip onto his shoulders, my nails digging into his skin. "Dion!" I cry out.

He slides my shorts and lacey underwear off. A gasp escapes my lips as he tugs me closer, his tongue expertly flicking against my pulsating clit. I toss my head back, breathing in short gasps. With each lick and lap of his tongue, I feel myself teetering on the edge of ecstasy.

"Damn! You taste better than champagne," Dion murmurs, reclining on his back and pulling me toward him. "Come here and sit on my face," he commands, his hands gripping my hips.

Hovering over his face, I slowly lower myself onto his tongue and ride until my body shudders with waves of ethereal pleasure. I throw my head back and shut my eyes, enjoying the sensation of his skilled mouth on me. My sensitive clit is throbbing and pulsating. Dion lifts me off his face, and unexpectedly inserts two fingers into my core, leaving me both startled and intrigued as I observe his actions. Using his other hand, he circles his thumb over my sensitive area, intensifying the pleasure as he continues to stimulate me until I reach another climax. My soft moans turn into louder cries as I reach my peak. The powerful waves of pleasure surge through me, causing my body to sway and tremble uncontrollably as if under some otherworldly influence. My hands clutch at the sheets, my chest rising and falling rapidly as I catch my breath.

He dips his head low to my sex once more and gives my clit one final lick. "I could eat you out every day," he murmurs in my ear, and I roll on top of him to return the favor.

"My turn," I whisper back, and he helps me slide off his jeans and boxers before I straddle him, feeling his hardness pressing against me.

Lowering myself onto him, I clamp my mouth shut to stifle my moans as he guides me with his hands on my hips, setting a rhythm that has us both gasping. I ride him harder and faster, relishing the sound of our skins slapping together.

"I want you to shout my name, Reign," he groans, his grip on my hips tightening.

My pussy squeezes around his girth, refusing to let him have the upper hand. With a smirk, I lean down to his ear and whisper, "Make me."

His eyes darken with desire as he spins us over to doggy style, fully aware that's my favorite position.

"Let me hear you say it," he groans, thrusting deeper and harder into me and hitting all the right spots.

Throwing my ass back, I am unable to contain my pleasure any longer and scream his name.

"Diooonnnn!" I shout at the top of my lungs.

"Yes, just like that," he growls, his movements becoming more intense at the sound of his name on my lips. I grip the sheets tight as he continues to drive me wild with each powerful thrust. Aware that he's getting close, I match his rhythm. With a final thrust, Dion lets out a guttural groan as we both reach the peak of ecstasy together, our bodies trembling in unison before collapsing in a tangled heap of limbs and heavy breathing.

We stare up at the ceiling, our chests rising and falling.

"I don't think I've ever had that many orgasms before," I admit breathlessly.

Dion's lips curl into a sexy smile. "Well, I aim to please, and I'm glad I could deliver," he replies, his voice deep with satisfaction.

I playfully swat his chest. "Oh, shut up!"

He chuckles, pulling me closer and planting a soft kiss on my forehead. Snuggling into his arms, I bask in the soft glow of moonlight filtering through my lavender curtains. Dion holds me tight, his steady heartbeat against my ear, lulling us into a peaceful sleep.

This was the best New Year's I've ever had.

Chapter 2: Dion

It's been a long time since I enjoyed New Year's with a woman. Reign Amara Brown has captured my soul in a way no other woman ever has. She is all I think about: morning, evening, and night. I play ball with her, confide in her, and share a bond that I never thought possible. Reign is the ideal woman for me, as if God made her just for me to love. She's intelligent, sexy, and independent. Reign doesn't need anything. She gets it on her own, and that is such a fucking turn-on. The thought of her makes my dick twitch under the sheets.

Over the holidays, I officially introduced her to my parents and disclosed that we were pretending to date but had fallen in love. My mother praised Reign, calling her delightful and appreciating that she is *willing* to deal with me. Can you believe that? My mom is something else, but I know she means well. My father gave me a fist pound and told me I did well for myself and not to mess it up.

Like I would ever want to.

The wedding in June that Reign asked me to accompany her to, paid off in ways I never thought possible. Impressed by my performance as the stand-in MC, the bride recommended me to some of her associates who needed an actor for wedding commercials, resulting in a series of ads where I portray the groom, working with my on-screen bride. While it is not nearly as much as I would like to make, it is helping me pay *some* of the bills. *Not my rent though, I'm so behind.*

Despite not being my first choice, this role will help me reach my career goals. I know the road to becoming a successful and well-known actor is paved with rejection, but the dream has been burning in my heart since childhood, and even though I have yet to land a significant role, I am determined to pursue it until I do. My dream requires unwavering dedication, and giving up now will almost certainly result in its failure.

Since the commercials began, others have contacted me, including Layla, the owner of the boutique that Reign and I visited. I'm optimistic that one of these contacts will soon lead me to a deal for a movie or television show. Being more visible increases the chances of catching a casting director's eye. I auditioned for a two-part fantasy series titled *Seventeen: Magic is Real Part I.* and *Earth: Magic is Real Part II.* in December, and I'm still waiting to hear back. The part is for a father who is keeping a big secret from his daughter, and I think it will be fun to play. I never considered auditioning for a fantasy story, but here we are. My ideal role would be to play someone in an action movie or comedy; however, securing this part will significantly boost my bank account.

My agent informed me that a response would take time. If I'm hired, filming is scheduled for July or August. Which means I won't be able to co-coach the Little League with Eddie.

My agent has also scheduled another audition, this time for a vampire story, which I'm excited about. She has been scheduling auditions for me every other week.

I glance over my shoulder at Reign's sleeping form; I want to make her breakfast before feasting on her again. Quietly getting out of bed, I slip on my boxers and walk to the bathroom to do my daily routine.

Heading to the kitchen, I gather two mixing bowls. Looking through the cabinets, I fish for all the ingredients for pancakes: all-purpose flour, baking powder, eggs, milk, sugar, vanilla extract, cinnamon, and butter. Reign does not cook much, so when I stay over, I make sure to keep the cabinets and fridge stocked, or we shop together. I don't make much, but I'm able to do that. My nostrils flare as the delicious scent of vanilla and cinnamon wafts through the air. Once the pancakes are done, I place them on the kitchen island to cool while I pour orange juice and champagne into a flute.

Taking a tray from the cupboard, I place the pancakes drizzled with strawberry syrup and the mimosa I prepared on it, then head to the bedroom. Upon entering the room, I see the sheets covering the bed, but Reign is not there. I place the tray of food on the dresser and check her closet to see if she's there. Empty. Walking down the hallway to the bathroom, I hear soft R&B music playing and gently knock on the door.

"Come in, babe," Reign's sultry voice calls over the music, making my cock twitch.

When I open the door, Reign is surrounded by bubbles up to her neck in the bathtub. The blood rushes to my dick, and I brush my hand over it to push it down before she notices. *Too late.*

"Would you like to join me?" she asks with a seductive smile, her eyes hungrily taking in my bulge.

"Don't have to ask me twice," I reply, removing my boxers and letting my thick and veiny cock spring free. Stepping into the tub, I settle into my spot. Reign leans back against my chest, her soft skin pressing against mine, and we relax in the warm water.

As I lather a washcloth with her favorite vanilla-scented soap and gently wash her back, she tells me all about her plans for her boutique. She hired someone new to replace Skylar and promoted Nancy to manager. She also hired two additional women and will interview two or more candidates. Her business is expanding, and she recently signed a new lease for a larger boutique. I am so proud of my girl.

The water stirs as Reign swiftly turns to face me. She straddles my lap, my dick hardening against her.

"Reign… what are you doing?" I ask with restraint, brushing her hair out of her face.

She laughs, wiggling her pussy on my dick. "What do you think I'm doing?"

"Fuck," I mutter under my breath. "I made break—"

Reign cuts me off by descending onto my cock, her lips parting with a moan. She throws her head back and moves on top of me, causing tiny ripples in the water. My fingers run along her brown nubs as she rides me harder and faster. Sucking on her erect nipples, moans escape her lips as she grinds against me. I press my thumb over her swollen clit to push her over the edge, causing ragged breaths and shudders to wrack her body. When she comes down from her high, she pulls the plug from the tub, and the swirling water slowly disappears down the drain. Standing up, her sexy ass body glistens with water droplets.

"Come on, let's take this to the bedroom," she says, grasping my hand and leading me out of the bathroom.

The bedroom door closes behind us, and her lips curve into a huge smile.

"You made breakfast!"

I purse my lips in a deliberate pout. "Yes, and now it's cold."

Reign squeezes my cheeks between her fingers. "I'll make it up to you."

"Oh yeah? How?" I playfully challenge her, raising an eyebrow.

She lowers her hand down to my hard cock. "Get on the bed and I'll show you."

"I love it when you take charge," I comply with a smirk.

Reclining on the bed with my hands behind my head, she gets on all fours and crawls to me slowly and seductively, stopping at my dick. Gripping her hands firmly around my shaft, she looks up at me with a mischievous smile before stroking me up and down. Her fierce gaze focused on me the entire time has me so close to losing my shit, and she knows it. She spits on my cock and deep-throats me while flicking her wrist in a circling motion, a single tear forming in her eye as I fuck her mouth.

"Shit, Reign," I groan.

The sucking noises from her juicy lips are driving me wild. Each stroke, suck, and lick of my dick sends me closer to the edge. My release covers her chin and tongue as I throw my head back, fixing my eyes on the ceiling. She licks every bit of it and smiles at me, pleased with herself.

"Come here," I growl, gripping her neck to press my mouth against hers, the familiar taste of myself mingling with her sweet lips. Her playful tongue engages in a game of dominance with mine, fueling the fire between us even more.

Three weeks later…

I wake up ten minutes after the irritating sound of my alarm has faded, the buzz still ringing in my ears. If I don't get in the shower within two minutes, I'll be late for this audition. Normally, I am more punctual; however, recently, I've been a bit distracted trying to spend some quality time with my girl. Reign has been extremely busy over the last three weeks, which I understand, but she has not responded to any of my messages or calls. I feel like one of those thirsty men who can't take a hint after the first rejection. Stepping over the pile of clothes in my bedroom, I head out of the room and make my way down the hall to the bathroom. After quickly going through my usual routine, I grab a bagel on my way out the door.

With two minutes to spare, I make it to my audition on time. Walking through the doors with pride, I'm greeted by an olive-skinned gentleman with a salt-and-pepper beard.

"Are you Mr. James?"

"Yes, that's me."

"Great! Please follow me."

He leads me down a narrow hallway to a waiting area; there must be at least thirty other people auditioning.

Another man approaches me and hands me a stack of papers. "Please turn to page forty for your lines."

Nodding, I move to the back of the room, flipping through the packet. I am auditioning for the role of Raheem, the middle brother in a trio of dangerous vampires. I will be acting out a scene where the brothers are preparing for war. Hmm… for this scene, I need to dig deep and channel specific past experiences that have upset me. *How would I feel if I were preparing for war?* Angry.

I reflect on my past experiences that have ever upset me, like losing a game of 2K or losing a part to someone else. Losing to Eddie in 2K does not put me in the right mindset for this role, and if I do not get it, perhaps this role may not be for me. *This might be a little difficult.* I need to think of something more impactful to help me get in character before they call my name. I've always been a positive and relaxed kind of dude, so things don't typically get under my skin, which is why I need to tap into something deeper. Reign ghosting me? No. *Let me dig deeper.*

I think back to when I was in middle school in Mrs. Gover's class, and a white kid called me the N-word. Yeah, that word, and not with the "A" at the end for "endearment," but the "ER" with force behind it. My parents taught me never to use the word because of what it represents, and despite the fact that it is used in everyday language across several cultures during conversations, I chose not to add it to my vocabulary, so when that boy called me one, I flipped on him and got suspended from school. My mother taught me to love everyone, regardless of race or religious beliefs, and to stay high when an ignorant person goes low. God would handle them, but at that moment, my fist *handled* him just fine.

Growing up in the South, my parents experienced the end of segregation as children, which significantly influenced their childhood and made it more guarded. After I had been suspended, they decided to have "the talk" with me. You know what talk I am referring to—the *Black talk*. They needed to explain what it means to be a Black man in this country and how people will look at me and assume I'm a drug dealer, gang member, or thug. They have had difficult conversations with me about the police and how society perceives Black men. My father shared a story with me about a march he joined in Mississippi that was not documented in history books or mainstream media. My mother recounted her upbringing in Alabama, including her experiences with school integration. I could never imagine dealing with the racial discrimination and challenges my parents faced. However, the memory of that incident with the kid still boils my blood, but it's not sufficient to fuel the anger I need for this role.

I rub my fingers in a circular motion against my temples. *Ahh.* Okay, let me think. Closing my eyes, I recall working in IT. The company purchased a new system for us to use, which I needed more training on. I sent several messages and emails to my boss, requesting a meeting to discuss the new system. My manager treated me as if I were a burden; asking him for assistance was too much, and it appeared that it was not his job. Finally, he set up a meeting and stated, *"I can teach, but I can't teach common sense or critical thinking."* And I thought to myself, what the fuck was that supposed to mean exactly? We were using a new system that I was unfamiliar with, one in which he had extensive training but I did not, so how could critical thinking or common sense be applied to something I didn't understand? He was clearly being a dick. If I didn't care about jail time, I would have punched him in the nose for insulting my intelligence, but I digress. I reported that jackass to HR and quit three months later to pursue my acting career full-time. Later, one of my former coworkers informed me that he was sued for sexual harassment and subsequently fired. Good for him!

By the time my name is called, I am mentally in the headspace for the part. I probably should have thought of that incident first.

"Hello, Mr. James. My name is Marco, and this is Ronnie. We will be rehearsing the script with you."

"Nice to meet you both," I reply, shaking Marco's hand and exchanging a nod with Ronnie.

"Let's begin," Marco says, prompting me to start.

I inhale and exhale sharply, channeling the memory of the idiot who insulted my intelligence, and I'm ready for my scene.

"Action!" The casting director's voice roars through the room.

I immediately get into character.

"Raheem, what the hell is wrong with you?" Marco shouts at the top of his lungs.

"What do you mean, what the hell is wrong with me? We need to handle this shit now!" I respond, reciting my lines with ease.

"You can't expect our troops to be ready to wage war in the middle of the night," Ronnie argues.

I slap my right hand against my left palm. *"What the Remi Clan did was unacceptable! We must retaliate now!"*

"Raheem, Jacob is right! We need time to prepare," Ronnie reasons, nudging my chest.

Shoving him back, I flare my nostrils. *"Both of you are useless! I will have my revenge and kill every last one of them with or without you!"* I storm off in the opposite direction.

"End scene!" The casting director calls out with a resounding clap of his hands.

I take a deep breath and decompress for a few moments to ground myself, releasing Raheem's emotions to reconnect with reality. Acting is an art that sometimes requires a lot of energy. Transitioning between the character's emotions and my own requires a conscious shift in mindset.

"That was great, Mr. James! My people will be in touch with your agent," the casting director compliments.

Nodding, I give a slight smile. "Thank you for your time and consideration."

"Wassup, bro? How's it going?" Eddie greets me as I walk into his apartment. We're going to unwind and play some 2K.

Looking around, I notice gold, glitter, and sparkling accents all over his apartment. My face must have given away my thoughts because he looks at me sheepishly.

Trying to bite back my laugh, I ask, "Does Scarlette live here now?"

He tosses one of the throw blankets onto the armrest of his sofa. "Yeah, uh, it seems like it."

I burst out laughing, and Eddie joins in. "Is that what you want?"

"I don't mind it. I just don't know when it happened, really. Like, one day, I woke up, and all her girly shit was here."

"I never thought you would be so pussy-whipped, bro."

He throws one of the smaller, fluffy pillows at my head. "Shut the hell up, man. You were whipped first."

Reign's beautiful face pops into my head, reminding me that I haven't seen her in three weeks. *Get a grip. It's only been three weeks.* I dismiss the thought and grab the controller, settling back in the recliner chair to choose a team.

Eddie's eyes narrow. "How are things with you and Reign?"

Trying to downplay his question, I shrug nonchalantly. "Fine, I guess."

He gives me an expectant look. "You guess?"

"Yeah, we're good."

Eddie grabs a controller and selects his team, not convinced by my response.

"I haven't seen her in three weeks."

He stops and looks at me with a raised eyebrow. "Three weeks? That's a long time, man. Scarlette and I see each other every day."

"Scarlette lives here."

Eddie laughs, "True, but still. Aren't you and Reign exclusive? Why haven't you two seen each other?"

"She's been busy with the move to a larger boutique," I reply, adjusting my settings for the game.

I expected her to reply to a text message or join my parents and me for lunch last Wednesday. Maybe I am overthinking this. We went months without seeing each other, but we weren't official then.

"I don't know, bro, it's been a minute since I've been in a serious relationship. What's the proper protocol for this type of shit?"

"Dude, I don't know. I can't help you. But can you hurry up and finish adjusting your settings so we can play?"

"Man, why are you rushing me? Let me do my thing. Damn," I reply with a chuckle.

Eddie shakes his head and throws back his beer.

We're two minutes into the second quarter of the game, and the crowd's roar can be heard over the speakers. The sharp click of the door bolt disrupts the game, causing both of us to turn our heads. No one other than Scarlette stands in the doorway.

"She has a key?" I whisper-shout to Eddie, who shrugs in response.

"You have a key to Reign's place too."

Touché.

"*Hola*, Dioonnnn," Scarlette shrieks, stretching out my name and rushing to me for a hug.

I pause the game to hug her back. "Hi Scarlette, how are you?"

"*Estoy muy cansada*," she sighs.

Scarlette kisses Eddie on the cheek before heading to the kitchen. Being around Scarlette has taught me more Spanish than I have ever learned in school. I still can't speak it, but I understand a little better now. When she is tired, she always sighs and says the same phrase.

"Long day at work?"

"*Sí*, work has been kicking my butt. My fake dating app has taken off, and now I'm developing some new features."

She unpacks the shopping bag onto the counter. "I'm making curry chicken, rice, and peas. Are you staying for dinner, Dion?"

I check my phone for any responses from Reign or my agent, but find no new notifications.

"Don't mind if I do," I respond with a goofy grin on my face.

During the holidays, she made *Croquetas de Jamón*. They are small, lightly breaded, and fried béchamel fritters, and they are delicious. She wrote down the recipe for me, and I plan to make them one of these days.

While Eddie and I continue playing our game, Scarlette bangs pots and pans in the kitchen, preparing a meal I already know will be delicious.

"Oh shit!" She exclaims suddenly, causing Eddie and me to pause our game.

"What happened?" We ask in unison.

"Darcy just sent me a DM on Instagram."

Eddie and I exchange confused glances before Scarlette continues, "No, you don't understand. She never reaches out to me directly. I wonder what she wants."

Eddie nudges me. "Women."

I nudge him back with a smirk.

"Oh wow, Darcy sent me a long message saying she hasn't heard from Skylar since the wedding."

Eddie and I look at one another, eyebrows raised. *The wedding was in October.*

"That's strange," I comment, immediately calling Reign, but of course, she doesn't answer. "Scarlette, I haven't spoken to Reign in three weeks. Can you try calling her on your phone?"

"What? Are you serious?" She asks, a crease forming on her forehead.

"Yes, she hasn't been responding to my calls or messages. Have you spoken to her?"

Scarlette's worried expression mirrors my concern. "Not really. I spoke with her briefly last week, and she said she was super tired and would call me back, which she didn't," she realizes, reaching for her phone to call Reign. The line rings and goes straight to voicemail. Now I am starting to get worried. Maybe I should go check on her at her place.

Scarlette leaves a voicemail, "Aye, what the fuck is up? You can't be *that* busy." She hangs up, saying, "I'm going to reach out to Nancy. I'll be right back," before leaving the room.

As she disappears to the bedroom, unease settles in the pit of my stomach during the fifteen minutes she's gone. *What if something happened to Reign?*

"I spoke with Nancy, Reign is fine." Scarlette reassures me as she returns from the bedroom, and I let out a sigh of relief.

"They have been busy with the boutique. The move hasn't been as smooth as they had hoped. She only answered because I had never called her before and assumed it was important. I told her that Darcy hasn't heard from Skylar and to let Reign know. She said Reign was most likely asleep at home because they had spent the day packing and moving boxes from the old location to the new one. She mentioned they would be finished next weekend."

Thank God Reign is okay, but what's going on with Skylar?

Eddie speaks my exact thoughts. "Damn, what's going on with Skylar?"

Scarlette bellows, "Hell, if I know, but if she hasn't spoken to Darcy, something is definitely up." She turns to me and explains, "Reign has been like this before, getting so focused on her job that she isolates herself from others. She will reach out when she is less stressed, Dion."

I thank Scarlette for the update. She then excuses herself to the bedroom to call August and inform her on what's going on with Skylar.

Chapter 3: Reign

Beep-beep-beep.

The jarring sound of my alarm jolts me awake, and in my still-sleep-fogged state, I fumble around, hitting and knocking everything off of my nightstand. With a groan, I finally manage to silence the alarm. *Urgh!* Rubbing the sleep from my eyes, I notice ten missed calls from Dion, Scarlette, and August, along with three voicemails. I haven't been in the mood to talk to anyone because I've been fully focused on relocating my boutique. It doesn't make it right, of course. This is just how I operate—I can only focus on one thing at a time, and that one thing was my business relocation.

My friend April Brown, who I met through Scarlette works in real estate with her mom. *Brown is such a common last name.* April and her mom helped me find a place, although April doesn't like working in real estate. She's a talented artist and hopes to own her own gallery one day, but she's damn good at her job. As a thank you for helping me, I plan on purchasing some of her work once I settle into my new location. We all hit it off so well with April that August invited her, along with Jieun, who is Edwin's wife, to brunch today. Edwin and Scarlette are cousins. So, Scarlette's *cousin-in-law?* Is that a thing? I'm sure it is. Anyway, I've known Jieun for a few years now. Jieun Lee, better known as Mrs. Rodriguez now is a scientist and is living her dream.

Last year, she married Edwin during the week of Christmas. I love them together! They wanted their wedding to be small and intimate because Edwin is saving for his physical therapy practice. I would have planned their wedding if it weren't near the holidays. Thanksgiving, Christmas, and Valentine week are my block-off dates, now that I'm in a serious relationship.

Finding a location for my new store was a smooth process; the moving company I hired was not. They didn't show up. Luckily, I hadn't made a payment. Nancy and I moved everything ourselves with the help of the other workers. It was exhausting, with Nancy and me doing the majority of the heavy lifting. With the move finally being done, we are still unpacking and organizing everything in the new location. We are located in the city, but it's closer to where I live. I ordered a bright neon sign for the storefront that will say, *"Event Planning with Reign."* Yeah, I know it's a bit much, but it's me.

March is jam-packed with four weddings scheduled in just two days. Naturally, it's just my luck that three of the weddings fall on the same day. I managed to strategically convince the brides to have their ceremonies at the same venue. Luck was on my side because that almost never happens. April and May are equally busy months for planning spring weddings. The good news is that during those months, I won't have three weddings in one day. Moving forward, I will only handle two weddings per day.

Seeing Dion's name on my screen makes me feel like a terrible girlfriend. My poor Dion, he probably hates me now. I haven't responded to any of his calls or text messages because I've been so swamped with everything. I tend to shut down when I'm stressed out, which is no excuse. I am in a committed relationship with a wonderful, supportive, and sexy man. *Do better, girl!*

I contemplate what to say to him.

What can I say?

What is there to say?

How do I tell him I'm an awful girlfriend for ignoring all of his calls and texts because I've been so busy, as if he doesn't have his own life and still makes the time to contact me? I suck doesn't quite cut it.

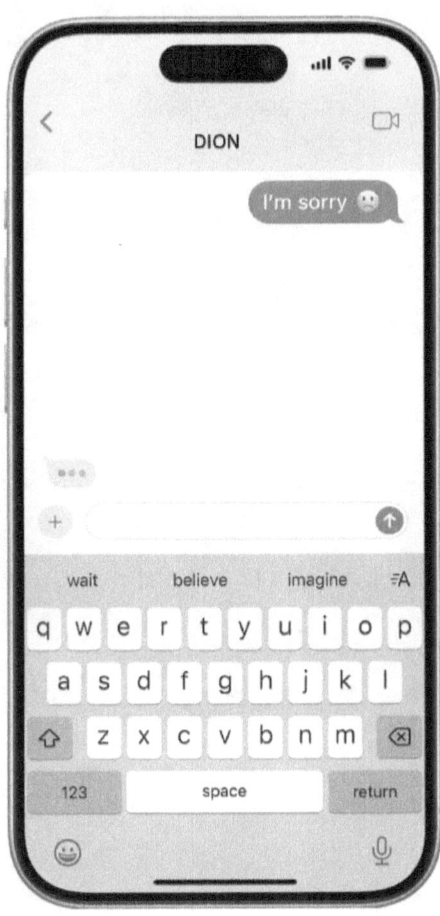

My thoughts are a jumbled mess, so those two words are all I can manage. If there was an award for the worst girlfriend, my face would be on the trophy.

Three dots appear briefly on the screen before disappearing, then reappearing, and disappearing again.

Dots appear again, and I hold my breath.

I let out a sharp exhale. He doesn't entirely hate me... *yet*.

My phone rings in my hand, and I pause before answering.

Me: "Hey, Dion."
Dion: "Hey, Reign. Have you heard from your sister?"

My sister? I don't remember the last time I spoke to her. I tried to contact her last month, but I assumed she was too preoccupied with her new husband and life as a stay-at-home wife, tending to her husband's every need—no disrespect intended.

Me: "Uh, no, I haven't, actually."

Dion: "I think you need to get in touch with her."
Me: "What's going on? Is everything okay?"

Maybe I should have listened to their voicemails first.

Dion: "Scarlette told Eddie and me last week that Darcy sent her a DM on Instagram saying that she hadn't heard from Skylar since the wedding. Scarlette called you to see if you had spoken to her, but you didn't answer. Which brings me to what the hell, Reign? Why haven't you been returning my calls or messages?"

An icy dread washes over me as my heart falls from my chest into an endless black hole, stealing my breath. His stern and concerned tone leaves me speechless, a pang of guilt settling in my chest. I've been single for so long that I completely forgot to communicate with Dion. *Reign, you're a grown woman in an adult relationship. Start acting like it!*

Open communication is crucial for healthy relationships as it promotes understanding, growth, and deeper connections between partners. I know this, so I have no excuse for my actions.

Me: "Dion, I'm so sorry I've been M.I.A lately. I've been so focused and busy at work that I've lost track of time, and by the time I got home, I passed out. I haven't spoken to anyone, and the last time I talked to Skylar was over a month ago, maybe around the holidays."

Dion sighs on the other end of the phone.

Dion: "Scarlette is worried about Skylar. Don't you find it

odd that you haven't spoken to her in a while?"

I recall the last few "unread" text messages I've sent her. With the demands of my relationship with Dion, work, and daily life, I haven't had the chance to think about Skylar, and I realize we haven't spoken since the Christmas Eve party. *Great!* Not only am I a horrible girlfriend, but I'm also a terrible sister. *What the hell, Reign?*

> *Me: "Yes, you're right. I'm sorry. I've been stuck in my little world, but I'm done with my move. I'll give Skylar a call to check in on her after we get off, and I want to see you soon. I miss you."*
> *Dion: "Call Sky and let me know how she's doing. And I want to see you too, Reign."*
> *Me: "I'm having brunch with the girls today. I'll call Sky to invite her to join us. Do you want to come over later?"*
> *Dion: "Sure, I can come over. We'll talk later."*
> *Me: "Okay, I love you, Dion, and I'm really sorry for being so caught up in my move."*
> *Dion: "It's okay, Reign. I love you too."*

Apologizing to Dion lifts a weight off my shoulders, yet a new concern surfaces as I begin to worry about Skylar. What the hell is going on with her? I dial her number, and it goes straight to voicemail.

> *Me: "Hey Sky, what's going on? Why aren't you replying or calling any of us back? I know I should be the last person saying this, but like Sky, call me back, please. I'm going over to August's place today for brunch. Maybe you can*

*meet me there, and we can talk about what's been going on.
I love you, sis. Talk to you soon!"*

After unsuccessfully attempting to reach Skylar, I listen to Dion and Scarlette's voicemails, rubbing my temples at their annoyed tones. August sighed and hung up. I fucked up here. I scroll through my contacts for Peter's name and hit dial. I don't feel comfortable reaching out to him, but I'm left with no choice.

Peter: "Hello?"

His deep voice startles me inexplicably.

*Me: "Hi Peter, it's Reign. Sorry to bother you, but I'm trying
to reach Sky. Can you please put her on the phone? I
haven't heard from her in the longest."*

Silence stretches between us for at least a minute, which seems to last a lifetime before he responds.

Peter: "Sure, let me get her."

It comes out almost forced, and I wrinkle my eyebrows. Something feels off.

Skylar: "Hi, Reign."

Her voice sounds strained and unusually tense.

*Me: "Hey sis, it's been a while. What's up with you? Why
haven't you been responding? Is everything okay?"*
*Skylar: "Everything is fine. My phone is broken, and I
haven't gotten a new one yet. Sorry about that."*

Me: "Oh, okay. We've been worried about you."
Skylar: "I'm fine, Reign."

There's a slight ruffling sound before silence falls over the line. She must have put me on mute.

Me: "Skylar, are you there?"

One-minute passes, and then another. I check my screen to make sure that the call is still connected; it is.

Me: "Skylar!"

I practically scream into the phone.

Skylar: "I'm here, Reign. What do you want?"

She shouts back, sounding far away. *Why is she being so weird?*

Me: "Sky, we just want to make sure you're okay. You don't seem like yourself. Are you sure you're okay?"

Skylar sighs heavily on the other end of the line.

Skylar: "I'm... I'm fine. I'll talk to you later."

The words tumble out quickly, and before I can respond, she hangs up. *What the hell was that about?* My soul is filled with a deep unease that I can't quite put into words. Sky hung up before I could get any information or invite her to brunch. She basically rushed me off of the phone, but why?

A chilling wind whips past me, raising goosebumps on my arms as I arrive at August and Calvin's home. Honking taxis, distant sirens, and chattering pedestrians create a symphony of city life around their brownstone on the Upper East Side. They live near luxury shops, high-end boutiques, and other notable stores. Calvin is a neurologist at the hospital where my father works. With Calvin working until 10 p.m. tonight and August having the weekend off, today is perfect for brunch.

"Reign, my girl!" August exclaims, inviting me inside and pulling me into a warm hug.

Wrapping my arms around her, I inhale her familiar scent of lavender and citrus. "August! I've missed you."

"I heard you've been too busy even for your man," she says, shaking her head with her silver hoops gently swaying.

I smile sheepishly, admitting, "Guilty as charged."

As August chastises me, I look around her living room. It features a neutral boho style with cream and beige tones, abstract patterns, and accent color throw pillows. The walls are adorned with a vast collection of vintage-inspired paintings, some small and some large, each with its own texture and faded colors. If you ask me, the color scheme is rather dull—a monotonous expanse of white, cream, and beige that stands in stark contrast to my vibrant purple. The word I would use to articulate August and Calvin's taste in décor would be...*interesting*.

"Reign, are you even listening to me?" August's voice snaps me back. "You've been single for seven years, so you may be out of the loop, but when you're in a relationship, you should at least be communicating with *yo* man."

"Yo?"

"Mhmm *yo!* You see what you're doing to me. I can't even speak proper English anymore."

Leave it to August to tell me exactly how she feels and act like a dramatic fake Southern belle.

"I hope you have something planned for Dion!" She continues to lecture me, her eyes narrowing.

"Yes, yes, yes, I know I fucked up. I will fix it, I promise."

Her face lights up with approval, and she ushers me to the bar to pour us both a drink. The worn wood of the barstool feels cool beneath me as I sigh.

Exchanging a sad look, we say in unison, "Skylar?"

August asks, "What's going on?" as she grabs a stainless-steel wing corkscrew from the drawer.

"I'm not sure. I called Peter before coming here."

"What did he say? Did you speak to Sky? Is she okay?" August fires off questions, leaving no room for me to respond or even breathe.

"August, I don't know. Yes, I spoke to her, and she seemed off but wouldn't tell me what was wrong. She told me her phone was broken and she hadn't fixed it yet, and then she rushed me off the phone. I think—*no*, I'm pretty sure something is up."

August twists the corkscrew into the bottle of champagne. I watch *the arms*—as I like to call them—lift at the sides. *POP!* Sizzling bubbles fizzle as she pours us each a glass.

"Maybe we should head over there after brunch with the ladies," I suggest, taking a sip of the champagne.

"Of course," she replies, a worried look in her eyes. "I just hope everything is okay with her."

A warm and bubbly laughter wraps around me from behind, a comforting sound that eases my own worries. Love Williams enters; her gorgeous goddess braids meticulously arranged in a high bun on top of her head. We met at one of August's brunches in 2021 and have stayed in touch since. She has been through so much and is so strong because of it. *But that's not my story to tell.* Love lives on Long Island and owns an indie bookstore that August sometimes sends her staff to clean. They've known each other for about five years.

Her best friend, Kimi Choi, a successful indie author known for her intricate plots and vivid descriptions, is accompanying her. She received an award for her steamy Vampire Clan Trilogy, a series known for its sensual and passionate scenes. I devoured the first two books. Some scenes were so spicy they left me breathless and wanting Rocky—*my vibrator.* She's currently working on a sizzling fairytale that I can't wait to read when it is released.

"Hi, ladies," I greet them, enveloping Love and Kimi in a hug, their cherry blossom scent filling my senses. "How have you both been?"

"Wassup Reign! I'm good. I've been waiting to kick it with y'all for a minute now," Love exclaims, with a wide grin.

Kimi is the same height as Love and wears her dark wavy hair in a messy bun. She bobs her head when she speaks. "Reign, my love," she says, kissing both of my cheeks. "I've been buried in work lately, but I am so ready to drink. I mean *eat,*" she corrects herself with a playful wink. "August! You know how much I love my cocktails, girl!"

August laughs, hugging both Love and Kimi as Scarlette enters, holding her phone to her ear. She's yelling at someone in Spanish— *actually*—a mix between Spanish and English. *Spanglish.*

"No. Me. Importa." She spits through gritted teeth. *"Necesitas...* Figure it out!" She ends the call abruptly and shoves it into her bag. *"Hola,* Reign. *Besos, besos,"* she says, kissing me from cheek to

cheek.

"Do I want to know?" I ask, raising an eyebrow at Scarlette's phone call.

She sighs and throws her arms around me. "There's a major problem with the new app's configuration—it's throwing all sorts of unexpected errors, making the app unusable." Her words were muffled against my shoulder. "I thought everything was running smoothly."

Scarlette's burning anger gradually subsided, but then she pointed her finger at me and shook her head.

April appears, with Jieun trailing closely behind her, providing a welcome distraction from what I know will be a tell-off from Scarlette.

April rushes toward me, arms outstretched, and embraces me tightly. "Girl, I'm so happy we found a place for your business! And if you're interested in artwork, I can always paint you something for free," she offers, holding her hand over her chest.

"I was already thinking about buying some of your artwork. Like, girl, I'm going to pay you!"

Despite her successful career in real estate, April's true passion will always be art. She needs to save a substantial amount of money—enough for a down payment, renovations, and the initial gallery setup—before purchasing a suitable property for her life's work. With my commission, she'll be a little closer to achieving her goal. I'm always rooting for women to win at their ambitions, and I try my best to help in any way that I can, especially Black women, because we have to work twice as hard at everything that we do! Or minorities in general.

"We finally finished moving yesterday, but now we have to unpack everything while planning four weddings for March." I hold out three fingers and wiggle them dramatically. "And three of them are in one day," I add, sighing heavily.

April's brows furrow with a grimace, and her facial expression changes to one of clear disapproval or amusement. "Well, damn girl, that sucks!"

I start laughing. "Yes, I know it sucks, but you definitely didn't have to say it straight like that."

A nervous chuckle escapes April's lips, and she quickly backtracks, saying, "I mean, it's just a lot to handle all at once. But I know you'll pull it off with your usual grace and style."

"April never thinks before she speaks. She just blurts out whatever comes to mind," Jieun adds, swaying her dark, pencil-straight hair.

"What the hell is going on with Skylar? And why the hell are you being a bitch towards my wonderful and amazing friend Dion? *¿Estás loca?*" Scarlette shouts out of nowhere, her arms crossed and a scowl on her face.

Scarlette is another who speaks without filter, but it warms my heart to see how well she and Dion get along.

I nudge her into the corner of the room, away from the others. "I promise you, Scarlette, I am not crazy. And I called Peter's phone and spoke to Sky—"

"Wait... what?" She cuts me off, her long lashes fluttering in surprise. "You spoke to Skylar on Peter's phone?"

"Yes! I spoke to her, and she said her phone was broken... But Scarlette..."

Her eyes are fixed on my lips, holding her breath for me to continue.

"But then there was silence on the line."

Her eyes dart nervously, her fingers tapping anxiously on her arm. "Silence?"

Dread rises in my chest, threatening to consume me.

"Yes, it's like she put me on mute or something, and then she came back on to rush me off like I was the ugly, stupid stepchild."

Scarlette's lips twitch into a small smile. "Reign, I can't stand you!" She laughs lightly before covering her mouth with disgust. "This is a serious matter, and something is clearly going on with your sister. Don't make me laugh. *¡Qué pesada eres!*" She scolds, the fiery tones of her strong Spanish accent adding weight to her words.

I let out a small laugh, which faded quickly as I recomposed myself and resumed my serious demeanor. "No, I agree. I was telling August we should go there after brunch."

"Yes, we should," she agrees, linking her arm with mine, returning to the bar and joining the rest of the ladies.

August serves us mimosas and makes a fruity cocktail for Jieun. She has a tray on the counter piled high with various types of pancakes: blueberry, strawberry, banana, and more, topped with a colorful array of berries, cherries, and grapes. There's eggs, biscuits, and sausages. She most definitely had this food catered. August can cook her ass off, but she wouldn't make all this for us, not with her schedule.

"*Bon appétit,* ladies!" August shrieks, breaking through the chitter-chatter.

The spread looks absolutely delicious, and we all dig in, the room droning with a low hum of conversation, peppered by sighs and complaints about long hours and the desperate need for a vacation.

Love mentions needing to hire more workers for her store to help with inventory because she has an audit coming up soon. She has two options: books to buy and books to "borrow," which she used her personal funds to buy. Now that business is booming, she's worked out deals with indie authors to ensure her store carries their books.

Kimi's next book deadline is approaching, and she wants to take a trip to de-stress before locking herself away for a month of intensive writing. April discusses some paintings she wants to work on for a show next month, while Jieun discusses samples that need to be processed in her lab and an instrument she needs repaired. Scarlette is complaining that her staff is struggling to grasp the functionality of the new app she's implementing. I know nothing about creating apps, so I can't offer an opinion.

Sitting next to Scarlette, savoring my strawberry pancakes and mimosa, I nod and agree with everyone, gradually zoning out, only to be brought back to attention when Love suggests a couples trip for Valentine's Day weekend. The chit-chatting comes to a halt. *Couples trip?*

"Seriously, Love? That's so unexpected and last minute," Kimi says deadpan, her lips forming a thin and tight line.

"I think we should do it," Scarlette agrees with Love. She looks to me to back up her and Love's crazy idea, knowing that I have four weddings coming up.

I shoot daggers at her, silently cursing their timing. "I don't know if—"

Scarlette waves her hand, cutting me off. "Hear me out, ladies. You've all mentioned being tired. I'm tired too. I need a break to recharge, and I think you do too. So how about a couple's trip for Valentine's Day? We deserve it. Say yes, and I can have it booked in thirty minutes—twenty if I'm lucky."

Love claps her hands. "Yes, yes, a thousand times yes! I'm down, and I know my boo will be up for it too. I'm texting him now."

The rest of us exchange glances, all silently agreeing, knowing damn well we deserve it.

"Let me move some things around and call Dante real quick. I don't know if we'll be able to make it, but I'm going to try," Kimi says, excusing herself to the balcony to make a phone call.

August is smiling and wiggling her brows at me. "Calvin is off for Valentine's Day weekend and the entire week, and I know you are too."

She's right. Since I'm in a relationship with Dion, I've made it a point to inform my potential clients that I'll be unavailable that week.

My lips press into a thin, hard line as I roll my eyes and return my attention on Scarlette. "Where do you want to go this late in the game?"

Valentine's Day weekend is one of the worst times to plan anything because everything is either booked or costs a fortune. This is our first Valentine's Day together, so maybe I want to celebrate it with only Dion. Besides, I'm a planner, and I have to plan my events, vacations, or whatever, six months in advance, not *two* weeks.

Jieun adds, "What place isn't fully booked by now?"

"Valentine's Day is in two weeks. Most places are already booked, or they will charge outrageous prices, and I doubt Richard and I will be able to make it. He has an important meeting coming up—I forget which day," April says with a sigh.

Scarlette hops off the barstool and suggests, "Let's go to the Poconos! My uncle has a ten-bedroom cabin there that we could Airbnb. I'll give him a call."

August notices my silence and wraps her arms around me. "What is it, Reign?"

I shake my head, my eyes heavy with unspoken guilt.

August gently directs my gaze back to her understanding

face. "Is it Sky? Dion?"

Honestly, I don't know how I feel right now. I need to find out what's going on with my sister and her new husband... there is something off that I can't quite put my finger on. I don't like how the conversation ended. *What is he doing to you, Sky?* I overthink so many things, but I have no idea what to do with this. It doesn't feel right. And then I feel bad for pretty much ghosting Dion the entire time I've been moving from one location to the next. I have a one-track mind.

"It's nothing, August. I just have a lot on my mind right now."

She squeezes my hand reassuringly. "That's why we need this last-minute getaway. It will be good for all of us."

"That's only if Scarlette can pull it off and arrange a place for us to stay," I say, tapping August on the nose.

"This is Escarletta Lucia Rodriguez. If anyone is going to get it done, it's her."

I giggle and nod in agreement. "She's a force to be reckoned with, that's for sure."

Twenty minutes later…

"Guess what, ladies?" Scarlette returns from her phone call with a radiant smile on her face and announces, "We're going to the Poconos! My uncle agreed to let us stay at his cabin from the day after Valentine's Day through Wednesday morning. I may have mentioned that my lovely cousin-in-law," she looks at Jieun, "wanted to celebrate her honeymoon."

Jieun starts laughing. "So, you used me and Edwin as bait to sway your uncle into letting us stay at his place?"

Scarlette grins. "Desperate times call for desperate measures, right? We have to pay for at least one night because he's losing money by letting us stay. You know he doesn't like to lose money." She rolls her eyes. "But hey, consider this your very late wedding gift from Uncle Rico."

Jieun chuckles and shakes her head. "Did you talk to Edwin about this?"

Scarlette waves her hand dismissively. *"Pronto, pronto,"* she says, which means soon.

"Are we traveling together, or will we meet up there?" Love asks excitedly.

Realizing that my Valentine's Day plans had already been made for me, I quickly text Nancy to let her know about the changes. Of course, I could just say no, but who are we kidding? I need a break! Dion won't be happy with this last-minute trip; if anything, I'll cover the extra expenses and make it up to him later.

August suggests, "Maybe we can meet up there?"

"Or we could rent a party bus?" Kimi smirks, her shit-eating grin widening.

Love and Scarlette's eyes light up at the idea.

"Yes!" They say in unison.

"What do you think, Reign?" August asks, turning to me with a hopeful expression.

I shrug my shoulders. "Sure, why not."

"Atta girl!" August exclaims, hugging me tightly.

"I just spoke to Richard. He confirmed that he has a meeting on that Monday," April says, a look of disappointment etched on her dark brown-skinned features. "I hope you guys have a great time without us."

"We'll miss you," Scarlette says, pouting, and April nudges her playfully.

August gets her laptop so the ladies can look up party buses together.

Later, I'll have to find a way to tell Dion about my plans for us to spend Valentine's weekend with my friends, some of whom he hasn't met yet. *That should go over well.*

Scarlette looks up from her phone. "Okay, we'll split the cost by twelve. We also need food. Are we doing take-out or cooking?"

"Make that ten," Jieun interjects. "Edwin just texted me back saying he has to cover someone's shift that Sunday. It was last-minute, and he agreed to do it before we decided on this trip."

Disappointment is evident on Scarlette's face as she processes the news. "Oh no, that changes things," she murmurs. "The only reason Uncle Rico is letting us stay there at a discount is because I told him we were celebrating you two."

Jieun shrugs her shoulders, "I'm sorry. Will he be there? He doesn't have to know we won't be there. Or maybe tell him at the last minute we couldn't make it."

"Ay dios mío," Scarlette shakes her head and takes out her phone. She adds a string of Spanish words to her previous statement to express her frustration. "Okay, Uncle Rico said he wouldn't charge us for all four nights, but we have to pay for three now instead of one."

Wow! Scarlette wasn't joking when she said her uncle hates losing money. I get it, though. We all have businesses to run, and sometimes families take advantage of this, always expecting a discount.

"Take out or order in?" Scarlette asks, bringing the question back up.

"Take out," Love answers.

August suggests, "Let's cook one night."

"Who the hell wants to cook while on vacation?" Kimi says deadpan, and we all expect August to agree.

She makes a face. "I love to cook. Maybe I'll hook you girls up with a gourmet meal one night."

"Oh yeah! August is going to show us why she's been married all these years." Love teases, causing everyone to laugh.

"Damn right," August laughs.

With the plans settled, I now have to break the news to Dion tonight.

Chapter 4: Reign

Skylar and Peter's brownstone is not that far from August's. August, Scarlette, Love, and Kimi accompany me to pay them a visit. We walk down the tree-lined street, and as we get closer to their house, I pause on the grand stoop leading to their door, filled with trepidation at what awaits us inside. My heart pounds wildly in my chest, my mouth as dry as a desert.

Love clears her throat, and with caution in her tone, asks, "So, what exactly is going on?"

Exhaling sharply, I trail off, "Umm… I'm not sure, really." My voice trembles with uncertainty. Maybe I'm misinterpreting something.

"Let's press the intercom," August suggests as I hover my hand over the button, uncertainty washing over me.

Feeling Scarlette's comforting rub on my back, I gain the confidence to press the intercom buzzer. My heart is racing as we wait for a response.

"Hello?" Peter's deep voice crackles through the speaker.

"Hey," I say in an unnaturally high-pitched tone, and Scarlette's eyes widen. "It's Reign. We were in the neighborhood and decided to stop by."

"Why would you stop by without calling first?" Peter's tone is icy, unlike his charming self, and it sends a shiver down my spine.

Scarlette cuts in, *"Hola,* Peter, it's Scarlette. Listen, we want to see you and Sky. It's been a while. Let us in, okay?" She basically demands.

It's hard not to laugh at her insistent and bossy tone, but I quickly stifle it as Peter's silence on the other end of the line grows uncomfortable. The buzzer finally rings, unlocking the door. I mouth a "thank you" to Scarlette, and she nods.

My legs feel like noodles as I push open the deep red door, stumbling a little. *I had one too many mimosas.* A chilling sense of dread washes over me, making my skin crawl, and when I pivot, I am met with pointed stares from my friends, their unspoken judgment pressing down on me like a physical force. Although she's silent, I can hear August's voice in my head, urging me, "Girl, take yo ass in there and see what's going on with your sister."

"This wasn't smart. Maybe I should come back when I'm sober."

"We're already here," Kimi says with a small smile. "Let's see what's up."

Rolling my shoulders back to shake off the nerves, I gather my bearings and head inside. Once through the threshold, we are met with the classic interior and high ceiling designs brownstones are known for. We walk across a beautiful hardwood floor, the polished wood smooth beneath our feet, and the burgundy walls, accented with tan and gold, sparkle softly in the light from the large windows. Peter's late mother used to live in this house. He only has a few close relatives in New York—his older brother, sister-in-law, and two nephews. His aunts, uncles, and cousins from his mother's side live in New Jersey. His father side of the family are from around the world and Skylar never mentioned any specifics. Peter inherited the lovely brownstone from his mother through her will; his brother was already cared for. Skylar mentioned that Peter's father was never a factor; his absence remained a mystery, and she didn't want to pry. I would want to know about my father-in-law. Like where is he? Is he dead or alive?

We make our way to the parlor; the smell of old books and polished wood hangs in the air. The ladies and I settle into the plush armchairs. Each tick of the grandfather clock echoes throughout the quiet room; the seconds—maybe even minutes—stretch out as we wait for Skylar and Peter to appear.

"Hi, Reign. What a pleasant surprise," Peter greets, his tone sharp and cold, sending an imaginary worm wiggling down my spine.

"Hi, Peter. Yeah, the girls and I were in the neighborhood and decided to stop by to see you guys." I keep my tone warm and friendly.

My friends bob their heads up and down, going along with my lie.

With a pointed expression, Peter turns quickly on his heels, the sound of his shoes clicking on the polished floor echoing down the hall. "I'll get Skylar," he says over his shoulder.

I exchange a nervous glance with my friends, alarmed that Peter's abrupt shift in demeanor is not a good sign. As we wait for Skylar to arrive, I can't shake the feeling that something is about to go terribly wrong.

"Hi, Reign," Skylar says in a quiet voice as she approaches us, her eyes darting between each of our faces.

What the hell is wrong with her, and why is she speaking to me like that?

When I reach out to hug her, she flinches slightly and her shoulders tense. She looks fragile and on edge, so unlike the confident and carefree Skylar we are used to.

"Are we interrupting something?" I ask, trying to keep my tone light and casual as my gaze moves from Skylar to Peter's face.

Peter stands possessively behind Skylar; arms tightly folded across his chest and a scowl on his face. "No, of course not. However, it would have been nice if you had called first before showing up to our home unexpectedly."

Choosing my words carefully, I apologize for the unannounced visit. "You're absolutely right. I—*we* came here uninvited. I am truly sorry. Please accept my apology."

Peter nods. "I'll give you some privacy," he says, leaning in to kiss Skylar's cheek while keeping an icy stare on me.

Time stood still as we waited for his footsteps to disappear down the hall.

Once the sound of his footsteps faded away, I suck in a breath, exhaling slowly. "Sky, is everything good?"

She looks over her shoulder and bites her bottom lip, deciding whether or not to speak. I can see the conflict in her eyes when she finally opens her mouth, but she rapidly blinks three times.

An icy chill seeps into my bones, and the hair on my neck prickles with unknown danger. She's far from fine. She's terrified of him.

When we were kids, I was disorganized and a mess, but

whenever my sister needed me, I was there for her, and vice versa. My mom favored Sky, so I would stay out all night at Scarlette's place to avoid the tension at home. Mostly on the nights my dad worked the night shift. When I was there, my mother did not want Skylar and me to talk. Why? I don't know, but we devised a secret language and signals that only we understand. Rapidly blinking twice indicated everything was fine, three blinks signaled trouble, and five blinks means you need help.

Skylar blinked three times, indicating that something is wrong, but she's unable to say why. *I don't know what to do.*

Do I play it off? Maybe I should try speaking in our secret language?

"Ba-is ba-e ba-urting ba-ou?"

Sky and I created a language by placing the sound B-A in front of a word, which sounds like a sheep saying, *"Baa."* The kids I went to private school with all had unique ways of speaking, with each clique making it their own.

Her eyes widen and flicker in recognition. I glance over my shoulder, and the girls are all confused.

Skylar hesitates for a moment before responding, *"Ba-es."*

My mind is spiraling. What do I do? What do I say? My heart breaks for my sister. All that shit I said about her and her wedding, the way she was acting the entire time. I noticed nothing. This asshole is hurting her. She was acting like a bitch when we were planning her wedding, which was unusual for her, but I figured she had the Bridezilla thing going on. How had I not noticed this before?

Scarlette meets my gaze, and she and August jerk their heads, signaling that Peter is approaching us.

Think. Think. Think. Poconos!

"Hey, Peter. I'm glad you're back. I was wondering if you guys would like to join us in the Poconos for Valentine's Day weekend.

We're doing a couple's trip."

Skylar looks to Peter for an answer. His thick brown brows shoot up, but a smirk spreads across his lips. "I already have something special planned for my beautiful wife and me," he declines, wrapping his arm around Skylar and drawing her closer to his chest.

Skylar blinks five times.

"Oh, no worries, Peter. Maybe next time then. Skylar, when do you plan to get your phone fixed so that I can text you?"

"Very soon," she replies, blinking five times more.

Think!

"I'm hosting a brunch tomorrow at my place. I insist you stop by," I blurt out.

Peter rubs the lower part of Skylar's back, and she replies, "No, not tomorrow. Peter and I have plans."

Scarlette's expression, a scowl directed at me, catches my attention. I channel my best friend's assertive attitude.

"You and Peter can stop by tomorrow after you finish whatever you're doing. I have not seen you in months. We need to catch up, and I won't take no for an answer."

Skylar opens her mouth to speak, but I cut her off. "I'll see you and Peter tomorrow."

Peter looks agitated. "Reign, we are—"

"Okay, we'll see you tomorrow," Skylar interrupts, cutting Peter off.

His scowl deepens. "Fine," he concedes.

I force a smile. "Great, I'll text you, Peter, since Sky's phone is broken."

He gives me a tight-lipped nod before we turn to leave. As we walk away, I can feel Peter's frustration radiating off of him. I know he's not happy about my sudden intrusion.

As we leave their home, we exchange confused glances. Did I just make matters worse or better for Sky? Shaking my head, I take my phone from my bag and send Nancy a few texts about the brunch I'm hosting tomorrow. All the ladies are invited, but only Love can make it.

Dion is fifteen minutes away. Now I'm rushing around my home, the smell of bleach and pine cleaner stinging my nostrils as I desperately try to make it look presentable. Due to my busy schedule in recent weeks, my penthouse has become quite untidy and needs a thorough cleaning; however, quickly straightening up will have to suffice. I'm thrilled with my thriving business, but why do all of the brides I book want their weddings around the same time? This reminds me: I must now include a clause in my contracts limiting bookings to two brides per day. This might cost me clients, but with Nancy and me handling every wedding detail, my well-being must come first. I cannot risk overworking myself or Nancy. This section should have already been in my contracts.

I don't know why I didn't think to include it before.

The other women I've hired assist with appointment scheduling, client scouting, and running errands: gathering dresses, accessories, and other items from various bridal stores. This gives Nancy and me the breathing room to brainstorm and design a unique wedding for each bride. My team is motivated to refer clients because each referral that leads to a booking increases their commission.

I have so much I need to tell Dion about Sky and the trip. *Oh shit!* The trip. He will probably be a little upset about the last-minute trip the girls planned. I've already sent Scarlette some money for food and will send her more for the party bus. Although Dion's earning more from acting in commercials, it's still insufficient to clear all his debts. I have no idea how badly in debt he is. I wish he'd let me help him. Because he is considered a low-level actor, he only receives a few thousand dollars for each commercial that airs. Still, I believe in my heart that he is truly talented, and that the right opportunity will present itself to him, and he *will* succeed.

The dishwasher hummed to a stop just as Dion quietly let himself in. His eyes bore into me, even though I hadn't looked behind me. Every hair on the back of my neck stands up, and a shiver runs down my spine. The electric pull between the two of us causes liquid to pool in my underwear and my nipples to peak. I can smell his delicious sandalwood cologne as his warm breath tickles the back of my neck, raising goosebumps on my skin. Dion's cock hardens and pokes me in the back. After a few beats, he spins me around, handing me a single black rose. *Damn!* My heart thumps against my chest like a trapped bird desperate for freedom. The way he makes me feel without even touching me is both exhilarating and frightening. There is no question, no doubt, no possibility of change—I am completely and irrevocably in love with Dion Atom James.

"My rose," he says in a deep and husky voice.

I inhale the rose's intense, spicy scent, a potent aroma that fills my nostrils with a seductive blend of warmth and zest. Each rose has a distinct fragrance, some sweet, some spicy, and all deeply hypnotic.

"I've missed you," he says, peppering tender kisses on my forehead, down the side of my neck, and down the outside of my arm until he reaches my elbow. He looks into my eyes intently, his large hands firmly but softly gripping both of my elbows. My lips naturally form a smile, but I feel guilty about being so focused on my job. Not to mention *Sky*.

"Dion, I'm sorry for everything and for not responding. I've been stressed out about the upcoming move and weddings, which left me with tunnel vision," I blurt out without taking a second to breathe. "I also need to secure clients for the summer and fall seasons soon."

Dion's expression softens as he listens to my explanation, his thumb gently caressing my cheek.

"And then there's Sky," I add, feeling a twinge of guilt as I twist and escape his grip to clear my mind. "She's in danger!"

His beautifully sculpted forehead is marked by the faintest lines, almost invisible against his handsome brown skin. He sighs, his broad shoulders droop slightly. His eyes dart back and forth, a thought crossing his face as he considers his response. "What happened to Skylar?"

My throat tightens as the weight of his question bears down on me. "I—I don't know," my heart swells.

"Reign?"

"I don't know, Dion. He's hurting her, that's all I know." The words tumble from my lips and scatter on the floor like rose petals.

Dion takes a deep breath, scratching the back of his head and running his hand through his hair. As the horrifying possibility that my sister is actually in trouble sinks in, a strangled sob rises in my chest, and I grapple with the implications.

Dion's eyes bore into mine. "That is a serious accusation, Reign. Did you speak to her? Did you see her?"

"Yes! The girls and I stopped by their place after brunch, and Dion, she seemed off. They both did..." My voice trails off as I consider sharing Sky and my unique silent communication with Dion, as well as confessing our childhood secret language. It sounds quite silly to say out loud.

Dion gently places his hands on my shoulders, the warmth

radiating through my tense muscles as he swipes away the imaginary bubble of stress that has clung to me. For a brief moment, I felt lighter and more at ease.

"She *what,* Reign? Did she say he is hurting her? You can tell me anything," he reassures me.

"We," I say hoarsely, a salty dryness coating my tongue and enveloping my mouth. I clear my throat and start over, trying not to freak out. "We communicated in our own way, and she pretty much told me she's in trouble and that he is hurting her." I watch as his expression changes. His eyes are wide and round like saucers, with a crease between his brows. "We're hosting a brunch tomorrow, and I'd like you to distract him while I talk to her alone."

Dion blinks a few times, as if he is thinking about something. "Reign, do you remember our disagreement in your office?"

Remembering our small tiff, I nod.

"I overheard Skylar on the phone saying she didn't want to do something or..." He shakes his head, trying to recall the incident. "Or something. Damn! I don't remember now!"

My brows pinch together in concentration. Who could she have been talking to? Darcy? My mother? Or was it, Peter? Maybe Shonda? *Urgh!* What didn't she want to do? *Maybe marry Peter.* But if that were true, why didn't she come to me and say something?

I've always done my best to be there for her whenever she needed me. What would make this time different? A knot forms in my throat, making it difficult to swallow. *My mother!* She sometimes kept Skylar away from me when we were kids out of fear that my behavior would have a negative influence on her.

As my hand clenches and releases around my throat, panic surges through me, my heart pounding rapidly and loudly in my chest.

"Reign, are you good? What's going on? What do you need?" Dion asks frantically.

Dark spots begin to dance before my eyes. I can't breathe. *I can't breathe.* What is happening to me? My vision is obscured by a blurry haze, and each shallow breath is a painful reminder of my fading strength.

Dion shakes me, his voice filled with urgency as he tries to snap me out of it. "Reign, focus on my voice. You're going to be okay," he reassures me, his hands gently gripping my shoulders. "Count to five with me. One, two, three, four, five."

I try to follow Dion's instructions. "One… two… three… four… five…" I repeat in a weak voice, trying to regulate my breathing. As I focus on Dion's voice and the counting, my panic slowly begins to subside, and the haze in my vision starts to clear.

"Come here," he says softly, pulling me into a comforting embrace. "You're safe with me."

I fall into his arms, melting into his thick and sexy form. I nuzzle my head deeper in the crook of his neck, the sandalwood scent enticing my senses.

"Did he hurt her?" I croak out, my voice barely audible. It's rhetorical. She already told me. *Or maybe he's not.* I second guess myself as Dion's arms tighten around me. Perhaps I got it all wrong. It's been decades since we've spoken that language or signaled one another. I don't know what to believe anymore.

The steady beat of Dion's heart, like a solid anchor holding me in place, calms my anxiety.

"I don't know, Reign, but we will figure it out." He lifts my chin up to meet his gaze head-on. "Together."

I nod, feeling reassured by his words.

"And Reign," he continues. "Our relationship is new for the both of us. We're on this ride together, so we must communicate, no matter how busy one of us is."

Nodding, I whisper, "hold me," burying my face in his chest, never wanting him to let go.

"Of course, baby," he murmurs, wrapping his arms around me protectively. "I've got you."

Chapter 5: Dion

Reign is curled up comfortably on the plush purple sofa, engrossed in a medium-sized black book, its cover adorned with red trimmings and smudged with gray markings that resemble smoke. The front cover features a vampire, and as I lower my head to read the title, "Rise of the Clan," the gold letters practically pop off the page. My brows shoot up in surprise because I've never seen her read anything other than wedding planning books. She is reading something that isn't her norm and completely lost in it. It must be good. The sight of her sitting motionless with her head buried in the book is sexy; the only sound is the delicate rustle of pages turning in the quiet room.

Sitting beside her, a playful tone in my voice, I ask, "What are you reading?"

She taps her finger on the pages and looks at me with a wide grin on her face. "I'm reading the third book in a trilogy written by my friend."

Folding my arms across my chest, "And here I thought I met all your friends," I tease, grinning when she pretends to swat at me.

"Excuse me, you don't know *everyone* I know," she says, mirroring my grin. "I do have other friends."

I blink twice.

She laughs and says, "Okay, Scarlette is my best friend. We are thick as thieves. And August is my girl. But I have other friends. We just don't see each other as often. You know how it goes once you're an adult."

Man, do I? Eddie is the only childhood friend I still have.

I peck her on the lips and say, "I guess I'll take a shower while you read. Do you want to watch a movie or something when I get out?"

I'm not really going to take a shower. I already took one, but she doesn't know that. I'm just trying to get her attention. My cock hasn't been inside her wet pussy for three weeks. I want, no, *need* to be inside her. I *have* to taste her. And please her.

She looks up from her book and points her finger to her chin, looking up at the ceiling. "Yeah, let's watch a movie on Netflix."

"Netflix and chill?" I suggest with a lighthearted tone, knowing damn well that I will be inside those wet folds before the movie even starts. There will be no mercy. I want her screaming my name for the next few hours.

She giggles and sets the open book to the side of her. "Sure, let's 'Netflix and chill,'" she says, gesturing air quotes.

"What's all that for?" I gesture air quotes back at her.

"When have we watched a movie on Netflix and actually chilled?" She asks, her voice thick with sarcasm.

When has anyone watched a movie on Netflix and actually chilled? It's not a real thing. Sex is always involved.

Knowing she's right, I drop my shorts to the floor, holding her gaze.

She parts her lips slightly. "What happened to you saying you were going to shower?"

I lift my shirt over my head, flexing my toned muscles, my gaze unwavering. "I already did."

She reaches to her right, grabs a bookmark, slips it into the book, and places it on the table next to the lamp. Her gaze never leaves mine. "Why did you lie about showering then?"

Oh yeah, I got her right where I want her. I lower my boxers to free my erect dick from its confinement. "I wanted your attention."

Reign watches me with hooded eyes, her long eyelashes fluttering. Her round, pouting lips are waiting to be filled by all of me. "Well, now you have it." She sits up on the sofa, slowly spreading her legs for me and biting her lower lip. She's tempting me. *Fuck!* Her nipples are hard, sexy brown pebbles that poke through the soft fabric of her top. Reign is a beautifully sculpted, brown-skinned queen created by God specifically for me.

"So, what movie are we pretending to watch tonight?" She purrs, her voice low and sultry.

Nodding toward the hallway, she stands up, taking my hand in hers and leading me to the room. It's been three weeks, and I'm going to take her in every position on that king-sized bed.

As she slowly removes some of her clothing, a deep fire burns within me, spreading throughout my entire being, surpassing the basic five senses—sight, hearing, smell, taste, and touch—she is igniting all of my senses, far exceeding anything we learned in school. Her mere presence disrupts my thermoception sense, causing my entire body to remain on fire, a blaze that only her touch can extinguish.

"Get on the bed," she commands, her voice a seductive melody that beckons me to surrender. She's not wearing a bra, and I can't help but grab a bud between my fingers before doing what I'm told.

Shit! She's taking control. While her taking charge is sexy, I will lead when the time is right.

I obey, acutely aware of the sandpaper-like dryness in my mouth. The only thing that can quench my insatiable thirst for her is the juice from her pussy. I intend to savor every drop of the sweet and tangy nectar that drips into my mouth as I worship her with my tongue.

Reign grasps my large and stiff dick in between her hands and peppers the entire length with soft kisses; her gaze locked on mine. Her soft lips on my cock are just enough to send me over the edge, and she knows exactly what she's doing with that sexy mouth. When she's done teasing me, she traces the same path with her tongue, and I let out a groan. *Fuuccck!*

She licks up and down from the root to the crown, twisting her lips into a satisfied and mischievous grin. I'm at her mercy. For now. Reign strokes my dick slowly, gradually increasing the pace; I lean back against the headboard as she jerks me off harder and faster.

"Ssshit," I stammer through the pleasure.

My admiration prompts her to pop my cock into her mouth, positioning it until she is completely full of me and slightly gagging. She bobs her head up and down, quickening the pace before slowing down to spit on it. She rubs the spit up and down, repeating the process. This woman will be my undoing. Reign expertly swirls her tongue around the tip of my dick, licking the split while massaging my balls. *Shit, that feels so fucking good!* My proprioception sense is coming into full effect. Words cannot express my body's awareness of the pleasure that Reign is giving me. I'm about to explode. My chest rapidly rises and falls as I surf the orgasmic wave she has me on. She pops my dick out of her mouth, causing my member to jerk and squirt loads of my warm, thick seed all over the bed.

The remnant of my come drips from her mouth. She wipes it away with the back of her hand, a satisfied smile playing on her lips as she looks up at me with lust-filled eyes. I come down from my high and fixate on her with a penetrating stare; she is lying on the bed with her legs open, ready for me. Her lacy gray thong serves as a barrier between me and the folds I so badly want to kiss. Lowering my head between her legs, I blow on her, and she lets out a small moan. I reach up and take one of her nipples between my thumb and pointer finger. Biting down on the flimsy material, I pull her underwear down with my teeth. Her pussy is mine to take, and as much as I want to pounce on her like a lion waiting patiently and silently in tall grass for its prey, I don't. Instead, I reach for her nightstand to get her vibrator. Reign's eyes widen like saucers in anticipation of my actions with her toy.

"Lick it," I command, holding the vibrator out to her.

She opens her mouth instantaneously and licks and sucks on the rubbery cock. Gently sliding the vibrator into her soaked pussy, I note how her body arches up and her legs spread even wider. I slowly pull it out and thrust it back in, causing her to yelp with delight. With dilated pupils and a throaty moan, she throws her head back, her hands gripping the sheets tightly. She writhes in pleasure as I rub her swollen clit with my thumb and repeatedly push the vibrator back and forth until it is saturated with her essence. Her body trembles in response to the powerful sensations of her first orgasm. Her fingers glide down her wet opening, gathering the juices, and she spreads the warm fluid along the edge of my mouth. I lick my lips slowly, a sly grin spreading across my face, deepening my left dimple.

"Make love to me," she pants.

"I intend to," I promise, turning on the vibrator and pressing it on her swollen nerve.

The pleasure overtakes her, and she rocks forward, grinding against the toy. She twists and explodes with pleasure, her eyes rolling to the back of her head. But I'm not done yet. Lowering my nose to her slick entrance, I inhale her scent. *Fuck!* My tongue darts out, licking, sucking, and paying close attention to her clit as she grabs my head and pushes me further into her pussy. I alternate between kissing, sucking, and licking. Nibbling to inflict a little pain and licking to subside it. Her lips emit pleased hums, followed by massive trembling. She lets out desperate and filthy sounds, as well as a few cuss words.

"Ahh. Yes! D-damn. Diooonnn!" she shouts, her body shaking uncontrollably. She tries to move, but I hold her in place, allowing her to ride out her orgasm on my tongue. She screams, and before she can react, I shove my cock into her hard and unwaveringly, with no warning. After a few thrusts, I turn her around on all fours to pound her from behind.

"Yes, Dion, yes, just like that!"

I pound in and out of her; the wet sounds of our love-making reverberating through the room. Fuck, she's so wet for me. She matches my pace, throwing that fat ass back while I slap and squeeze it, admiring it. It's so round and juicy. Just as I'm about to reach my peak, her body convulses with another orgasm. I pull out and pump myself, another load of seed spilling onto the bed. She flips on her back, eyes low and pleased.

Little did I know that when I agreed to play her fake boyfriend, it would lead us to this point where we are naked, content, and deeply in love with each other.

Wrapping my arms around her, we drift off to sleep. Our arrangement started as fake, but now it feels more real than anything I've ever experienced.

Sunday…

A high-pitched beep from Reign's phone alarm cut through the silence of my sleep, sending a rush of panic through me as I awoke. I've stayed overnight many times, but I've never heard that sound before. It wasn't the usual gentle melody; instead, it was a metallic screech that made me jump.

"What the hell, Reign?" I lightly shake her to turn the damn thing off.

She groggily reaches for her phone, squinting at the screen. "Sorry about that. I changed the alarm tone to make sure I woke up on time to order some groceries for brunch today." She apologizes, typing away on her phone and swiping through the apps.

Oh shit, I forgot about that.

I check my phone; I haven't checked it since I arrived at Reign's yesterday. I see two missed calls from my agent: one from yesterday and another from today. She did not leave a voicemail, but there were a few text messages. I updated her contact information to "Agent Tina" after signing a new contract and legally appointing her to be my agent. I was paying her off the books before. She's been good to me as long as I pay her on time.

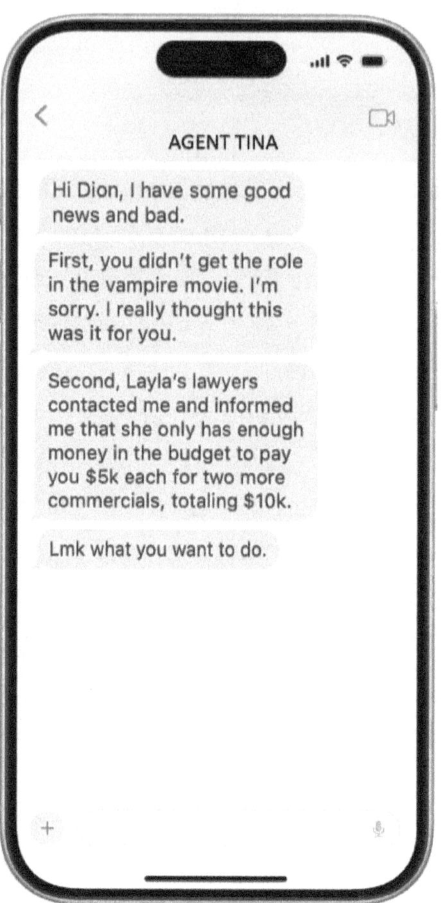

Is a ten-thousand-dollar budget for two commercials considered *good* news? I deserve to be paid more than that. At eight years old, I earned 20Gs for a single commercial that changed my life. I felt like the wealthiest person alive, holding that check in my hands. Yeah, at eight years old, I was already making more than what Layla is offering now.

My mom said, "Look, just cause you have some money now don't mean jack. You still going to college." Her "improper" tone was only used at home. Mom used her "proper" tone in public because a Black woman's voice was easily dismissed or ignored at the time. She often spoke softly to avoid being labeled as "ghetto" or the derogatory term "angry Black woman." I'm glad I wasn't around when my parents were children, dealing with segregation and other bullshit. I know for a fact I wouldn't have survived. Then again, this generation has seen its fair share of *fuckery*.

Same shit, different day or decade, depending on how you look at it.

"What's wrong?" Reign's gentle voice brings me back to reality.

Shaking my head, I reply, "You remember that vampire audition I went to?"

Her eyebrows furrow, and she nods her head yes.

"I didn't get the part," I sigh, my shoulders slumping in defeat.

Reign strokes my shoulder gently and says, "It's their loss, not yours. You'll get the next one."

"I hope so," I mutter, reclining back on the bed and typing a response to my agent.

"Are you okay?" Reign asks softly.

I nod, forcing a smile. "Yeah, I'm good."

She isn't convinced, but she doesn't press on.

She's up early on a Sunday, but when is she not? Tina is one of the hardest-working women I've ever known.

The suspense is killing me, Tina!

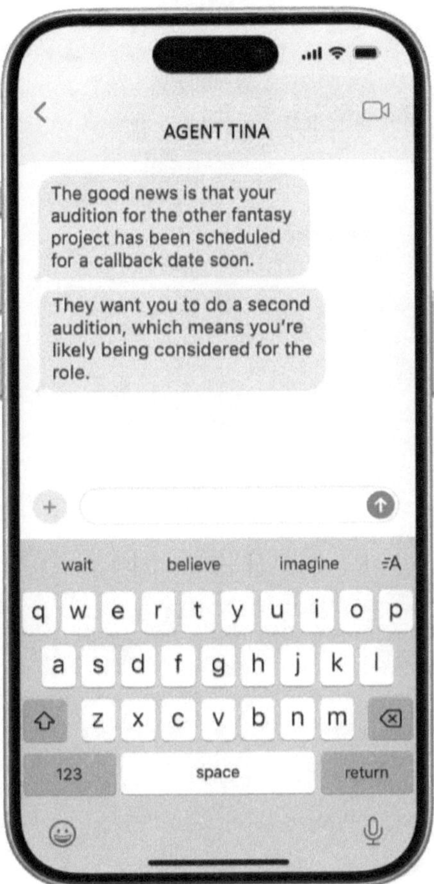

I don't want to get my hopes up, though Tina could be right. Why call me back for another audition if they weren't seriously considering me for the role? However, other actors have been called back for a second, and sometimes even a third audition and are still not hired.

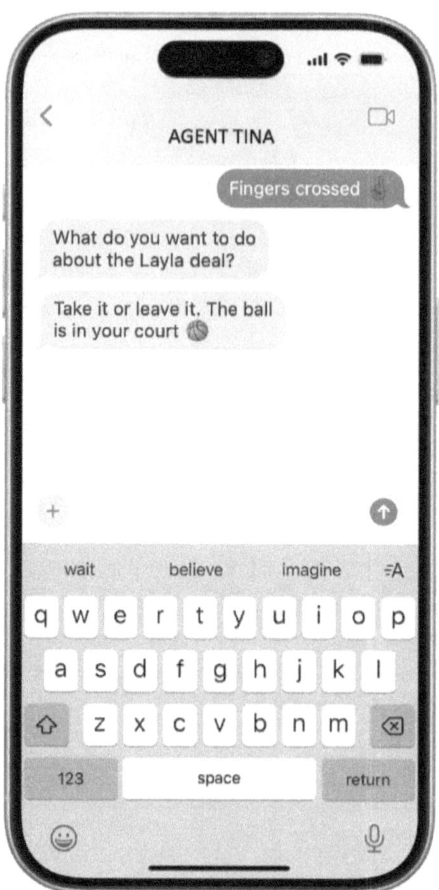

Ha! Tina made a basketball reference.

On a serious note, I haven't told Reign, Eddie, or my parents, but if I don't start making more money soon, I'll lose my apartment. The landlord has already begun the eviction process, his words sharp and cold as he detailed my past-due rent. Tearing up those checks last year put me in a hole. I was at least keeping up with rent when Reign was paying me to be her pretend boyfriend. I don't regret it, but my debt remains overwhelmingly high, with earnings from my commercials doing little to alleviate my financial burden. Forty-plus thousand dollars in debt hangs over me like a dark cloud. The system is rigged against people like me, favoring only a privileged few. *And you already know who I'm talking about.* Why the hell am I shelling out $2,200 for a tiny, one-bedroom, one-bathroom apartment? It doesn't make any sense. *Ten-thousand dollars is still better than nothing, I guess.*

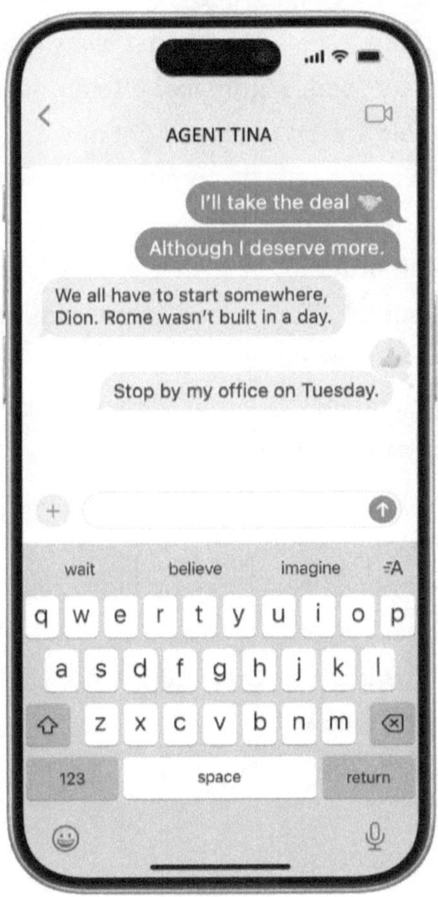

And with that, I set my phone on the nightstand. Damn, man, I really wanted that part. *When will I catch a break in this industry?*

"Any good news?" Reign asks, looking at me with hopeful eyes.

"If you call getting a call-back for another audition good news,"

I respond, slightly irritated. I catch my tone and quickly correct myself, "I'm sorry."

I had hoped to receive a phone call informing me that I had been given the part, not a second audition.

She nods sympathetically and leans over to press her lips on mine. "You'll get your big break soon. I know it."

My lips meet hers. "Thanks, babe."

"We have to clean," she adds, pulling away to start her day. Leaning back on the bed, I grimace. "Reign, it's eight in the morning. Why would I want to clean right now?"

She frowns, "We have guests coming over today. My friend Love and her boyfriend, Trent, will be here around 11 a.m. I just want things to be in order for brunch. Let's go, let's go!"

Reign's voice sounds like an endless stream of words. *We? Love? Trent? Who are these people?*

"Why are they coming so early? Haven't they heard of CP time?" I groan, covering my head with a pillow.

Reign pulls the pillow from my face. "Come on, Dion."

I bury my head again under the pillow. "Nah, seriously. They shouldn't be here until at least three or something."

"Not all Black people are late to events, you know."

"Every event I've been to, they are always late," I retort, my voice muffled by the pillow.

Reign takes the pillow from my face and throws it on the floor.

"Was that really necessary?"

She gives me a pointed look. "Yes, get up. Love and Trent are coming early to discuss the game plan."

I don't budge.

"Come on," she urges, shaking me by the shoulders.

Groaning, I reluctantly sit up, swinging my legs to the side of the bed and pulling on my boxers.

Her light brown eyes dart from me to the floor.

"What is it?" I ask, pulling a white T-shirt over my head.

She chews on her bottom lip, nervously fiddling with her cuticle. "Reign?"

"I… umm… made plans for us."

I untie my durag and toss it on the bed. "Yeah, this brunch, right?"

She hesitates before nodding, "Yes, but also... Valentine's Day plans."

Here I thought this brunch was the only plan she made for us. "What type of Valentine's Day plans?"

She shifts uncomfortably. "We're going to the Poconos for Valentine's Day weekend."

I freeze. Rooted to the ground like a tree, unable to move a muscle. I struggle to hide my irritation as I search for a calm and rational way to express my feelings. Reign planned a trip for us. It's sweet and thoughtful. *Right?* But also, expensive.

I knew when Reign and I decided to take our relationship to the next level that she had a lot more money than me. She is a strong and independent woman who does not rely on anyone or any man to care for her. She can get anything she wants on her own. That's what attracted me to her. It was also the fact that she could play ball, though she cheated that day in the gym by brushing her fingers along my abs. My lips form a faint smile. Her strength, courage, mind, work ethic, and body attracted me to her. She turns me on in more ways than one, causing my cock to twitch beneath the fabric of my boxers. I silently chastise my manhood. *This is not the time!*

"Dion?" Reign's voice is soft and hesitant.

Reign, my love, my rose. I know she means well, and I love her for planning something for us. I just wish she didn't have to pay for everything herself.

I heave a deep sigh. "What do I owe you for my half?"

"You owe me nothing. Don't worry about it."

I shake my head, feeling guilty for not being able to contribute financially. Reign's understanding and generosity make me love her even more, and while her words are sweet, they carry a sharp sting, much like bee venom.

"Reign, I will pay you back. I don't feel comfortable with you shouldering all the expenses."

She wraps her arm around my neck, brushing her fingers through my hair. "Dion, you would do the same for me if our situations were reversed. It's fine. I promise you."

I'm hopeful this won't be my forever. Living paycheck to paycheck is not sustainable. This can't be my life. I'm gifted. I know it in my heart. I live, breathe, and eat acting. It is my calling. Acting is what I was meant to do. One day the right opportunity will present itself. I just know it.

I plant a soft kiss on her forehead before moving down to her luscious and inviting lips. She tastes delicious, and my dick hardens.

"Babe, I have one more detail to add," she says, pulling away slightly.

Pushing down my cock in my shorts, "What is it?"

She feigns innocence, using my growing arousal to her advantage. "It's a couple's trip."

I groan inwardly, my lips pursed. "What?"

"The ladies and I planned a Valentine's Day trip for our men. Me, Scarlette, Love, August, and Kimi."

Why hasn't Eddie texted me about this yet? *He's just as whipped for Scarlette as I am for Reign.*

Reign looks up at me expectantly, her eyes searching for a

reaction.

Despite my initial annoyance, Valentine's Day in the Poconos with my girl is starting to sound pretty good.

Reign smiles as I kiss her lips, knowing she has won me over with the idea.

Chapter 6: Dion

I am met with stares from unfamiliar faces as I enter the kitchen. Reign's hips sway purposefully toward me, the soft clicking of her slippers on the wooden floor breaking the awkward silence. Damn, she is so fine. *Focus.*

She links arms with me, her light brown eyes crinkling at the corners. "Dion, I would like for you to meet Love and—"

"Trent Collins!" I exclaim, realizing who he is and cutting Reign off. "*The* Trent Collins, wow, what an honor to meet you!"

Trent stands to his full length from the bar stool to shake my hand.

"I guess my reputation precedes me," he says with a chuckle. "Nice to meet you, Dion."

Reign's eyes dart between me and Trent, sharp and assessing. "Am I missing something?"

Love's laughter bubbles up and spills into her cupped hands, and Reign's brow furrows in confusion.

I've been following Trent Collins's story for years, ever since the tragedy unfolded. Despite facing unimaginable hardships that few can understand, he stands before us as a self-made billionaire. If I remember correctly from an article, he was alone until he sought refuge with an extended family member. He has a photographic memory, recalling the details with unnerving accuracy, and graduated from high school at fourteen, showcasing his exceptional intelligence. In addition to owning Tren Corporation, one of New York's top security firms, he also develops technology to protect businesses from cyberattacks. There are rumors that he can make people disappear, but I wouldn't dare confirm or investigate such claims.

"Man, Trent, I feel awful about what you've been through, but it's inspiring how you've come from nothing and turned your business into a goldmine," I reply, kissing my fingertips.

Reign absentmindedly scratches the back of her neck, trying to gauge the situation.

"Reign, Trent is a billionaire!" I nearly combust.

In stark contrast to Trent's smug grin, she responds with a dramatic roll of her eyes and a shake of her head to show that she is unimpressed by money.

"Well, Love, this is my boyfriend Dion, who appears to be a fan of *your* boyfriend."

My gaze shifts between Love and Reign, and Love bites her lip to stifle a laugh. Very poorly, might I add. She extends her hand for a handshake. "Nice to meet you, Dion."

I'm not a fan of Trent Collins. I just *admire* him; there's nothing wrong with one man admiring another.

Nothing at all. *Nope.*

I take Love's hand, giving it a gentle shake. "Nice to meet you too, Love."

Reign claps her hands together, adopting a direct and assertive tone. "All right, now that we're all acquainted, let's cut to the chase.

I invited you guys here early to discuss my sister's... uh... dilemma with her husband."

Love glances at Trent, who raises an eyebrow. "Baby, something seemed off when we visited Reign's sister yesterday."

Reign nods, her expression serious. "Something was definitely off."

Trent crosses his arms. "Would you like me to conduct a thorough background check on her husband... what was his name again?"

"Peter Peterson," Reign and Love say in unison.

Reign continues, "Yes, that would be helpful. Thank you, Trent."

Trent nods, "Consider it done. I'll get started right away. Let me make a few phone calls."

Trent steps away from us, and Reign turns to Love. "What does he do?"

"Well, he—" I begin to say as Love starts to say, "So, he—"

We both pause and look at each other, amusement visible in Love's dark hazel eyes, and I gesture for her to tell his story.

Reign eyes me warily before redirecting her attention back to Love. I scratch the back of my head, feeling a bit sheepish. *Reign was obviously asking Love about her man, not me.* I'm curious about how they ended up together, though. According to an article about the rise of the Long Island billionaire, Trent Collins is in his forties and is completely dedicated to his work and the advancement of his company.

"Trent owns a security firm. He also designs software and tech for other businesses. Consider all things security, and he's your guy."

"Does he work for the government?" Reign asks.

"I can't confirm if he does or doesn't," Love replies, wiggling her brows.

"Interesting," I interject, and Reign shoots me a glare. I should stop talking.

"After the incident, he installed a cutting-edge, custom-designed security system in my apartment." Love clears her throat and continues, "The system is top-notch."

What incident?

"If anyone can dig up something that doesn't want to be found, it's him. My baby is amazing," Love gushes, a faint pink color tinting her light brown cheeks.

She is so in love with Trent. It's written all over her face. I wonder if this is how Reign and I look to others.

Reign smiles as she looks at Love, who is totally smitten with Trent, or her "baby," as she affectionately refers to him.

"That's great, Love! Sky and Peter will be here soon. I'm going to pry her away from Peter to get to the bottom of the warning she gave me yesterday."

We nod in agreement with the game plan.

Trent rejoins us in the kitchen. "My guy will have everything there is to know about this Peter Peterson by the end of the month," he assures us. "And I mean everything. Like if he took a shit last Thursday at 3 p.m., we'll know about it."

"What do we do if he is hurting her..." Reign trails off, placing her forehead in her hands.

My eyes harden, and Love and Trent exchange a knowing look.

"Come here," I say, pulling Reign into my arms. Her body melts against mine as she lets out a shaky breath. "We'll cross that bridge when we come to it."

Ding-dong.

Our gaze is drawn to the door, and unease slowly seeps into my bloodstream. I hope Skylar isn't in pain because of him. *God, please.*

Peter didn't strike me as someone who would mistreat Skylar, but appearances can be deceiving. Abusive men often put on a charming and caring front in public and show their true colors behind closed doors. There's a special place in hell for people like that.

My mother's advice was straightforward: never lay a hand on a woman and never tolerate abuse from a woman. The painful truth is that male victims of abuse are often dismissed, because how can a woman abuse a man? Not many people would believe that. Still, in my experience, most men refuse to admit to being abused. My mother's words echo in my mind. *"The best defense is to run unless they're armed; then I'd pray for God's protection and hire a lawyer."* Who would believe that a man of my size could be attacked by a woman half his size?

Love and Trent exchange another glance.

"Do we have a plan?" Trent's hushed voice breaks the tense silence.

"You and Dion keep Peter busy while I talk with my sister," Reign whispers.

"I will help in any way I can," Love offers.

Reign nods, then sprints to the door and unlatches it.

Time seemed to stand still as Peter and Skylar walked through the door, their faces uninviting and somber. Reign wants us to distract Peter. How? We barely spoke the last time I saw him at Reign's parents' house, maybe exchanged a few jokes here and there. He was mostly with Reign's cousins and their spouses: Shonda, the older sister, and her husband, Ronald; Raquel, the middle sister, and her husband, Allan; and last of the not-so-lovely bunch, Robyn and her husband—whatever his name is. They all seem to fit together perfectly, a clique of rude and entitled individuals. I didn't think much of the husbands when I first met them, and after the Christmas Eve party, it was enough for me. I haven't seen them since December, but that still isn't long enough.

I already had my hands full waiting to hear what Max, Reign's disgusting ex-boyfriend, had to say. When he found out that Reign and I were dating, although we were pretending at the time, he removed his son from the Little League team that I co-coach with Eddie. Typical. He told his ex-girlfriend that he didn't think I was a good enough coach for their son, so he should leave the team. *Liar!* The poor kid was devastated, but there was nothing I could say or do. I still don't understand how Mrs. Brown could stay in touch with a man who cheated on Reign. She was unaware that he had a six or seven-year-old son the entire time they were together.

Who does that?

Reign walked in on him fucking some chick bent over his bed, and he had the nerve to finish inside the woman before—I don't know—*apologizing* to Reign. I've said it before, and I'll say it again: why cheat? If you're not happy, just leave. I would never cheat on Reign. She deserves the world, and I hope that one day I'll be able to give it to her. She deserves so much for dealing with such a terrible family, a toxic ex-boyfriend, and the foulest mother. Which mother would stay in touch with an ex who clearly cheated on her child?

Back to Peter: I find it difficult to connect with him, and maybe there's a reason for that. Yet, I shouldn't judge him without getting to know him. Skylar and I also have a strained relationship. She was consistently rude, especially when she was with her friend Darcy. I'm so confused by her that I don't know what to think. However, she is still Reign's baby sister, and she loves her, so I will eventually grow to love her as well—and I will do whatever Reign asks of me in regard to her sister.

"Hi, Sky," Reign greets, opening her arms wide for an embrace.

Skylar hesitates for a brief moment; it's so subtle that I doubt anyone notices. She quickly recovers and steps into Reign's hug, but her body language remains guarded. She doesn't seem to want to be here, and Peter stands beside her, sticking out like a red apple in an orange field. Awkward. It reminds me of the first time I met Ronald, when Reign joked about him standing like a statue or was it Frankenstein? I can't remember now. Either way, Peter mimics the same rigid posture, looking weird and out of place.

Skylar and Reign have similar features, but Skylar's face is more oval-shaped, and her brown eyes are just a tad bit lighter. They look distant, like she's been through a lot. She doesn't seem as vibrant as before, and her demeanor is less rude. A silent question arises and takes shape within the confines of my thoughts.

What's going on with you, Sky? If only she could hear my unspoken concern and share what's been happening. We lock eyes for a split second, only for her gaze to shift away almost immediately. Her black curly hair is styled in a sleek high bun, emphasizing the soft baby hairs that frame her face. She's dressed in all black, with a pearl necklace around her neck to match the pearls elegantly displayed on her wrist. The light from the oversized windows shines brightly on her finger, making the diamond ring sparkle so brightly that it is nearly blinding. Peter is dressed in a sharp black suit with crisp fabric, and his dark brown spiky hair has grown out since I last saw him. Are they going to or coming from a funeral? What the hell?

"Hey, man," I say, walking up to Peter, who extends his hand for a firm shake. "How's it going?" I ask, trying to drum up a conversation.

His emerald eyes quickly move between faces, scanning the room intently. A brief silence hangs in the air, and you could hear a pin drop before he responds.

"Good, and you?" He replies with a tight smile; his piercing gaze fixed on Reign as she and Skylar disappear down the long hallway to her bedroom.

Something is definitely up with this creepy dude. I look back at Trent, who silently nods in understanding.

"Hello, my name is Trent, and this is my girl, Love," he says, resting his hand on the small of Love's back.

Love smiles politely. "Hi, again."

Again? Oh yeah, they sort of met yesterday.

Peter turns his attention back to Trent and Love, a calculating expression on his face. "Nice to meet you both," he says, extending a hand to Trent, his gaze flickering back down the hall.

"How about we get started?" I suggest diverting Peter's attention away from the hallway. "Are you hungry?"

Peter shakes his head, still focused down the hall, and responds in a distracted tone, "No, I'm fine."

I exchange a concerned glance with Trent as we follow Peter's gaze back down the—you guessed it—*hallway*. I don't know how Reign expects me to distract him when I can't even get him to look at me.

Love hands me a glass of mimosa.

"Thank you," I say, nodding my head in appreciation.

She hands one to Trent, who accepts it with a grateful grin and kisses her cheek. His green eyes sparkle with an affection as bright as the summer sun. Love beams at him, her own eyes reflecting the same adoration. She pours another mimosa and offers it to Peter, who declines with a shake of the head.

"Oh! I insist," Love says, holding out the glass. "We're not going to drink all this ourselves." She points to the three unopened bottles on top of the granite countertops. Reign bought four bottles of champagne and orange juice.

"Love, how about you join the rest of the ladies for a chat while the men discuss business?" Trent takes the mimosa from her and hands it to Peter, who reluctantly accepts.

Perhaps Trent is better at distracting him than I am because I'm about ready for him to leave—*weird ass.*

"I'll leave you boys to your boring business talk," Love says, walking away to join Reign and Skylar in the bedroom.

Peter grudgingly follows us to the sofa but remains fixated on where Love just disappeared. What the hell is his problem? His relentless staring is making my skin crawl. If he really is abusing Skylar in some way, he is the lowest of the low. A scoundrel, a repugnant creature that ought to be crushed.

Woah! Where did that come from?

This mood reminds me of the part I was auditioning for.

And they thought I wasn't good enough.

Peter sips the mimosa. "I don't usually drink these," he says, eliciting an awkward laugh.

Trent nods, his Haitian accent thick as he responds, "Me neither, but hey, whatever my *Cheri* wants, she gets."

Where did that come from? I discreetly google the word "*cheri*" on my phone, which translates to *sweetheart.* I downloaded the Translate app to help me understand when Scarlette switches between English and Spanish during our conversations.

Raising my glass, I toast, "To pleasing our ladies."

"Cheers to that," Trent says, he and Peter clinking their glasses against mine.

"So, Peter," I begin, trying to steer the conversation to small talk. "What's been going on with you? We haven't seen you two in a while. Since the Christmas Eve party, actually."

Peter takes another sip before replying, "Yeah, just been busy with work and stuff."

Trent sets his glass on the lavender coaster, leaning back on the sofa. "What do you do for a living?"

That's a great question. I know he's wealthy, but what does he do exactly for a living? I wait for his response too.

He clears his throat before answering, "I'm a partner at Peterson & Traymen, but I took a few months off to spend with my beautiful wife."

Didn't he just say he was "busy with work" not too long ago, or am I losing my mind?

"That must be demanding," I comment, trying to maintain the facade of casual conversation.

"It can be," Peter replies, standing to his feet. "I should go check on Skylar."

"Reign is probably showing Sky and Love some of the dresses she ordered for her upcoming wedding events," I lie with ease through my teeth.

He chuckles dryly, "Is that right?"

"Yeah, man, you know how women are. They love showing off their designer shit," I say, rubbing my chin hairs.

"Love is always showing her *bestie*, Kimi, shoes, accessories, all the shit I don't care about," Trent adds.

Peter continues to stare at the hallway before he finally nods and sits back down. A prolonged and excruciatingly uncomfortable silence ensues, forming a palpable barrier in the conversation.

"So," I clear my throat, my voice like a sharp-pointed knife cutting through the tension. Trent and Peter look at me expectantly. "How about that couple's trip the women planned?"

"Love won't stop talking about it," Trent remarks, shaking his head. "Are you and Skylar joining us?"

I glance at Peter, who avoids my eyes. "No, we're not going. I'm going back to work on that Monday, so we won't be able to make it."

Trent speaks up, "That's a shame. It would have been nice to have you both there."

I force a smile, the stillness growing heavier. This conversation is going nowhere. Peter's unsettling demeanor and responses are making me uncomfortable. Things are chill and easy between Eddie and me; we've been cool for years. I'm not getting anywhere with Peter; his brows are furrowed in a deep scowl, his lips curled into a sneer, and I can practically feel the hostility emanating from him. You know that fake smile you give when the photographer yells, "Say cheese!?" That's precisely the expression plastered on his face, strained and artificial.

This is so awkward. How do women do this? Come up with topics and chat about them forever.

I look at Trent, who is openly scrutinizing Peter, trying to figure out his motives. Trent, see, I like him. He's a cool dude. I can see us becoming friends—or at least great acquaintances.

Trent and I exchange a glance, silently communicating our mutual discomfort.

"So," I start again. This seems to be the only word I can think of to begin a conversation right now. Peter doesn't seem to want to talk—I'll talk to Trent instead. "How did you and Love meet?"

Trent's eyes light up, and he lets out a chuckle. "Love and I didn't start out liking one another; we couldn't stand each other."

My interest is piqued, and in my peripheral vision, I see Peter still staring down the hallway toward Reign's bedroom with a strange expression.

"Nah, really?" The way those two look at each other, eyes full of adoration, you'd never guess they got off on the wrong foot.

"Yep, she was in a bit of a bind. I offered her my services, but she was a tough client. She did not listen to any of my advice."

My eyes widen. "You two started in a business relationship too?"

Trent mirrors my expression. "*Too?* Did you and Reign have a business relationship as well?"

A small smile tugs at my lips. I recall Reign describing our situation as a *professionalship*, a word she made up.

"You could say that. I'm an actor, and Reign hired me to be her boyfriend."

Peter's eyes widen in shock, and a cold dread grips me as I realize the mistake I made. August and Calvin learned of our arrangement at Skylar and Peter's wedding, but Reign has yet to tell Skylar.

I quickly backtrack, trying to cover up my slip up. I add hastily, "We were in a pretend relationship, and then we ended up falling in love for real."

That didn't help.

Peter returns his attention to the hallway, now uninterested.

"Those Brown women are something else," I say, jerking my head at Peter, who gives a slight nod and returns his gaze to that damn hallway.

"*Vre lanmou,*" Trent says in a thick Haitian accent.

I nod, not knowing what he said but trying to play it cool.

Trent grins, "It means true love in Creole."

"Oh, nice. You speak more than one language?"

"Five, actually. I'm mixed and grew up learning more than one language. My primary language is English. Creole is my second."

I rub my chin hairs, impressed. "That's cool, man. I did read somewhere that you were Haitian."

Trent chuckles, "Yeah, I am. My mother was Dominican and Black. My father was Haitian."

Taking in the information, I furrow my brow slightly.

"I need to use the restroom," Peter says abruptly, leaving the conversation.

Trent and I exchange uneasy glances, discreetly watching Peter's retreating figure. He must pass Reign's bedroom to get to the bathroom, and I'm sure he can feel our eyes on his back. When I first met him last year, I thought he was an okay dude, but I don't know now, something feels off about him.

Chapter 7: Reign

Skylar's brown eyes are distant, clouded with unshed tears. What is going on with my baby sister? The once bright and playful glimmer in her eyes has vanished, now dull and lifeless. She is not the same woman as she was several months ago. She seemed different at the Christmas Eve party, but I was too focused on Max and his new wife, and my bitch of a mother to notice. I'm an awful big sister. I promised Skylar I'd be there for her when we were little. Where was I when she needed me the most? Our bond remained strong, defying my mother's attempts to keep us apart. Skylar's incredible personality shines through when she is not surrounded by our dysfunctional cousins or the woman who raised us. The person in front of me was not my sister; it was her ghost—a stranger with chilling and empty eyes that froze me still for a beat.

A cold dread creeps into my bones as unfamiliar arms tremble around me, like a silent plea for help. Her touch felt alien, sharply contrasting with the familiar comfort of my sister, Skylar Brown.

Dion steps forward, firmly shaking Peter's hand to assert himself. I quickly steer Skylar away to have a private conversation, locking arms with her for support as we walk to my bedroom. I open the door to my walk-in closet, and usher her to the elegant accent chair at the center, closing the door behind us for privacy. Leaning my head against the wooden door, I collect my thoughts before posing my question.

"Sky?" A bubble forms in the pit of my stomach, obstructing my ability to speak clearly.

Skylar looks up from her lap, her eyes silently pleading for me to stop. Her fear reflects on me, causing my own anxiety to spike. She doesn't want me to ask the dreaded question.

"What the hell is going on with you and Peter?" The question tumbles out in a burst of high-pitched panic, like a bird startled into flight.

Skylar nervously picks at her cuticles. "Nothing, we're fine," she mumbles, not looking up to meet my eyes. Her statement lacks sincerity and conviction.

"You're lying, Sky. I asked if he was hurting you yesterday, and you said yes! *Ba-es* means yes. Did I misunderstand you? Is he really hurting you?" My voice cracks with emotion, and I'm losing the little patience that I have.

Skylar avoids eye contact, fidgeting with her hands.

"Are you going to sit there and say nothing to me?" There is no way I misunderstood her. He's hurting her, and she is unwilling to admit it. "You can tell me the truth, Sky. He can't hear you from my closet."

She remains silent, playing with her cuticles. When she lied as a child, she would nervously play with her cuticles. Now, as an adult, she continues to do the same habit. I know she's lying, but I don't know how to approach her when she won't confide in me.

The door creaks open, and Skylar flinches, both of us turning to see Love standing in the doorway. Skylar visibly relaxes as Love closes the door behind her, her fruity perfume wafting in the air.

Love says, "Hey, guys. What's going on in here?"

Skylar quickly looks away.

"I'm not getting anywhere with her," I snarl under my breath.

Love gives me a knowing look before turning to Skylar and gently asking, "Hey Sky, I know we don't know each other very well, but from the few times we've met, you didn't seem like yourself yesterday. Is everything okay?" Love's tone is gentle and reassuring, like a soft breeze on a warm day.

My sister gives Love a weak smile, something she hasn't done with me. I don't know if Love instinctively understands how to approach Skylar or if it's just her natural warmth that puts people at ease.

"I'm sorry if I gave you the impression that something was wrong. I am a newly married woman navigating my life. Everything is different, but I can assure you both that my relationship with Peter is peachy."

Love's smile falters slightly, and we exchange knowing glances. *Peachy?*

What the hell does that even mean? *Peachy?*

I repeat the word in my head, trying to make sense of it.

Who uses the word peachy?

"Sky, are you—"

A loud pounding on my bedroom door startles Skylar to her feet and cuts off my question. I glance at Love, who looks just as scared as I am.

"Skylar, are you ready to go?" A cold, sharp voice, dripping with malice like a poisoned dagger, carries from behind my bedroom door to my closet. *Peter.* His brash, obnoxious tone is like nails on a chalkboard.

Skylar's face pales, and she quickly races to the door to open it, avoiding eye contact with Love and me.

My heart sinks to the pit of my stomach as I watch her rush to the door with such haste, as if any delay would have dire consequences. I exchange a worried glance with Love before following Skylar out of the closet.

Peter's sharp, green eyes bore into me with a coldness that chills me to the bone. "Skylar, are you ready?" He repeats impatiently.

I can see the tension in Skylar's body as she nods quickly.

How do I play this?

What do I do?

What can Skylar do?

Skylar follows Peter's brisk strides down the hallway. Love and I follow closely behind to the living room.

Dion's worried face appears as we enter the room, his eyes darting between Skylar and Peter. Peter glances back at me, a mocking smile playing on his lips. "Reign, will you be at the family dinner next Saturday? We haven't seen you at a family dinner since before the wedding." He says, in a deliberate and sarcastic tone that sharply contrasts with his charming and friendly demeanor before marrying my sister.

Dion tightens his jaw and creates a much-needed barrier that separates Peter and me. "Reign and I will be there," he interjects firmly. "See you both then." Dion nods at the door, casting a pointed look at Peter.

We will?

Peter dips his head low, giving an imaginary tip of the hat, his smirk wide as he takes Skylar's hand and leads her to the door. Skylar exits my penthouse without a word or a glance, the echo of her clicking heels slowly fading into the distance.

"How badly is he hurting her?" I ask no one in particular.

"He's abusing her, either verbally or physically," Love mutters, her expression grim.

"I didn't notice any bruises on her," I add, furrowing my brow.

"How would you? She was wearing long sleeves and dress pants," Trent points out, scrolling through his phone.

Love wraps her arms around Trent's lower half. He is a full foot taller than she is. He has to be at least six feet two—no, taller.

"I was thinking of contacting my cousin Dante to see if we could get some eyes on that man," Trent suggests. "Reign, do you want my company and me to get involved?"

I gaze up at Dion with anticipation, my heart racing in my chest.

"You saw what I saw. We can't just sit back and do nothing."

Dion's words resonate with me, and Trent looks to me for confirmation. My head bobs up and down as my mouth fails to form the word he is looking for—*yes*.

"I'll contact Dante," Trent says firmly, tightening his hold on Love's waist. He adds, "You ready?"

Love nods and grabs her and Trent's belongings. "I'll see you soon," she says, hugging me and Dion.

"We will get his ass, I promise," Trent says, hugging me. He turns to Dion and gives him a fist pound. "Good meeting you, man."

"You too. We should definitely link up."

"For sure," he replies, before turning to leave with Love.

Leaning against the door, I meet Dion's gaze, his outstretched arms inviting me into his warm embrace. I relax into his form, comforted by the familiar scent of sandalwood that surrounds me, bringing a moment of peace.

Saturday

February 8th, 2025

I sense an impending doom in the air—so severe and detrimental that it seems almost inevitable—and I feel completely overwhelmed and powerless.

Dion stands tall and beautifully sculpted in front of the floor-to-ceiling mirror, wearing a blue button-up dress shirt and black slacks. His gaze meets mine in the reflection, noticing the distress in my eyes. "Are you okay?" He asks, his voice smooth like butter.

His question hangs in the air for a few beats before I muster a response. "Sure."

He turns to face me, his light brown eyes boring into mine. "Reign, we don't have to go if you don't want to."

"No, it's okay. I'm okay. I want to go. I *need* to go. You heard the way Peter asked if I would be there."

"Yeah, like he didn't—"

"Want me there." I finish his sentence while slipping on a royal blue half-shoulder top to complement my black dress pants.

The soft cotton top and cool silk pants feel good on my skin. I smooth down the fabric, checking out my back view in the mirror. Dion and I love to match when we attend events together.

He gently takes my hand and twirls me to face him. "Damn, that ass is—"

"Please do not finish that sentence," I playfully scold him, swatting his hand away.

He flashes his infamous sexy grin, revealing his left dimple, and licks his lips, weakening my knees.

"And please do not give me that look. We have to go."

"We could get a quickie in before we leave," he suggests, smacking my ass.

I roll my eyes, knowing he's only half serious, and request an Uber to the Upper West Side. In less than thirty minutes, we arrive at my parents' five-story, six-bedroom lavish home. My bitch of a mother would not be here if my father had not dedicated his life to medicine, eventually becoming one of the top pediatric surgeons in the tristate area.

"You got this," Dion whispers in my ear, squeezing my hand before we walk through the front door.

Two people greet us at the door, taking our jackets and hanging them on the coat hanger.

"Right this way," says a young woman, leading us to the grand dining room where my parents and everyone else are already seated.

All conversations cease, and a hush falls over the room as all eyes turn towards us in silence. Dion squeezes my hand reassuringly as we move to the far end of the table, closest to the second exit and away from my mother, ex-boyfriend, and his wife.

My mother smiles tightly, a fiery edge sharpening in her tone as she greets us, "So nice of you to finally join us. It's been what? A few months since you last *graced* us with your presence." She pauses for dramatic effect, her eyes narrowing as she adds, "What brings you into the company of our divine presence?"

Divine presence? Her passive-aggressive comment pierces through me like a burning blade, igniting a furious inferno within me.

Dion whispers so only I can hear, "Reign. My rose. Remember why we are here."

I take a deep breath. His voice, a quiet, steady stream, caresses my ears, drawing my bubbling anger back in.

"I thought the door was always open—or was I mistaken?" I quip back with a poised smile.

She stands to her feet, her icy brown eyes locking onto mine. "You are our daughter. You are always welcome here. Please have a seat." Only my mother can make those words sound like a threat.

We settle into our seats. Skylar and Peter sit across from me, Raquel and Allan to my left, with Shonda and Ronald beside them. Their parents, Aunt Shirl, and her husband are seated beside my ex's wife and her asshole husband. Aside from my father and Dion, the room is full of arrogant pricks.

I look at my dad across the table and quietly mouth, "Hi, Daddy."

He warmly smiles back at me. I know he's on my side, no matter what. I'm Daddy's little girl. We've always had a strong bond, but I haven't seen him in months because of my unpleasant and hostile feelings toward the rest of my family.

I try to meet Skylar's gaze, but she avoids eye contact. Peter gives me a smug look, and I resist the urge to roll my eyes.

The aroma of freshly baked bread fills the air as waiters and waitresses politely take our orders. My parents hired Lyric, one of NYC's new and upcoming private chefs, to prepare our meals for tonight. The main course consists of crispy duck breast, accompanied by a choice of two sides: roasted root vegetables or Brussels sprouts. I choose Brussels sprouts, and Dion chooses roasted root vegetables. Next, we select the starchy side dishes. The side dish options include wild rice, farro—a nutty grain that complements duck meat well—and creamy mashed potatoes known as potato puree.

"Which one are you getting?" Dion asks, looking up from the

menu.

"Hmm… I'm going with the rice."

He nods and tells the waiter he would like the wild rice too.

The room buzzes with hushed conversations and cold glares. Dion and I are mostly silent, an awkward stillness while we wait for our food.

I take a long sip of my ice-cold water, the condensation clinging to the glass. Meanwhile, Raquel eyes me warily, holding a glass of bubbly liquid in her hand. She clinks her glass two times. "I would like to take this opportunity to congratulate Shonda and Ronald on their pregnancy."

She's pregnant? I hadn't even noticed. The room erupts in a storm of applause, peppered by excited murmurs of "congratulations" from everyone except Dion and me.

"Mind your manners," my mother warns, her tone venomous.

I bite into the warm, soft bread, tuning out her words, unsure who she's speaking to.

"Reign," she says sharply, causing me to look up from my bread.

"You are being rude," she scolds, her gaze hardening.

I swallow hard, folding my arms on the table. "How so?" I'm challenging her by placing my elbows on *her* dinner table—*she didn't pay for it herself.*

My mother's lips thin in annoyance. "Your cousin is pregnant. You need to congratulate her," she scolds, exaggerating each syllable.

I couldn't care less about it. I don't want to participate in the charade.

"It's okay, Aunt Loretta. You know Reign doesn't have any class," Shonda remarks.

I roll my eyes at her comment.

"That's why she's with a broke, failed actor," Raquel adds,

nodding toward Dion.

I clench my jaw, heat rising to my cheeks.

"She paid him to pretend to be her boyfriend," Robyn smirks.

My mouth falls open at Robyn's comment. *How do they know?*

I turn to Dion, feeling exposed and humiliated, and guilt is written all over his face. He looked almost as white as a ghost.

"How do they know?" I whisper-yell at him.

Dion opens and closes his mouth.

"How pathetic is she to hire a boyfriend?" Shonda snorts.

"And still pretend," Raquel chimes in.

"So sad," Robyn adds.

Dion finally speaks up, standing tall and firm. "I'm not pretending to be Reign's boyfriend! We are in a relationship, and I love her!"

Shonda rolls her eyes, unimpressed. "Sure, you do," she scoffs. Raquel and Robyn exchange knowing glances, clearly not convinced.

Peter sits back in his chair, watching the drama unfold with a smirk. Skylar looks down at her lap. My mother looks at me with scorn, while my father offers me a sympathetic smile. Everyone else in the room falls silent, stunned by the revelation.

"Believe what you want, but it's the truth," Dion adds. "I'm not here to convince anyone."

Peter chuckles under his breath, and Skylar remains silent.

Raquel doesn't buy Dion's words, shaking her head. "Give it a rest. Peter told us Reign hired you to be her boyfriend. The act is up."

Shonda throws her hands up. "Yeah, give it a rest. You should probably be paid for overtime," she quips, eliciting a few chuckles from the group. "No one in their right mind would be with someone so pathetic. Reign sucks."

"How could you stoop so low?" My mother chimes in, laughing in my face. "What a shame not being able to find true love without having to pay for it." Her laugh grates against my already wounded pride; the shrill sound makes me feel even more humiliated.

Everyone, except for my father and Dion, laughs at my expense, even Skylar.

Sucking my teeth, I look at their mocking faces. As coldly as possible, I respond, "At least I can pay him with my hard-earned money rather than waiting for an allowance."

The room falls silent.

My mother stands up abruptly, seething with anger. "What did you say to me?"

Standing tall, I hold my ground and meet her furious gaze with defiance. I shout at the top of my lungs, "At. Least. I. Can. Pay. Him. With. My. Hard-earned. Money." *Bitch*.

My mother's face turns red with anger, slamming her hands on the table. The silverware clatters loudly, and the glasses emit a sharp rattle. "You ungrateful child! How dare you speak to me like that in my own house! I'm so sick of your entitled—"

My father intervenes. "That's enough, dear. You need to relax."

"No, let her finish," I insist, unflinching at my mother's outburst.

"You are a burden to this family," she spits out, shaking my resolve and severing me in two.

My father's eyes soften as he looks at me, caught between his loyalty to his wife and his love for his child.

"A burden, huh?" I retort with a steely gaze.

"Yes! A *burden*," my mother repeats. "I had no idea what it was like to truly love a child until I had Skylar."

I feel a sharp pang of hurt at her words, realizing the harsh reality that my own mother, the one who brought me into this world, never loved me.

That hurt cuts deep and turns my heart to ice. Raw anger and fiery heat consumed me, unleashing an uncontrollable wave of fury. Turning to face my father, I let out a roar that cut my throat: "That man—sitting at your table—that you have always welcomed into your home—molested me twenty years ago!"

Chapter 8: Reign

Have you ever noticed how a beautiful sunny sky can suddenly darken to an eerie greenish hue?

The air suddenly shifts, carrying the scent of pine and damp earth, along with a bone-chilling gust of wind. A monstrous roar, heavy with the threat of destruction, drowns out all other sounds in that fleeting, suspended moment.

A massive, dark funnel cloud appeared in the dining room, resembling a forming tornado. Its terrifying presence resonated with a low, guttural rumble, signaling its readiness to destroy everything in its path.

The storm was me.

Fueled by rage, I unleash my fury, hurling the wine glass with such force that it shatters against the wall. Dion tries to take my hand, but I jerk away, feeling his touch linger on my skin like a phantom. A hushed silence fills the room, broken only by the quiet echo of the shattered glass falling to the ground, and all eyes are on me.

"Have you lost your ever-loving mind!?" My mother shouts.

I stand there, chest heaving, breaths short and angry, body

trembling with pent-up rage.

"Reign?" My father's voice is stern and sorrowful. He never calls me Reign unless it's serious. To him, I've always been Amara, a name passed down from his mother. I look at him, my eyes blazing with emotion. His gaze shifts from me to my mother and then to *him*.

The monster.

The repulsive, insidious asshole who had stolen my innocence all those years ago.

"William," Dad says in a low, dangerous tone. My father's eyes bore into him with a look that could cut through steel.

"I—I have no idea what she's talking about," he stammers, his eyes darting nervously between my father and me.

"Lies!" I let out a deafening scream, causing the kitchen staff to stop dead in their tracks, clinging to their glasses in terror as all movement ceased.

His face visibly pales, beads of sweat forming on his forehead. "I—I didn't do anything. I—I swear, I didn't touch her."

My father's fists are clenched at his sides; his jaw is tight with anger. "Then explain why she is accusing you of molesting her, William. Explain that!"

That man's mouth opens and closes like a fish out of water; the truth caught in his throat.

"Tell me what happened, Reign," my father asks, gently but firmly.

My eyes flicker between my aunt's husband and my father, the tension in the room thickening with each passing second. "When I was a little girl and you worked overnight on weekends, I'd spend the night at their house," I say, my voice quivering as I point to my Aunt Shirl and cousins. "One night, while they were sleeping, I went to the bathroom to pee, and he walked in on me. Instead of leaving like a normal person, he stood there watching me and instructed me to clean myself slowly."

My father's face contorts with rage as he lunges forward, grabbing that man by the collar and shoving him against the wall. "You sick bastard," he growls with disgust.

Dion says with a steely glare at my aunt's husband, "She's not finished."

My father tightens his grip on my aunt's husband's collar before releasing and pushing him away.

"He forced me to lie down while he examined my private parts, touching and staring at me as if I were a piece of meat. He—"

Shonda interrupts abruptly, shouting, "No, I will not stand here and listen to these false accusations against my father! You are a liar!"

Ronald pleads with Shonda, "Please remain calm for the baby's sake."

She points an accusatory finger at me. "This bitch is lying! I will not let you slander my father's name!"

"Shonda, please don't let that woman upset you or the baby," Robyn begs.

"This can't be true," Raquel whispers, her face pale and her eyes wide with disbelief.

Aunt Shirl tries to shout, "My husband never touched you," but her weak and unconvincing voice falters.

Emotions overwhelm me, causing tears to well up in my eyes, blurring my vision and making it difficult to see. "I am not lying," I choke out, my voice cracking. "He molested me. He touched me, and then he..." I trail off, looking at Dion, who nods for me to continue. "He jerked off in front of me, letting his fluids drip on my skin." I close my eyes, trembling as I relive the traumatic memory.

Skylar gasps in horror, covering her mouth with her hand, as

Peter stands next to her, eyes wide and mouth agape. My ex and his wife quietly leave the table, their faces tight with shock. Dion's jaw clenches in anger, and tears threaten to escape from my father's eyes.

Regret for my silence binds my heart like a barbed wire, consuming me with its bitter taste. Sadly, many women are victims of assault and suffer in silence, never sharing their experiences.

I'm one of them.

And, whether or not my sister admits it, she is too. I fiercely guarded my pain and vulnerability to avoid appearing weak, burying it deep inside me in a misguided effort to erase it forever.

Not anymore.

Today, I reclaim my power.

My strength comes from breaking free from the chains he tried to bind me with. *You no longer have control over me!* My therapist would be proud of me.

"Leave. Now." Dad's voice is as cold as ice, allowing no room for discussion.

"What!?" My cousins, aunt, and mother all speak at once, their voices overlapping.

"Get the fuck out of my house! And don't ever show your faces here again!"

I stand there, shocked by the volume of my father's tone. I've never heard him raise his voice like that before.

"Steven, you can't be serious!" My mother bellows.

"I am dead serious, Loretta. This is my house, and I won't tolerate any abuse towards my daughters!"

"We are family, Steven!" My mother screeches.

"I don't care, Loretta. If you or anyone else harm our daughters, they are not welcome here!"

In my peripheral vision, I notice Peter loosening his tie in response to my father's words. *What has you so choked up, Peter?*

The intensity of my mother's glare makes me flinch. If looks could kill, I would be dead on the spot.

"Did you know?" Dad asks my mother, his voice nearly an octave higher.

My mother's face falls flat, her eyes shifting anxiously from me to Skylar, who avoids her gaze and shakes her head in silent disapproval. I never told Sky about this.

"Answer me, Loretta. Did. You. Know?"

"Uh, yes! But—"

"Get out!" Dad's voice is sharp and cutting, causing my mother to stumble backwards in shock.

"What?" She blinks rapidly, clutching her imaginary pearls.

"Get out of my house, Loretta. I can't believe you hid this from me!"

"But Stevie…" She reaches out to touch my father's arm, dipping her voice low in an attempt to seduce him into forgiveness, but he remains unmoved.

"Get. Out. Of. My. House." Dad spits through gritted teeth. "I want you and your family gone before I call the police."

My mother straightens her shoulders and gathers her composure. She takes a deep breath and tries another approach. "Stevie, let's talk about this."

"There is nothing to talk about, Loretta. I've sat back and ignored you and Amara's bickering for far too long. This is unforgivable. You knew, and you lied to me for years. She is your daughter, for fuck's sake! I can't even look at you!"

My mother extends her hand, but he brushes past her without a second glance, stomping out of the dining room in a trail of seething rage. She is left stunned.

I stand motionless, *paralyzed*. Dion is beside me, offering silent support by gently squeezing my hand. My cousins, aunt, and her husband rush out of the dining room, their hushed voices and scrutinizing stares making me uneasy as I remain in my spot, bewildered.

My mother slowly turns toward me, a dark scowl on her face and lips pressed into a thin line. Her right hand strikes my face with a sharp sting, jolting me out of my shock. "You little bitch!"

Skylar gasps, her eyes wide with disbelief, and I stumble back, my hand flying to my cheek.

She raises her hand once more, but Dion grabs her wrist. "You will not lay a hand on her again," he says firmly, standing between us.

"Let go of me, you pathetic, broke little worm!" My mother hisses against his grip, turning up her nose at him.

"I may be those things, but the person I love didn't just kick me out of the home we built together," Dion retorts, releasing her from his grip. He raises his hands in surrender and steps back to create space between them.

Her eyes narrow as she glares at him, a look of pure contempt on her face, before gathering her things to leave.

I bite back a smile. *My hero.*

Peter clears his throat. "Let's go too, Sky."

Skylar nods, making brief eye contact with me and wiping a single tear from her cheek. She and Peter leave the townhouse holding hands, with my mother trailing behind.

I watch them go.

"Are you okay?" Dion's concerned gaze meets mine, and I struggle to hold back tears.

"No, but I will be," I reply, forcing a minor smile.

Dion opens his mouth to apologize, but I hold up a hand to stop him. "It's okay," I say softly.

"No, Reign. I slipped up, and I'm sorry."

I grin slightly and shake my head. "Thank you for defending me."

His eyes soften as he looks at me. "I'm sorry I couldn't do more," he says, referring to the incident.

He opens his mouth to say something else, but I place a finger over his lips. "You're here now," I interrupt gently, "and that's what matters. Thank you for being here for me."

Dion smiles, wrapping me in a warm embrace. "I'll always be here for you, Reign. No matter what."

His cologne, a soothing blend of sandalwood and spice, calms me instantly, providing a sense of comfort and warmth. We stand in silence, holding each other, only the gentle rhythm of our breaths breaking the quiet.

My father clears his throat with a deep rumble, causing Dion and me to separate.

"Amara..." he trails off, struggling to find the right words, the hurt in his eyes evident.

There are none. What *can* he say? I know that my father is hurting too. I can see the pain etched in his expression, a mirror of my own.

He whispers, "I'm sorry," tears falling silently down his cheeks. My heart aches at the sight of his pain. His strong and familiar arms envelop me, the uneven drumbeat of his broken heart echoing in my ear as our tears mingle. "I'm so, so sorry," he repeats.

Three days have passed since the tense family dinner where I disclosed the actions of my aunt's husband. My phone has been flooded with a flurry of calls and texts from my father, each one expressing a worried inquiry about my well-being. He is crippled with regret and blames himself for what happened to me. He wishes he had been more perceptive and stepped in sooner to help with the issues between my mother and me. Dad was unaware of the true extent of our problems. He simply dismissed our issues as typical mother-daughter conflicts, underestimating the severity of our actual situation. My mother hates me, and her animosity will forever leave a hollow hole in my heart.

She is staying with my cousin Shonda and her husband after Dad kicked her out. He is furious with her for keeping such a secret from him and allowing that man into our home for over two decades. Now that the truth has come to light, he doesn't know how they'll move past it. My mother, on the other hand, is trying her hardest to reel him back in.

I wish her luck. She's going to need it.

Despite sending her several text messages, I haven't heard back from Skylar. I would have thought she wanted to talk about what I disclosed or… just talk. How hasn't she replaced her phone yet? *Peter!* My intuition is telling me that Peter is manipulating her in some way. My heart and soul feels it.

I recall her desperate, almost panicked rush to the door as Peter's frantic knocking shook my bedroom and closet. She was terrified as she scrambled to the door, fearing for her safety, her eyes wide with panic, her breath catching in her throat. I feel so hopeless. *What can I do?* Even if I go to the authorities or confide in someone else, I'll need proof.

Shaking off the thought, I reassure myself that today will be a great day. A busy one, but a great one. I don't want to think about Skylar, my mom, or my cousins. With confidence and a clear mind, I stride into my boutique bright and early. The great thing about the new location is that I no longer have a forty-five-minute commute.

My boutique is just a quick ten-minute drive from my home. *Won't he do it!*

Stephanie beams and steps forward, handing me a caramel latte just the way I like it. She's an excellent replacement for Nancy, providing the same incredible assistance while adding her own flair.

"Good morning, Ms. Brown. How are you feeling today?" She asks, her long auburn hair gently swaying.

I take a sip of the latte and savor the rich flavor, feeling grateful for life's small joys. "Good morning, Stephanie. I'm feeling good."

She nods. "I'm glad to hear that."

"Good morning, Ms. Brown," Kandace greets me with a grin as she walks in.

"Good morning, Kandace," I respond, returning her smile.

She greets Stephanie and goes to the back to store her belongings. I hired Kandace to assist Stephanie with the front desk, handling appointments, bookings, and vendor meetings. All of the women contribute to the success of my business.

When I walk into my office, Nancy and Bonnie are bustling around, unpacking duffel bags filled with wedding essentials for the Wilson-Jean bridal party. They arrange the items on the foldable tables, ensuring that everything is organized for the bride and groom to select from. Today, we'll review the wedding checklist to ensure that everything is in order for the big day next month. With Valentine's Day this weekend, finalizing the wedding checklist is time-sensitive and needs to be completed today.

Nancy breathes a sigh of relief as she places the final item, a medium-sized silver welcome frame, on the cluttered table labeled "Wedding Essentials/Venue Supplies." We have two tables. The second table, labeled "Accessories," is for items such as the cake knife, toasting glasses, bridal party gifts, the wedding cake topper, centerpieces, the garter, and wedding favors for the guests. The bridal shop contracted by the venue will supply both the boutonniere and the bridal bouquet for the event. In addition, the services they provide are more affordable compared to my usual recommendation.

After selecting the bride's ivory mermaid gown and the bridesmaids' wine-red halter mermaid dresses, the team is now focusing on the finer details to ensure the wedding is perfect. All the groomsmen will wear fitted black tuxedos with burgundy accents, beautifully complementing the groom's all-ivory suit. To ensure the bride has a stress-free and enjoyable wedding, I handle any problems that may arise. My team and I oversee every aspect of the wedding planning process. When the happy couple arrives, they just need to approve or reject our ideas.

I run the tip of my pen down the checklist, marking off all of the items we've already completed. The phone on my desk rings, and I hit the speaker button. "Yes?"

"Mr. Ward and Ms. Cox canceled their meeting for today and would like to reschedule for next Wednesday," Stephanie informs me.

Biting my bottom lip, I quickly check my calendar. Next Wednesday is no good; I'll be just getting back from my Valentine's Day trip and I gave myself the week off, anyway.

"Please ask them if they can do the following Thursday or Friday instead. Thank you."

"Of course, I'll let them know. Also, Mr. Wilson and Ms. Jean will be here in five minutes."

"Great, send them straight to my office when they arrive."

"Will do," Stephanie responds before hanging up.

Retrieving the binder from my desk drawer, I lay it open on the desk. I provide each couple with a customized binder and a set of duffle bags to make all materials easily accessible and efficiently managed.

Turning towards Nancy and Bonnie, I ask, "How are you ladies feeling today?"

Nancy responds, "I'm feeling good. Once we finalize the Wilson-Jean wedding checklist, I'll be able to focus on our clients for April and May."

"I'm sure they'll be pleased with everything we've selected for them," Bonnie adds confidently, clapping her hands together.

A knock at the door immediately draws my attention, prompting Nancy to spring into action. She rushes to the door to open it, and Bonnie follows close behind.

"Good morning, ladies," Ms. Jean greets us as she enters the room, her thin lips curving into a smile.

"How's it going?" Mr. Wilson enters behind her, slightly dipping his head to enter my office. He is so tall.

"Welcome, welcome, please have a seat," I say, gesturing towards the two chairs in front of my desk.

The click of Ms. Jean's black heels echoes in the room as she takes a seat. Mr. Wilson settles into the chair beside her, stretching his long legs out in front of him.

"How are you two feeling today?" I ask, flicking my gaze between them.

"We're doing well," Ms. Jean answers on behalf of both of them. Mr. Wilson nods his head in agreement with his future wife.

"Great! Let's get started. Please follow me." I lead them to the Wedding Essentials/Venue Supplies table. Glancing at the checklist, I suggest we review it first. "I want to discuss what my team and I still need to finalize for your wedding."

The couple's determined gazes meet mine, nodding in agreement.

"We had a personalized Welcome Sign made for the entrance,"

I inform them. The couple preferred not to request a sign from the venue, so I arranged for a personalized one to be made. "Next, we have selected three wedding pillows for you to choose from for the ring bearer based on your answers from the questionnaire." I review the list to ensure I haven't overlooked any items.

"We also selected two baskets for you to choose for the flower girl," Nancy adds.

"Yes, of course. Thank you, Nancy," I respond with a nod. Gesturing at the table with the options, I invite the couple to take a look and make their selection. "We have a guest book, pens and markers, and a box for cards." I always recommend my clients buy a card box for their cards to ensure a smooth end to their reception. This avoids any last-minute scrambling to collect and return the box to the venue.

The couple carefully examines the items on the table, quietly discussing them with each other. With only two card box options and no preference from the bride and groom, I offered a wine-red box with ivory accents and an ivory box with wine-red accents for them to choose from.

Ms. Jean shrieks with excitement, "Oh, I adore the wine-red box!" She holds the beautiful box, twisting it around in her hands.

My gaze shifts to Mr. Wilson, who nods. "I'm good with whatever my lovely soon-to-be wife decides," he says, gently pressing his lips to her forehead.

Her cheeks flush beet red as she carefully lifts the small, wine-red embroidered ring bearer pillow. "I like this one," she says, running her fingers over the intricate stitching.

While Ms. Jean makes her selections, Nancy is placing the chosen products on my desk, and Bonnie is arranging the remaining items in the returns box. Mr. Wilson gazes at the ivory basket adorned with a burgundy bow on its side. He smiles at Ms.

Jean, who nods her head yes. "We like this one," he says.

"Excellent choices," I remark, leading them to the second table. "After discussing the wedding accessories, you will be all set to go."

A furrow between Ms. Jean's brows appears. "Wait… Where is the aisle runner for the wedding ceremony?"

Nancy quickly locates the questionnaire binder and flips through its pages until she finds the aisle runner page. I use colorful tabs to divide the binder into sections for better organization. Nancy's subtly arched eyebrows suggest we might have overlooked a crucial step. I squint, inquiring if the bride chose a color for the aisle runner. She responds with a shake of her head, indicating a "no" to my question.

"Of course! What color would you like for the aisle runner?" I ask to rectify the oversight.

Aisle runners are optional, and venues may supply them, especially when the ceremony and reception are in the same location. This could be why we missed it. Moving forward, I will review the questionnaire once again and confirm with the couples before the showing deadline.

Ms. Jean looks up at Mr. Wilson. "What color would you like?"

He shrugs and responds, "I don't know. Either ivory or the wine looking one would work."

Ms. Jean presses the tips of her fingers to her chin. "Hmm… what do you think, Reign?"

"I think you should go with the wine-red aisle runner."

Her lips curve into a radiant smile. "Wine-red it is."

The decision is made, and I give Bonnie a subtle nod. She reacts by taking out her phone and typing away on it; securing the aisle runner will be a task for her to handle.

"Great! Did you have any other questions?" I ask, glancing at Ms. Jean.

"What should we go with for the wedding accessories?" She inquires, looking at the table of options laid out in front of her.

"In the past, couples have chosen personalized cake knives, toasting glasses, and a custom wedding cake topper."

Ms. Jean listens intently, nodding eagerly.

"You selected custom, so we have two designs for each of those items for you to choose from," I explain, pointing to the photos.

"Honey, which cake knife do you prefer? The one with the 'W' on it in the middle of the handle or the one with 'L&F' for our initials?"

Mr. Wilson examines the two options carefully before responding, "I like the one with the 'W.'"

Nancy circles their choice with a red marker. Next, they select the toasting glasses with their initials on them and then choose a gift for the wedding party and guests. Ms. Jean selects two ivory-laced garters. One garter is for a lucky single woman, while she will keep the other for herself. Finally, the couple decides on a cake topper, choosing the one with "Wilson" written on it. With the final items on their checklist now complete, the joyous couple left my office with grins on their faces, excited for their upcoming wedding day.

After analyzing the financial reports, I confirmed that I can hire four more staff members, which is a testament to our collective hard work. Still, I have chosen to grow my team cautiously by hiring two more employees now and keeping the option to hire two more later, depending on how things progress with the economy.

I scroll through my emails, the endless stream of resumes blurring before my eyes, hoping to find a few great candidates to schedule an interview with Nancy. She'll conduct the initial interview, and I'll interview her top choices, making the final hiring decision. My phone lights up, and the name *Darcy* flashes across my screen. I roll my eyes.

What the hell does she want?

Where do I start with Darcy?

Her mean-spirited actions and nasty comments toward me and my friends have made it impossible for me to like her. I never understood why Skylar was friends with her.

Inhaling and exhaling a sharp breath. *Therapy!* Or could it be that my mother's love and respect for Darcy is more genuine, making me feel less valued? She's Skylar's best friend and a constant presence in our family, and my mother adores her. Perhaps my mother wishes Darcy were her daughter instead of me because Darcy lives at home, spending her trust fund on frivolous things. I have a session with Carol after work, and I'll share my progress on self-reflection. The process of identifying why I react to people the way I do is insightful and often uncomfortable. The task feels like pushing a boulder uphill, each step a struggle against the weight and resistance. Shrugging my shoulders, I'll admit that I am still evolving and a work in progress. The last time I saw Darcy was at Skylar's wedding, where she was complaining and called me a bitch under her breath.

What does she want?

It must be serious if she's reaching out to me.

A knock on my door diverts my attention from the email containing three resumes meant for Nancy to interview.

Darcy walks into my office. Her blonde hair is tied back in a side bun, her cheeks are rosy-pink, and a stern expression is etched on her face. "Hey, Reign. How are you?"

I close my laptop and set it aside, gesturing for her to take a seat. "I'm doing okay. What is this about?"

She sits in front of me and crosses her legs, tilting forward on her knee. "It's about Sky," she says, leaning back and closing her hands together in a tight fist on her lap.

"What about her?" I ask cautiously.

"She's not replying to me. I have called, texted, and reached out to her on all social media platforms. It's as if she's a ghost. The only reason I know she is alive is because Peter recently posted a photo of them together on Instagram." She blurts out her words without pausing to catch her breath. Her olive-green eyes glisten with unshed tears, one tear threatening to spill down her cheek. I guess Scarlette didn't inform her that Skylar *was* alive.

There is no secret that Darcy and I are not friends. I don't like her. However, the sheer pain imprinted on what were once serene features is undeniable. Her face is pale, and her lips are drawn together in a tight line. When I don't reply, a single tear tracks down her cheek, and she quickly looks away, her hand wiping at the evidence of her sadness.

Taking a deep breath. "I spoke with her, and she said her phone is broken and she hasn't replaced it yet."

Darcy's shoulders slump, releasing the tension she'd been holding, and a long sigh escapes her lips. "I thought I did something to her or ..." she trails off, avoiding eye contact. "What is it? Is something wrong with me? She told me we would still be close after she got married. I know sometimes the relationship dynamic changes once you're married, but it's not like this. She must be upset with me, but I don't know what I did."

What I want to tell Darcy is that her behavior and personality contain a plethora of flaws, and she can be incredibly irritating. Recalling last year's incident, when she questioned the nature of my relationship with Dion in front of my girls, implying that it conveniently happened "all of a sudden"—which it did, but it was none of her business.

Okay, focus, Reign!

I'm carrying a heavy burden of hurt and pain caused by others, and I need to find a way to forgive and move on. My peace of mind depends on it.

Nobody owes you shit, Reign! Everybody is going through something, not just you!

It must have been complicated for Darcy to reach out, especially since she'd already contacted Scarlette—the reason we were at Peter and Skylar's in the first place, all thanks to Darcy's initial communication.

"I don't think that's the issue, Darcy," I reply softly, attempting to keep my voice steady.

"So, what is it? She must have a new phone by now. Did she change her number or something?"

I chew on my bottom lip, the taste of anxiety flooding my mouth as I consider whether to tell Darcy what I think about Peter.

"Reign?" She probes.

"I—I think Peter is abusing her," I stammer.

"What? Why would you say... *think* that?"

"Because, Darcy, shit is not adding up. Women don't just disappear after getting married. I mean, some do, but this is Sky we're talking about. Yeah, you have the honeymoon, vacation, and all that, but once that is done, you don't just disappear. As far as I can tell, she's only been to family dinners, and that's it. She hasn't even reached out to me, and despite our brief animosity toward each other during the wedding planning and—"

"And you leaving the wedding early," Darcy adds, cutting me off.

Rolling my eyes, "I left early for a reason."

I told Skylar that Dion and I were going to get it in; Darcy doesn't need to know that.

"Your *only* sister got married, and you thought, hey, why won't I leave when they cut the cake?" She leans back against the chair, folding her arms across her chest, an aggressive eye roll following.

"You know what—"

"What?" she taunts, her green eyes glowering at me.

See, this is why I can't stand this…

Shaking my head, I collect my thoughts. "I think Peter is either controlling her or abusing her." I throw my hands up. "I went to their house after you reached out to Scarlette, and not only was Peter rude, but Sky also seemed off."

Darcy's stern features soften as my words hang in the air. "Okay," she inhales and exhales slowly. "What do we do?"

"*We* don't do anything. I'm taking care of it."

"What are *you* going to do?" With a dramatic roll of her eyes once again and a sharp suck of her teeth. "Hire someone to fix the problem?" She remarks in a low, sarcastic tone.

"Why are you such a bitch?" I ask, not even hiding my frustration.

"It takes one to know one," she retorts.

"Look!" My tone is sharp. "I don't have time for this. Why did you come here again?"

She exhales and gestures her hands back and forth, pretending to wave a white flag. "Okay, there's no secret that we don't get along."

"I can't stand you," I say simply, with no remorse.

She pauses for a few heartbeats, her cold gaze meeting mine. "The feeling is mutual. However, we both love Sky, and clearly, something is going on."

Finally, something we can both agree on. I nod my head for her to continue.

"If you don't mind me asking, how are you handling it?"

"My friend's boyfriend is running a background check on Peter, and once he gets back to me, I'll be sure to let you know if anything significant comes up."

Darcy averts her gaze. "And what if ..."

"Skylar loves you, Darcy. Trust me when I say something is up with Peter."

Her muscles relax, and she gathers her bearings. "Okay, well, *nice* talk," she says, her voice sharp with returning rudeness.

Chapter 9: Reign

I arrive at my therapist Carol's office ten minutes early, and the soothing scent of lavender fills the air as I scroll through Instagram. Darcy was right. Peter posted photos from Saturday night with Skylar, captioning them *"My babe."* He tagged Skylar as a collaborator on the post, so it also shows up on her profile. Tapping on her page, I scroll through her feed, growing increasingly uneasy. Every post is tagged by Peter from the Saturday night dinners with my family. This is strange. Skylar hasn't created her own post since her birthday in October. That's odd, right? The more I stare at her pictures, the more I wonder. How did I miss this? He creates all the posts, and Skylar barely smiles in any of them. In every photo, Peter beams with an ear-to-ear smile, looking like the happiest man in the world. His wide emerald-green eyes and toothy grin give off an unsettling vibe. Who smiles like that? In contrast to Skylar's distant, lifeless light brown eyes, her expression remained blank and neutral.

Last year, on my birthday, when she ostentatiously showed off her dazzling diamond ring at the bar, I must admit, I felt a twinge of jealousy. I couldn't believe my baby sister was getting married before me, even though I wasn't in a relationship. I hadn't even considered dating anyone in seven years after walking in on that jackass Max fucking some chick in his bed. I never worried about finding love until Skylar's sudden announcement of her marriage after barely making it a year of dating Peter. My mother's excitement gave her more ammunition to use against me, and my cousins had a field day teasing me. But then I remember how her wedding announcement led me to meet Dion.

Every negative experience or situation has a lesson to be learned.

The positive lesson: I confronted my unhealthy obsession with my mother's approval, realizing how much I dislike her. This was a lesson I learned through difficult self-reflection. In a previous session, Carol pointed out the connection between me hiring a boyfriend and my need to please my mother. Her words carried weight, laden with unspoken truths.

My thoughts turn to the day my mother demanded that I use my resources to plan Skylar and Peter's wedding for free. Luckily, Dad covered all the expenses. I don't understand how he fell for a woman like her. *Bitch.* Rolling my eyes, I recall Peter politely conveying his and Skylar's enthusiasm for me to plan their wedding. He did so with a gracious nod and a gentle smile. His warm, honey-like voice back then was a stark contrast to the harsh tone he used at my place.

I stop at the black-and-white photo Skylar posted the week before their wedding, with the caption *"Wife to be"* and three dots following it. Her lips are pressed together in a thin line, and her eyes have a faraway look in them. It's unusual and disheartening to see a woman about to marry her soulmate looking so sad. Shouldn't she be radiating happiness instead? Why haven't I noticed this before?

"Hello, Reign, come on back," Carol calls out, jolting me out of my probing.

"Hi, Carol," I reply. Exiting out of Skylar's Instagram page, making sure not to double-tap on anything, I put my phone away.

Carol takes a folder from the top shelf and her notepad from her desk. She re-decorated her office in royal blue and silver, giving it a luxurious and sophisticated feel. The colors are rich and stylish.

"I love what you did with your office," I compliment.

"Why, thank you, Reign," she says. Carol then takes a seat in her chair, gesturing for me to sit across from her. "I figured it was time to spruce things up after the New Year."

She opens her notepad, pen poised and ready to write, as I settle into the chair. "So, Reign, tell me. How have you been?"

I mull over her question. To anyone else, it's a simple "I'm okay" response, but I don't know what to say. A second stretches into a minute, then another, until the only sound in the room is the rhythmic tick-tock of her clock. She clears her throat softly, a gentle smile on her face. After a few more beats of very uncomfortable silence, I open my mouth to speak, but nothing comes out. I nervously touch my throat, trying to soothe the lump forming as I grapple to find the right words.

"Reign, are you okay?" She asks. "Do you need water?"

Shaking my head no, I gather my bearings. "I'm sorry, Carol. I— I am trying to find the right words to express how I feel."

Carol nods with understanding, scribbling in her notepad. "Take your time," she says, raising her pen. "But not too much time. We don't want to waste precious dollars." She offers a little grin in an attempt to lighten the mood. "Okay, how about we start with your day today? How has it been so far?"

Filling my lungs and causing my chest to rise noticeably, I take a sharp breath. Carol's gaze remains fixed and unwavering. Should I mention Darcy? Peter? Or Skylar? *No, I probably shouldn't.* I suspect Peter is abusing Skylar, but I don't have concrete proof that would hold up in the court of law. While Carol is not meant to judge, I don't think it's wise to mention that. I'm having a hard time. Any other occasion, I have plenty to say, but now that I'm here with someone who will listen and not judge—I'm mute. I have so much to unpack: my aunt's husband, the aftermath, my father—

"How are things with you and Dion? Last we spoke, you said you two were doing great."

Okay, I can talk about Dion; he's been the best thing that has happened to me, besides my successful career. "Yes, Dion and I are doing so good." I look down at my cuticles and continue, "Well, we had a minor hiccup. I've been so focused on work that I kind of ghosted him in a way."

She scribbles something in her notepad before her hazel eyes meet mine. "You ghosted him?"

"In a way," I correct.

"How did you ghost him? *In a way?* As you phrase it."

I shift uncomfortably in my seat, feeling guilty for neglecting Dion. "We didn't see each other in three weeks, and I didn't respond to his calls and texts."

She nods, scribbling some more.

"I say 'in a way' because I didn't mean to ignore him. It was more or less. I needed time to finish moving from one location to another."

"That's right! You upgraded to a bigger place," she remarks, looking up from her notes.

"Yes, I did. It was a hectic time, and I just didn't have the time to respond," I explain sheepishly.

"Reign, life gets busy, and it's normal for things to slip through the cracks." Carol gives me a pointed look. "But communication is key, and a relationship consists of two individuals communicating with each other."

"No, I know. Dion said the same thing. I apologized to him, and he forgave me, but then I dropped the ball again."

She flips to another page, pen poised. "How so?"

"I planned a couple's trip for us for this weekend, and I'm covering all the expenses."

"That's a thoughtful gesture," she acknowledges, jotting down notes in that damn notepad.

"I don't mind paying for everything. We come from different worlds, and I know he's not using me. I guess it does something to his manhood and..." I trail off, trying to figure out what to say.

"Go on," she encourages, her pen ready to capture my thoughts.

"He has so much debt, and I want to help him, but he doesn't want my help."

Carol stops writing and looks at me. "Reign, do you consider yourself an independent woman?"

Taken aback by her question, I furrow my brows. Of course, I'm an independent woman, and she knows this. Why ask me this question? Sitting up straight in my chair, attempting to project confidence but failing miserably. "Yes," I say, lowering my voice an octave.

The corners of her mouth turn up slightly. "You *are* an independent woman," she states firmly.

"Yes, yes, I am. I *am* an independent woman," I repeat, trying to mirror her tone.

"Is it possible that Dion is an independent man who doesn't want handouts from his rich girlfriend?"

Ouch! I blink once, then twice. Is that a rhetorical question? How do I respond to that? That was a bit rude—wasn't it?

"Hear me out," she says, gesturing with her glossy, crimson nails. "I remember from a past session that Dion hesitated to share his feelings with you due to your status. In his eyes, you were…" She flips through the pages in her notepad. "I'm sorry, you *are* too good for him. That's what you shared with me, correct?"

Thinking back to that December day, just before Christmas. The squeak of our sneakers on the polished rec center floor in Freeport faded as we took a break from our one-on-one game. That's when he confessed I was too good for him, but he couldn't imagine life without me. He probably brought that up because he didn't have much money to get me a fancy Christmas gift. However, I'm not materialistic. I wear what's nice, and I love supporting new designers like Kia. I worked hard for my penthouse and used my trust fund to furnish it. As for the catering, private chef, and trips… *Focus, Reign!*

Bobbing my head, "That's correct."

Carol continues, "Dion, like you, is an independent man who does not want his girlfriend to provide for him. I'm sure it took courage for him to put his pride aside and pursue you."

A small smile graces my lips. "Yes, he's very driven and determined, and I admire that about him. But the trip was a last-minute thing my girls planned, and I think it'll be fun for both of us to get away for a bit. His friend Eddie will be there too."

"How does Dion feel about the trip now?"

"He's… okay with it. I'm spending the night at his place tonight."

I haven't really stayed over at Dion's place since we started dating. He mainly comes to mine. He was embarrassed about his apartment at first, but when I saw it, let's just say it was… something.

"That's great!" Carol exclaims. "When we last spoke, you said you didn't want to sleep there. What changed?"

"I guess I just wanted to show him that I'm comfortable being in his space too," I explain. "I'm in a relationship with a man I love. I *need* to be a part of his world more."

Nodding her head. "It's important to share those experiences and spaces with each other."

"He has lunch with his parents every Wednesday, and I've been to a few of them. His mother is such a beautiful and kind soul, and so is his father. They were nice to me. We grew up in very different ways, you know? His family is so loving and welcoming." Averting my gaze, "Unlike my stupid family," I say under my breath.

"What was that?" Carol questions.

Sighing, I reply, "My family sucks."

"I see," she observes, glancing at the clock. "Do you want to talk about your family? What's been going on with Skylar? Have you heard from her yet?"

My heart sinks at the mention of my sister's name. What do I say? *My twenty-five-year-old sister is in an abusive relationship, and I don't have any proof.*

"Yes, I heard from her. She said her phone was broken."

Carol eyes me warily but doesn't press. "What about your mother?"

"I saw her on Saturday."

Carol jots something down in her notepad. "How did that go?"

"Badly."

Her eyes widen. "Do you want to talk about it?"

"Dion and I went to family dinner, and I told everyone what my aunt's husband did to me, and my father kicked everyone out, including my mother," I tell her, matter-of-factly. *Sorry, not sorry.*

She quickly scribbles something in her notepad; her expression softens as she looks up at me. "I'm so proud of you for speaking your truth. How do you feel now that you've got such a significant and traumatic experience off your chest?"

Thinking about Carol's words, I lean back in my seat and look up at the ceiling. How does it make me feel? Relieved? Better?

Healed? I don't feel any of those things. I despise him for what he did and how it made me feel. My mother making me hide it and my aunt ignoring it enrage me. The dismissal of my pain felt like a cold slap to the face. My feelings were shoved aside with such cruelty that the memory still stings. *Hate. Anger. Bitterness.*

"Reign?" Carol's voice is soft.

"I hate that man, Carol. I hate my family," I confess, my voice cracking with emotion.

She finishes jotting down notes and directs her gaze back to me. "How did your mother react?"

Tears fall from my eyes as I recount the way the woman who gave birth to me dismissed my pain. All she cared about was her husband and how he looked at her. "She didn't care about my feelings, only my father's."

Carol glances at the clock again. We only have about ten minutes before this session is over. "Reign," she says gently. "What was *his* reaction when you spoke your truth?"

She knows I don't refer to that man as my uncle. She knows my disdain toward him, so when she says *his,* I know exactly who she is referring to. "He told my father he had no idea what I was talking about," I reply bitterly, folding my arms across my chest like a child.

"Reign, I know this will be hard for you to hear," she starts slowly.

So don't say it.

"One day, you will have to find it in your heart to forgive your aunt, your cousins, and your mother. But first, let's start with him."

My blood boils at the mere mention of forgiveness. I look away, blinking back the tears threatening to spill over.

"Forgiving these people is crucial for your well-being, not theirs. Holding onto anger and resentment will only continue to hurt you in the long run." She closes her notepad and looks at me with a gentle expression. "If you're ever feeling up for it, we can consider a family session with you, your mother, father, and maybe Skylar. However, I would like to meet with them all separately before doing a family session." She searches through her drawer and hands me three business cards. "For your homework, start by forgiving the person who caused you the least pain, then move on from there."

"Who hurt me the least?" I snort.

"Your aunt, her husband, your cousins, and your mother—they have all hurt you, correct?"

"Yes!" I reply, a hint of attitude coloring my tone.

"Which person do you feel has hurt you the least?" she asks again, her tone firm yet gentle.

How do I even begin to answer that? They have all hurt me. I hate all of them… equally. Don't I?

"You could start by reflecting on who might have hurt you the least. Once you decide, focus on forgiving them, not for their sake, but for your own. Holding onto the pain they caused won't help you."

Nodding my head, I ask, "I know you're right, but how can I forgive any of them?"

"Continuing to hold onto anger will only weigh you down. Forgiveness is the key to releasing that burden," she replies, writing down our next visit in her calendar.

A bittersweet smile plays on my lips as I collect my belongings and leave her office, the weight of her words settling on my heart like a heavy stone.

Chapter 10: Reign

After my therapy session, I head home to get ready to spend the night at Dion's. Usually, he comes to my penthouse since the hot water at his place quickly turns ice-cold, unlike what I'm used to. I don't like that my showers have to be quick. Dion joked about me being *boujee*, just because I love taking hot showers. There's nothing wrong with that, and, yes, even in the summer. I don't care how warm it is outside; I'm taking a hot shower. Besides, my penthouse is usually cold with the central air running. Sometimes, I have to turn it off or lower it, depending on how I feel. Don't judge me. That doesn't make me *boujee*. Clearly, Dion doesn't understand the term correctly. Then there's his neighborhood. Although not as bad as some I've heard of, I wouldn't walk alone at night. Honestly, I wouldn't feel safe walking alone at night anywhere, but that's just me.

While stepping into the shower, thoughts of my family and the trauma they caused flood my mind. Turning away from the showerhead, I let the hot water wash away the painful recollections.

Carol and Dion were right. I need to forgive all of them. I need to let go and let God... right? Perhaps I should try giving all my issues and problems to God, like Dion does. But then I consider all the things my mother has done to me and how she has made me feel for as long as I can remember.

How can I let go of that? How can I forgive her?

A mother who never attended my basketball games when I was a child.

A mother who wanted nothing to do with me, so she sent me to her sister's place on the weekends when my dad worked around the clock.

A mother who knew about what her sister's husband did to me but chose to ignore it.

The situation became even more ridiculous when Skylar was born. She kept sending me there, claiming it was *hard* for her to care for two children at once and that I wasn't very helpful with Skylar.

How can I forgive a woman who never acted like a mother to me? A mother who sided with my cheating ex-boyfriend. She still invites him around despite knowing what he did to me. Why is *she* my mother out of all the people in the world? She's a bitch. And if I forgive her or any of them, how can I be sure it's genuine? As I step out of the shower, I push aside the thoughts of resentment and focus on selecting a few outfits to bring to Dion's place. Quickly pulling on a pair of jeans and a top, I head out the door, arriving at his apartment an hour later.

Turning the key in the lock, it clicks with a satisfying sound. Stepping inside, I drop one of my bags on the brown two-seater sofa. I see he cleaned up a bit. Dion lives in a one-bedroom, one-bathroom apartment that he describes as a *shitty place*. It's not that bad; the apartment just needs a little work. The beige paint highlights every crack on the walls, where he has two signed photos of his favorite basketball players, Kyrie Irving and Jayson Tatum. *They are so fine.* Don't get me wrong, Dion is sexy as hell, hot—and more. But there's something about a man in a jersey that just does it for me. Every time we play one-on-one, I pounce on him like a cat in heat, especially when he's wearing one of his jerseys.

There are two windows with brown curtains, one in the kitchen and another in the living room with a partial view of the busy street. There's no dining room. Instead, there's a small brown coffee table in the center of the living room, with four beige coasters engraved with the letter "D." And a tall floor lamp nearby casting a warm, cozy glow over the room.

The brown hardwood floor creaks as I make my way to his room to put the rest of my things on a chair. The walls in his room match the living room's color, but he incorporated his favorite color, sunset, blending warm hues such as red, orange, and yellow with a touch of cooler blue tones. A smile tugs at my lips as I remember the day he shared his favorite color as sunset, and I clowned him about it. He did not care that I was laughing at him as he stood on business. *I love that man!*

My phone dings, with a new message from him.

A radiant smile blooms on my face. When he calls me his rose, my heart explodes in my chest, a warmth spreads through me like melting butter, and my stomach is a whirlwind of butterflies. Dion's acknowledgment of my love for velvety black roses warms my heart in a way that only he can.

DION
Hey, my rose
Where are you?
Hey babe, I'm at your place
Where are you?
I'm at the rec playing ball with my boys
Want to meet me here?
Everybody here

Everybody?

The girl at the front desk directs me to the gym when I arrive at the rec center. Cheers and screams fills my ears as I trudge down the narrow hallway.

"Reign!" Familiar faces of August, Love, and Kimi wave at me as I enter the bustling gym. Scarlette is holding up a makeshift scoreboard, with the teams "OLD HEADS" vs. "YOUNG BUCKS" scribbled on it.

This is exactly the distraction I need to take my mind off my family issues. I'm still worried about Skylar, but there isn't much I can do for her right now. She's not responding, and I won't show up unannounced again. *At least not for now.* I need to tell my dad about my concerns, especially after talking to Darcy. Maybe after my trip, I'll have Darcy meet me there. My poor father is so upset with my mother over what happened with my aunt's husband that I don't know how he'll react to my suspicions about Skylar. How do you tell him that you suspect your sister is being abused without any proof? What am I—

"*Hola*, Reign!" Scarlette squeaks, interrupting my thoughts.

"What are y'all doing here?" I walk over to the bleachers.

Scarlette lowers the sign blocking her face. "Unlike you, I visit my man!"

She is clearly a Long Island girl now, judging by the way she stays out here.

Rolling my eyes at her dramatics, I sit down next to her. "Whatever."

"Dion invited us," Love explains while pointing towards Trent on the court. "I didn't know Dion was from Freeport."

I watch Dion and Trent enjoying themselves on the court, laughing and joking around like old friends. That's a *bromance* I didn't see coming. *I like it.*

"We all from Strong Island," Kimi says, adjusting her sunglasses.

Now, why does she have on sunglasses?

"Well, not all of us," Love laughs, nudging August, whose arms are folded across her chest. "Some of us are *city* girls."

August scoffs, "I'm pretty much a member. Don't act like I don't be out here."

Squinting my eyes. "Strong Island?"

Love giggles with Kimi. "If you know, you know."

"I can't stand y'all!" I chirp, shaking my head with a smile.

"We thought we should hang out before the couple's trip this weekend. Besides, you are the only one who don't be coming out here, Reign," August quips, nudging me with her elbow.

"What do you mean? I do come out here," I protest, attempting to convince them and myself that I'm not a bad girlfriend.

"When was the last time you came out here?" August counters.

Pausing for a moment, I rack my brain for an answer.

Scarlette scolds, "She always makes my poor friend come to her," as all four women give me pointed looks.

Defeated, I slump my shoulders, a heavy sigh escaping my lips. There's no point in arguing when they're right. I need to be a better girlfriend. It's not fair for Dion to always travel to me—*even though I live in a better neighborhood.*

"Okay, okay. Can y'all stop looking at me like that? Damn! I will be a better girlfriend and come out here more. I mean, I'm spending the night tonight," I say defensively, turning my attention to the game.

"About damn time," Scarlette grumbles.

"Mhmm," August hums under her breath.

Catching Dion's eye, his lips curl into a sexy grin, revealing his infamous left dimple. Pointing at me, he winks, causing my face to flush as I can't help but smile back.

They are playing by ones and twos. Dante passes the ball to Dion, who dribbles up the court and signals Trent to cut to the basket. Trent understood the play and positioned himself to receive the ball.

"That's my man, my man, my man!" Love chants from the sidelines.

Trent blows a kiss at Love. She pretends to catch it, smiling and hovering her hands over her heart. *Aww, they are so cute.* The Young Bucks pass the ball in, but Dion steals the pass and goes for a layup. That's right, Dion! *My man is on fire.*

My favorite gold bracelet with the single black rose shimmers in the light reflecting from the large windows when I jump to my feet, clapping my hands as Dion scores.

"That's right, baby! Let's go, Old Heads!"

The game is played up to twenty-one points, and the current score stands at nineteen to sixteen. The Old Heads need two more points to win. Ivan, a promising twenty-year-old player, passed the ball to his teammate on the left. The kid spins away from Eddie and drives the ball to the net. *Swoosh.* Trent inbounds the ball to Dion while the opposing team is playing defense. Dion dribbles past half the court and calls for a pick; Dion uses the pick to drive the ball to the hole, but then he kicks it out to Calvin, standing at the corner by the three-point line. Calvin shoots and scores. That's game!

We praise our men for winning as if they were actual basketball players who just won a ring. The Young Bucks shake their heads, and one of them furrows his brow, his face all screwed up.

I shout, reminding him, "It's just a game!"

He shakes his head, walking off the court—*sore loser.*

Ivan greets me with a fist pound. "Wassup Reign, how ya been?"

"I've been good. How about you?"

"Just chilling. I've been wondering where you been at," he says, a smirk forming on his lips.

Dion rests his hands on my shoulders from behind. "Iight now, stop flirting with my girl."

"I mean, she don't be coming around. Perhaps she needs a real man," Ivan jokes, brushing imaginary dust off his shoulders.

Rolling my eyes. "You need to stop."

Ivan played on Dion and Eddie's Little League team. Now he is playing college basketball, and scouts have their eyes set on him.

Whenever I see him, he deliberately flirts with me to get under Dion's skin. Apparently, his baby sister had a small crush on Dion, and they've had this love-hate mentor-brother-type relationship since. *That is a mouthful.*

Ivan laughs. "Nah, it's all jokes. I'm just messing with you."

Dion clasps Ivan on the shoulder. "Perhaps you should joke with somebody else's girl."

Ivan smirks, dapping Dion up. "No doubt. It's all love. Y'all lucky," he says, eyeing our friend group. "Y'all got some fly women."

"They're off-limits, bro," Eddie adds, giving Ivan a fist pound. "Good game, though."

Ivan nods, flashing a charming smile. "Got it, got it. Respect."

The rest of the Young Bucks and Old Heads exchange fist pounds, saying "good game" as they head off the court.

After the game at the rec, we head back to Dion's place to get ready for dinner with his parents. Since his mother beat breast cancer, they have made it a tradition to have lunch every Wednesday at their favorite restaurant. Dion missed their lunch today because of an audition, so his mom decided to make dinner instead. His parents live so close to him, just a ten- to fifteen-minute drive. They live in a one-bedroom, one-bath apartment in a five-story senior citizen building with a white exterior, vertical geometric designs cascading down the sloping metal roof, and dormer windows on the upper floors. Additionally, the units and hallways have large windows for natural light, and a landscaped courtyard serves as the main communal area for residents.

We arrive on the fourth floor, the smell of dinner wafting up my nostrils.

"Hmmm, it smells so good from out here!" I bellow as we

approach their apartment door.

Dion gives one of his signature sexy grins before knocking on the door.

A loud, husky voice belonging to a woman with a strong southern drawl shouts, "I'll get it!"

The locks click, and the door swings open to reveal an older, brown-skinned woman I've never seen before.

Dion grins from ear to ear, his voice switching to a deep southern twang as he greets excitedly, "Heyyy Auntieee." They embrace one another, both laughing and chatting animatedly.

I stand back, my eyes almost bugging out of my head by the sudden change in his tone.

"And who might you be, sugar?" She asks kindly, putting me at ease.

Dion takes my hand in his and introduces me. "Auntie, this is my girlfriend, Reign."

Reaching out to shake her hand, I greet her with a smile. She, however, swats my hand away and pulls me into a warm hug.

"Chile please, give me a hug. You family!"

The scent of cinnamon fills my nose, as I fall into her warmth.

"You can call me Auntie Mavis," she says when she finally releases me from her embrace. "You know, we were startin' to think Dion didn't want women," she teases.

"Come on now, Auntie. Why'd you have to take it there?" Dion chuckles.

"Don't scare her off, Mavis," Dion's mom chimes in, approaching me with open arms.

"Hi, Mrs. James. It's good to see you again," I say, hugging her.

She pinches my cheek and says, "No formalities needed here. Call me Mom."

"Oh! Okay, M-Mom," I falter, blushing at the unexpected

gesture.

Mom. To be frank, she's been nicer to me than my own mother.

She smiles warmly at me, making me feel like part of the family, and invites us into the dining room.

"Hello, Reign," Dion's father greets me, his warm smile mirroring his wife's.

"Hi, Mr. James."

"Nonsense, Reign! Call me Dad. The way Dion talks about you, I know you two are in it for the long run."

"Okay, sure... D-Dad."

He chuckles and gestures to the man sitting beside him, introducing, "This here is my brother-in-law, Bernie, Mavis's husband."

"Nice to meet you, Uncle Bernie."

"Nice to meet you too, young lady," he grins.

Dion takes my hand and leads me to a table in the corner of the room with an elaborate spread of food on it. There's so much food that you would think it was Thanksgiving.

"It's only Wednesday," I whisper to Dion.

"My family loves to eat," he chuckles and points to a golden loaf on the table. "Auntie Mavis's homemade cornbread is so good. And don't even get me started on my mom's collard greens. She used smoked turkey neck instead of pork. We don't eat pork anymore. Well, my aunt still does."

My mouth waters in anticipation as Dion describes the delicious dishes. "These are my mom's famous crispy fried chicken and green beans. And her stuffing is to die for," he continues, gesturing towards the dishes with pride. "Auntie made the good banana pudding too. I've never had any better. It's so good it makes you wanna—"

"Smack yo momma," Dion and his aunt say in unison, laughing.

Mrs. James… I mean, *Mom* clears her throat and casts a stern gaze at Dion, who frowns.

"You're going to smack whose mother?" She folds her arms across her chest.

"Mary, leave my nephew alone. You know we just be fooling." Auntie Mavis looks my way and winks. "Ignore my annoying sister. She can't never take a joke."

Mom rolls her eyes at her sister and retorts, "Mavis, I am not annoying!"

"Girl, if you don't quit—" Mavis starts, and they walk back to the kitchen disputing with one another.

"Don't mind them," Dion whispers. "They are always arguing over something," he says, handing me a plate.

Everything looks so good. I'm not used to home-cooked meals. My mother always hired private chefs to make our dinner, and my father wasn't home in time for dinner most nights due to his shift. I hate to admit this, but I envy the relationship Dion has with his parents. Even his aunt. I *hate* my family. Okay, hate is a strong word… maybe I strongly dislike them. Yeah! That's it.

Dion fixes his plate and nods for me to do the same. I load up my plate with a little bit of everything, the rich aroma intensifying my hunger. I stop at a small wooden bowl. The smell is odd and is confusing compared to the other foods on the table. I can't tell if it smells good or bad.

"What is this?" I whisper to Dion.

A crease forms between his eyebrows as he looks at the bowl. "Chitterlings."

I bite my lip to stifle a laugh at the way Dion wrinkled his nose.

"You don't like chitterlings?"

"Definitely not my favorite. I don't know why she still cooks them," he grimaces.

"Who?" I question.

"That would be me," Auntie Mavis replies with a chuckle, pulling up a chair.

I sit next to Dion across from Auntie Mavis and M-Mom. *I have to get used to saying that.*

"Mavis, don't start," Mom chastises.

"This is what happens when you don't teach yo kids about home. They forget the significance of chitlins," Auntie Mavis scolds.

"Kids? Mavis, I only have one child," Mom corrects. "And he's not a kid anymore."

Auntie Mavis rolls her eyes and shoves a spoonful of green beans in her mouth.

I dare to ask, "What do you mean?"

Auntie Mavis' eyes almost bug out. "Reign, you don't know the significance of chitlins?"

Glancing around the table, I feel a bit embarrassed. "N-no."

Auntie Mavis sighs dramatically. "Well, chile, let me school you on a few things."

"Here she go," her husband mutters under his breath. "Mavis, don't you start!"

"You know she can't go a day without talking about Black history," Mom says.

"I would like to know," I say, feeling genuinely curious now, and Auntie Mavis's eyes light up with pride.

"Well, back when our people were slaves, they were given the scraps from the pig. And we were able to transform it into a delicious meal, showcasing our resourcefulness. You know, because we weren't worth nothing but a minute and were treated like animals... no, worse than animals. Today, people will cause outrage if a dog isn't being treated right. Let it be a Black man shot and killed for everyone to see and people don't give a flying fart about them—"

"Mavis! That's not true," Mom interjects, shaking her head.

Her chocolate brown eyes are tense, and she squints at her sister. "Ain't it?" she poses.

Mom throws her hands in the air and sighs.

"As I was saying before I was so rudely interrupted," she continues, side-eyeing Mom, who rolls her eyes. "Don't get me wrong, there are more people today than when I was younger who understand how this country has treated us poorly, but still. I mean I know that not all people are racist. However, race is the root of every damn thing in this country."

My eyebrows knit together. I know that race has been a major factor in everything. Yes, I had to work twice as hard to start my business, especially because there are more white women striving in my field than Black women, and yes, I had to dim my light in some cases to even be seen. Hell, I even permed my hair because of race. Still, there is so much history about my people that I am not aware of.

"Auntie Mavis, I would be happy to learn more about... us," I say, gesturing between her and myself. "There is so much I don't know, and I attended private school all my life with me being the minority. We were taught the basic Black History."

"Mhmm... of course you were. And now they want to erase everything. But as long as *we* are still alive, we will teach y'all everything you need to know. That way you can continue to share," she says, taking a bite of her food. "Where did you and my nephew meet?"

"Oh boy!" Dion blows out a breath.

I eye him warily. Although I hired Dion as my boyfriend last year and we fell in love, I tell people we met at Central Park. Why do I feel like Auntie Mavis is about to ruin my precious memory of one of my favorite places in the city?

"We met at Central Park..." I say cautiously.

Her eyes widened, and a hush fell over the table as everyone picked at their food.

She takes a sip of her water before dropping the bombshell. "Did you know Central Park used to be known as 'Seneca Village,' a thriving community of Black folks—"

"Whenever Black people are thriving, they always want to come and mess it up," Mom interjects, her fork scraping lightly against the plate as she spears a forkful of creamy mac and cheese.

"Mhmm... like Black Wall Street, but we ain't gon get into that," Auntie Mavis says, waving her hand back and forth. "Seneca Village was founded back in 1825. It was a small community, you know, that flourished. They had successful businesses, three major churches, schools, and more. But, as usual, when they see us doing well and not needing a damn thing from them—"

"Mavis! Your mouth," Mom scolds, cutting her sister off.

"Mary, sometimes I cuss; the Lord knows my heart. Now will you shut up so I can school this young lady!" Auntie Mavis continues, "As I was saying before I was once again so rudely interrupted by my baby sister, here they come, ruining sh—stuff." She corrects her language with a pointed look from Mom. "In 1857, the government used a law known as *'eminent domain'* to *forcefully* remove all the residents of Seneca Village. It had to be about three hundred of them—kicked out of their homes like they were nothing more than rats. And to add more salt to the wound, they audaciously began a campaign to change the public narrative. They labeled Blacks as *'tramps,' 'squatters,'* and *'thieves.'*"

I hang onto her every word; it's unlike anything I've ever heard. My father and the woman who gave birth to me didn't tell Skylar and me anything about their own childhood experiences. Apart from my grandmother on my mother's side, who expected her daughters to marry wealthy men, I know little about the rest of the family. My dad's parents are complete strangers to me. All I know is that my father moved from Mobile, Alabama, to New York when he was seven years old, and he was an only child. I don't know the ages of the woman whose body I was in for nine months and her sister when they moved here.

And since my private school education predominantly emphasized white perspectives, my knowledge of Black history is limited beyond what was taught in class. Our teachers taught us only the basics: Martin Luther King, Rosa Parks, George Washington Carver, and Madam C.J. Walker, among others. This story is entirely new to me.

During my school years, I wished for straight hair, believing it would help me belong among my white peers. Which is why I would get perms. Obviously, that mindset was foolish. Now, with my natural hair, I find it hard to believe I once thought that way. Yet, the feeling of running my fingers through silky, straight hair after getting a fresh perm gave me a sense of belonging. Prior to getting perms, what started as innocent requests from some students to play with my hair escalated into disrespect when their fingers got snagged, causing me pain and frustration and making me the brunt of nearly every damn offensive Black girl joke. At times, they would all gather around, mocking me about how nappy my hair was. I remember going home and demanding that my *mother* put a perm in my hair so I didn't have to deal with it anymore.

Auntie Mavis clears her throat. "Black folks were kicked out of the homes they built. They were forced to witness the destruction, rebuilding, and renaming of their community to Central Park. And for what? Why was this done? It doesn't matter because, in the end, they stole something from us, just like they've been doing! It's a damn shame. I'm seventy years old now, and while some things have changed, racism is still present. Till. This. Day." She states, pointing to the table for each word. "Had we stayed in Manila, Alabama, we probably wouldn't have had the same opportunities that we were blessed with today. Still, racial discrimination did hold us back. And don't get me started on the Black folk that think because they haven't experienced racism that it doesn't exist," she groans.

"We have faced more racism in this city than we did in our small town," Mom adds with a heavy sigh.

"I have never heard of Manila, Alabama," I admit.

"The town is now called 'Fools Acres,'" Mom explains, shaking her head.

"Mhmm, because a *fool* renamed it," Auntie Mavis quips.

"Mavis!" Mom scolds, but Auntie Mavis rolls her eyes. "It's a nickname for our home," Mom adds.

"Reign, if you wanna learn some more history, you could always attend one of my classes. I teach on Saturdays at the church." Her gaze zooms in on Dion. "You haven't told my new niece about my classes, have you?"

Dion looks up from his plate, his brows pinched together. "Auntie, you know not everyone wants to hear about the past all the time."

"Weeelll. Excuuussse me," she huffs dramatically. "I think it's important to know everything there is to know about our history. Them fools are already trying to erase it all to make themselves look better. Listen here, as someone who has faced racism and colorism, I will *always* teach about it for as long as God allows breath in my body."

"Do you know why they decided to desegregate?" I blurt out, unable to contain the question.

I wish my parents had taught us more about our history, although I could have looked it up myself. Having lived a different life, I didn't think about it too much. I learned about slavery and thought about how badly our ancestors were treated. They were raped, beaten, humiliated, and even eaten. The content was too overwhelming for me, so I never felt compelled to delve back into learning more about it. It's emotionally draining and heartbreaking. But my relationship with Dion and seeing his family and the neighborhood he lives in, along with the different life he has experienced, makes me want to learn more. It's pretty sad to want to learn more now, but it's never too late. Despite facing challenges like the mortifying hair incident, early business struggles, and the need to constantly prove myself, my life wasn't so bad thanks to my father's sacrifices. He ensured that our family never struggled.

Auntie Mavis frowns. "They didn't all of a sudden say, 'Hey, you know what? Black folk aren't less than animals. They *are* people. Maybe we should start treating them that way instead of lynching, raping, and doing unspeakable things to them. Let's desegregate!' No, it was to project an image of *'change'* to the rest of the world. Even though we were drinking from the same water fountain and going to school together, I could feel the hate in their eyes every time I walked into a room. People want to act as if segregation was so long ago, but I can remember it clear as day. I remember the first time I went to school with white children and how they looked at me as pure trash. What they don't want you to know is that we were fine being segregated. They painted this picture like we *wanted* this; we *needed* them, but we didn't. We had our own and were flourishing, but nope. Black folk can't be succeeding; they absorbed what we built and took it over! All because they saw how they were losing control over us. This is the history they don't want you to know." Her brows furrow in a deep frown, creating pronounced lines to ripple across her forehead. "Like I said, I teach classes on Saturdays; you're welcome to come."

"I would love to attend one of your classes and learn more. You should write a book."

The dining room fills with a deep, hearty laugh. "I should, shouldn't I? But chile, I don't have the time, and I'm too old to be typing on no computer."

"My friend is an author. Maybe we can figure something out. Do you have any written material that you use when teaching your classes?"

She points to her head. "My experiences are in here."

"Perhaps you could record some of your lessons, and I could look into finding someone to type it out for you."

Her eyes widen in excitement. "Hmm... okay, okay. I'm picking up what you're throwing."

"Great, I'll get back to you when I can. I think it is amazing that you teach these classes. Learning our history is important, especially because you have lived through some of these unspeakable experiences."

Mom nods in agreement, and Dion's light brown eyes meet mine with a sexy grin. I can tell he is pleased with me.

We continue to eat our lovely dinner while Auntie Mavis and Mom banter, with the husbands on the side chuckling softly, enjoying the delicious meals prepared by these incredible women.

Chapter 11: Reign

Friday

February 14th, 2025

Dion is cooking dinner for us tonight to celebrate our first Valentine's Day together. We had planned to go out but decided to stay in because restaurants are usually packed during this time of year. And I would prefer a home-cooked meal anyway, especially one prepared by my sexy man. He can cook his ass off.

We're not exchanging gifts because he doesn't want me spending any more money on him. He didn't exactly say those words, but I already know that's what he means. What he doesn't know is that I stopped by the store and got a new set of lingerie and handcuffs. I picked up some ideas from Kimi's spicy scenes. I'm hoping that tonight will help alleviate some of the tension he's been feeling with his lack of funds.

Looking at the time, I realize that Dion will be here in about fifteen minutes. We need to pick up a few more items for dinner at the grocery store. He is making seafood pasta with all of our favorites: shrimp and mussels, with crab legs on the side. Even just thinking about it makes my mouth water!

Throwing on a pair of sweatpants and a white T-shirt, I tie my hair up in a bun.

I hear the door shut, and Dion's deep voice calls out for me.

"Reign, are you ready?"

I check myself out in the mirror before meeting him in the living room.

"Yes, I'm ready to go."

He bites his knuckles as he looks me up and down appreciatively. "You don't even have to try hard to look sexy," he says with a grin.

A coy smile tugs at the corners of my lips. "I'm dressed in sweatpants."

"But you make them look so damn good," Dion replies, taking my hand and twirling me around. "I love your body in anything or nothing."

I playfully roll my eyes. "Of course you do. You're biased."

He pulls me closer and squeezes my ass. "I know what I like."

"You're lucky I like you too," I reply, enjoying our playful banter.

Dion plants a kiss on my lips before letting me go. "I got you a little something."

Surprised, I raise an eyebrow at the small silver gift bag he retrieves from the table and hands to me.

He notices my facial expression. "I know, I know, just open it."

Curious, I eagerly reach inside, my eyebrows shooting up in response to the contents. I shake my head as I look back at Dion, his lips splitting into a broad, goofy grin.

"What was your thought process behind this?" I ask, suspecting that this is his way of punishing me.

A sexy smile plays on his lips as he shrugs nonchalantly. "I saw it and thought of you."

Huh? I shake my head again. Of course he did, maybe I shouldn't have mentioned that spicy scene from Kimi's book. This man bought me a vibrating thong with a remote control.

Holding it up, I'm torn between feeling exhilarated and apprehensive about what to expect next.

"Put it on," Dion demands, asserting his dominance.

Furrowing my brows, "Ex—"

He smacks my ass, cutting off my protest. "I want you to put it on. Now."

Dion's dominant tone was both infuriating and strangely arousing. I comply with his request, his eyes following my every move as I deliberately pull down my sweatpants and slide off my underwear before slipping on the vibrating thong. Pulling up my sweatpants, a mischievous grin plays on his lips. He has me right where he wants me.

With a sly chuckle, Dion activates the remote control, sending a jolt of vibration through the thong. I nearly jump out of my skin with a surprised gasp.

His smirk widens as he watches my reaction, clearly pleased with himself.

"There are eleven different vibration modes," he informs me, toying with the remote. "Let's see which one you like best."

"D-Dion—" I warn, but my words are cut short by a particularly intense vibration that makes me squirm. "Shit!" I swear under my breath, kneeling over to grab my pussy to stifle the unexpected and overwhelming sensation.

The corner of his lips quirks up because he has the upper hand. "I will be controlling your orgasms today."

Glaring at him, I try to regain some control over the situation, but the pulsing pleasure between my legs makes it difficult to focus. Dion continues to experiment with the settings, each one eliciting a different reaction from me. As much as I try to resist, my body betrays me, and I feel myself edging closer to release, entirely at his mercy.

His eyes lock with mine, a wicked grin spreading across his face as he watches me unravel under his control. Just as I'm on the pinnacle of euphoria, he suddenly stops, leaving me teetering on the brink of release. My eyes snap open.

A devilish glint dances in his eyes. "Not yet."

My body still tingling, I let out a frustrated groan. "Dion! You can't be serious?"

"Oh, I'm very serious," he says, his voice dripping with satisfaction.

If blue balls were a thing for females, I'd be suffering right now. Why would Dion tease me like that? I was so close to my release, and he pulled the rug out from under me.

The entire car ride from my place to the store was a game of cat and mouse. Dion would relentlessly tease me and then abruptly stop every time I got close. What an asshole! But deep down, this shit is turning me on. Still, I have to figure out how to turn the tables on him. He is enjoying my frustration way too much.

We split up in the store to grab the items we still needed for dinner, like garlic, fresh parsley, butter, and white cooking wine. I approach a sales associate to ask for help finding the wine.

"Hi, can you point me in the direction of the white cooking w-wine?" I stammer out the last word as Dion approaches from behind with his items in a basket, cranking up the vibration again.

Heat rises to my cheeks as I struggle to keep my cool, and the worker looks at me like I have five heads. He points me in the direction of the wine aisle, and I quickly thank him before walking away, shooting a glare at Dion. A smirk forms on his face as he follows me down the aisle, and I try my best to maintain my poker face. When he stops the vibration long enough for me to grab the cooking wine from the top shelf, I seize the opportunity to get back at him when I catch him staring at my ass. I give him a little wiggle, and he sucks in a sharp breath.

"You shouldn't have done that," he warns, pressing that stupid button again.

Biting my lip, I suppress a moan as the vibrations buzz against my clit. He switches the mode to the tongue-licking setting, and I nearly lose my balance as my knees weaken. Holding onto the shelf for support, my eyes flutter open to meet Dion's smoldering gaze. More people walk down the aisle, glaring at me with disdain, but I can't bring myself to care. They have no idea how close I am to having an orgasm right here in the middle of the grocery store. I bite my lip harder, trying to stifle a gasp.

Dion's lips curl into a devilish smile as he decreases the vibrations to the lowest setting.

"Not yet," he says, taking the bottle out of my hand and placing it into the basket.

Leaning against the shelf. "Please, Dion," I beg, my words tumbling out more breathlessly than I wanted.

He presses against me, his hand discreetly slipping into my panties. "Soon. I will make you come more times than you can handle."

My breath catches in my throat, the thrill of being caught in such a public setting heightening the intensity of his promise.

The buzzing between my legs is at an all-time high, and I'm so horny now.

Stomping past Dion, I grab the bags from him and not so gently slam them on the kitchen counter.

"You good?" he questions, a smirk playing on his lips as he watches me fidget with the bags.

"I'm fine," I quip back, glaring at the remote control on the kitchen counter. I need to release this tension before I explode.

Dion's smirk widens as he steps behind me, and I shoot him a warning look. He just chuckles. His laugh only serves to heighten my frustration.

His hands reach past me to unpack the groceries, and my knuckles clench around the edge of the counter. I try to focus on unpacking the bags, but his proximity is distracting. His warm breath on my neck as he leans in to grab the wine from the bag makes it even harder to concentrate. When he is finally finished, he steps back and raises an eyebrow, silently challenging me to say something.

Ignoring his smug expression, I act as sous chef and begin prepping the ingredients for dinner for him to cook. We move around each other in the kitchen, and our usual banter continues, but every accidental brush of our bodies sends a jolt of electricity through me.

When dinner is ready, I slip into the bedroom to change out of the vibrating thong and toss it to the side. I've had enough of underwear today. I'm going commando, baby! I'm ready to turn the tables on Dion with a little seductive revenge.

Sauntering into the dining room, feeling confident and sexy, I sit pretty at the dinner table. As he takes in my lingerie, his smirk falters, and I know I've won this round.

"You look sexy," he comments, placing a plate of food in front of me.

I smile smugly. "Thank you." But I can tell by the way his eyes linger on me that he's already planning his next move.

The food was good as usual, and we enjoyed it over light conversation. As the night progresses, we load the dishwasher, and Dion settles on the sofa to watch Netflix. I bend over to pick up the remote, giving him a glimpse of what's underneath, or rather, the lack thereof. Dion's eyes widen, and his nostrils flare; I know I've got him right where I want him.

"No underwear?"

Sinking into the sofa, I spread my legs open to give him a better view. "Nope. You can't use the vibrator on me if I don't have any on."

Dion grins. "Well played," he concedes, dipping his head right over my entrance and blowing on it. "But there are other ways to make you squirm, Reign."

My breath catches in my throat, and I find it difficult to swallow. "Oh?"

He smirks, his fingers trailing lightly over my inner thighs. "Oh," he repeats. "I'll be right back," he says, standing up and heading towards the bedroom. "Don't move."

The anticipation builds in my chest, as I watch him go. When he returns, he wears nothing but a smile and his hard dick bouncing up and down.

My gaze lowers to his erection. "And here I thought we were actually going to watch a movie."

His mischievous grin widens as he approaches me, his hands discreetly hidden behind his back. "Who said we can't make a movie of our own?" Dion takes the handcuffs from his back and dangles them in front of me. "What are you doing with these?"

"I wanted you to use them on me."

Rubbing his chin hair, he looks around the room, considering the possibilities. I can tell when an idea pops into his head. There's a pole near my balcony that he could handcuff me to. We share a knowing look before he takes my hand and leads me over to the pole.

"Get on the floor," he orders in a low and husky tone. "I'm ready for my dessert."

I comply.

He lifts my hands above my head and handcuffs them to the pole, then spreads me open with his knees.

"When you have had enough, the safe word is purple."

Dion shoves his fingers into me without warning, and I arch my back in response.

"Damn, that pussy is so wet for me," he growls, withdrawing his fingers and sucking off the juices. "You taste so good, baby."

He dives back in with his mouth. His skilled tongue caresses and teases my swollen clit, igniting a rainbow of colors behind my closed eyelids. The suction of his mouth and the flick of his tongue blend with my soft moans. It doesn't take long before I reach my peak. A tingling sensation spreads through my body, intensifying the ecstasy pulsating through me and leaving me in a blissful state of surrender. With each wave of pleasure, the cold and unforgiving metal of the cuff bites into my wrist, tightening its grip as I struggle against it. The orgasmic release is so powerful that I feel detached as if my soul is watching from outside my body. I moan loudly, releasing my pent-up sexual frustration after hours of build-up.

"Dion, I—I"

He pauses, his eyes locked with mine. "Do you want me to stop?"

Biting my lip, I shake my head. Dion circles his tongue over my clit, sending shockwaves of pleasure that make me gasp for air. He skillfully inserts two fingers, curling them just right to hit that perfect spot inside me. Damn, that feels so good! As his tongue works its magic on my clit and his fingers continue their relentless assault, I feel myself teetering on the edge of another explosive climax. My body tenses, every nerve coming alive with pleasure as I let go completely, surrendering to the overwhelming waves of ecstasy. Moaning his name, I tilt my head back in pure bliss and fix my gaze on the patterns painted on the ceiling. I feel like I'm floating, lost in a sweet torment. My body quivers with each wave of pleasure, my breath coming in short gasps as I ride the intense sensations to an earth-shattering climax.

As I come down from the high, my body feels weak, and my mind is joyfully blank. Dion uncuffs my sore wrists and scoops me into his arms, carrying me to the bedroom.

He lays me down gently on the bed, straddling me with his hardened erection pressed against my thigh. His breath hitches as he pumps himself a few times before slowly and steadily inserting himself into my slick center, eliciting a tremble down my backbone.

With gentle precision, Dion moves in and out of me, setting a rhythm that builds with each thrust. He peels my lingerie off, exposing my breasts to the cool air. His thumb glides over my hardened nipple, eliciting a delicious numbness to spread. Gripping my hips firmly, his deliberate strokes pick up pace, the intoxicating sensations prompting a symphony of moans to escape my lips. Driven by a relentless desire, Dion continues to pound into me, the force of his thrusts making my body quiver with anticipation.

"Reign, your pussy is so good," he groans against my ear, thrusting harder and harder into me.

His thumb expertly rubs circles around my swollen clit, sending waves of electric pleasure coursing through me. My hands clutch at the sheets beneath me, my nails digging into the fabric as I arch my back in response to his movements. Every inch of my body quivers with the powerful surge of my orgasm as if a lightning bolt is coursing through me. We meet our release together, our bodies trembling in unison.

Dion collapses beside me, his heavy breaths mingling with mine.

The air is thick with the scent of sex and sweat as we hold each other, breathless and sated.

Chapter 12: Dion

The gentle warmth of the sun touching my eyelids wakes me up to a quiet morning. Looking over my shoulder, I gaze at Reign with deep appreciation, feeling grateful for her presence in my life. My heart beats in a new and exhilarating way when I'm with her. Her face is the first thing I think of in the morning and the last thing before I sleep at night. At times, especially in the quiet of the night, the reality of everything hits me, and I still can't believe she's real. Little did I know that agreeing to Eddie's absurd plan to fake date the stunning Reign Amara Brown would lead me not only to my soulmate but also Eddie to his. He swears he is not pussy-whipped, but considering how Scarlette basically lives with him, I'd say otherwise.

Scarlette is cool, though; she's like the sister I never thought I wanted. August is kind and upfront; even though I don't see her as often as Scarlette, she is definitely good people. I enjoy spending time with them and being a part of Reign's world. I'm even more glad that Reign is becoming more involved in my life too. *Finally*. I was initially embarrassed by my shitty apartment, but now I enjoy having her in my bed and in my circle.

Auntie Mavis sent me a few messages after dinner on Wednesday, saying she can't wait to see Reign again and hopefully meet her family. I guess she didn't catch the drift when my mother asked Reign if her parents could come for dinner one of these days; the deafening silence that followed was telling. My father gave me a knowing look. While I haven't mentioned Reign's horrible family business to my mother, I have shared some of what has happened with him. He explained that it can be hard for men to get along with their woman's mother. Loving someone may mean enduring almost anything, but it should never involve accepting disrespect. I never had the pleasure of meeting my grandmother, but Dad said she felt like he was taking her baby away. However, the dynamic with Reign and her mother is completely different. Based on what I've seen, she is a horrible mother figure to Reign, and Reign deserves so much better. She is kind, smart, sexy, and independent, yet she is cursed with a mother who is hateful and vile.

I want to give Reign the world, and one day I will give her everything she deserves and more. But how can I do that when she is fully capable of achieving it herself?

She looks peaceful as she sleeps soundly. Brushing the pad of my thumb over her plump lips, an electric energy courses through my veins and into her. Her body shivers slightly, but she doesn't wake up. I slowly remove the covers, and she stirs in response to the change in temperature. We slept naked last night, and now nothing is holding me back from devouring her for breakfast. Kneeling, I dip my head between her legs, inhaling her scent, my dick shuddering in response.

"Damn, Reign," I mutter under my breath before diving in.

I trace her lips with my tongue, working my way to her clit, her body beginning to twist and turn. She's waking up.

"Dion?" Reign murmurs, her voice hoarse. "What are you doing?"

"I'm having my breakfast," I reply before running my tongue over her swollen nub.

Her movements beneath my tongue are slow and deliberate as she trails her fingers from the back of my neck into my hair. As I suck on her clit, I gently insert my pointer finger, followed by my middle, and then my ring finger, eliciting a gasp of pleasure from her. There is no greater happiness for me than the feeling of her wet and warm sex gripping my fingers. The sensation is even more pleasurable around my shaft. I switch between quick, gentle strokes and tender suction on her pulsating nerve, feeling her hips move in rhythm. With a firm grip on my head, she vigorously rides my tongue, relishing the pleasure I'm giving her. Reign emits a soft hum as she closes her eyes, her muscles tense and quivering in anticipation. She's about to come; however, I want to come with her. Replacing my fingers with my erect dick elicited a loud "Yes!" from her.

With each slow thrust into her warmth, her tight core synchronizes perfectly with my movements. "Yes, Dion. Just like that," she shouts breathlessly.

I'll never get tired of this sweet and wonderful pussy. It's so fucking good! Feeling her reciprocate my passion and longing, I push into her with more speed and force. She wants me just as much as I want her. With each movement of the bed, the pleasure inside me reaches new heights. *Shit!* A wave of intense pleasure washes over her, causing her to shiver as she unravels beneath me. My pace quickens as my seed shoots through my pulsating cock, leaving a trail across the sheets.

Collapsing beside her on the bed. "Damn, Reign."

"Damn yourself," she breathes out.

Panting, we lie on the rumpled sheets, the ceiling above us appearing as a blurred white, our breaths quick and shallow.

As we catch our breath, my brows cluster together. "What time will the party bus be here?"

Reign sits up and gazes at me. "Why are you making that face?"

"Because why do we need a party bus to go to the Poconos? We could have just driven there."

She gets off the bed, and I watch as she walks to the door, her naked silhouette outlined by the light streaming in from the window.

"We wanted to arrive there together," she explains with a mischievous glint in her eye before leaving the room with a sexy sway of her hips.

Damn, that woman has me wrapped around her fingers.

"Wassup, bro?" Eddie greets, stepping down the stairs from the party bus.

I give him a fist pound. "How are you feeling, man?"

"Good, bro, everything is good. How are you really feeling about this trip?" He asks, opening the luggage compartment under the bus.

I shrug and start loading Reign's bags into the compartment. "I'm good."

"You sure?"

"Why are you asking, man?" I ask, sounding slightly annoyed.

"The ladies sprung this trip on us at the last minute. I wanted to make sure you were good *money-wise*," he lowers his voice.

Exhaling a sharp breath. "Eddie, I'm good. Reign paid, and I'll pay her back when I have it."

"Are you going to tell her how much in debt you are?"

Eddie is the only person who knows how much debt I'm actually in. All 40K plus worth of it.

"Hi, Eddie," Reign greets him as she approaches us. "Talking about me?"

Eddie quickly changes the subject, flashing a smile at Reign. "Just making sure our boy here loads up all your bags."

"I appreciate the help," Reign responds with a grateful smile and heads into the party bus.

"I thought we were only staying four nights. Why does she have so many bags?" Eddie asks as we load up the luggage.

"Man, you know how women are."

We finish loading the bags and get on. I nod my head to the driver and take in the interior. Trent and Dante are sitting in the front of the bus, across from each other. Scarlette, Love, Reign, and Kimi are seated at the back of the bus near the stripper pole. I wave at the ladies and sit on the black leather seat next to Trent, giving him a fist pound.

"Where are August and Calvin?"

"August had something come up at work, so Calvin went into work since August will be busy today," Trent explains, leaning back in his seat.

Scarlette stands and sways slightly as the sharp pop of the champagne bottle cuts through the bus. The scent of bubbly sweetness fills the air as she holds the bottle. "Okay, ladies! Let's get this party started."

A pulsating beat booms from the speakers, vibrating through the floor. Each woman grabs a glass and begins dancing, their movements fluid and energetic. Love and Kimi move seductively around the pole. Purple and white lights on the ceiling blink rapidly, in time with the pulse of the music, creating a mesmerizing strobe effect.

The music is loud with a thumping bass, but it doesn't drown out Eddie and Dante's conversation. They're locked in a heated discussion about the Knicks' performance last season versus this one.

Trent leans in and says, "I found out some info on dude."

I glance at Reign, who is smiling, laughing, and enjoying her time with her friends.

"Good or bad?"

"It's some fucked-up shit."

The muscles in my neck tense. I massage them absentmindedly, my gaze still on Reign. She catches my eye, and a dull ache follows with stiffness. I force a smile. Her light-brown eyes light up, and she winks, blowing me a kiss. Her friends exchange knowing glances, noticing our interaction, and playfully tease her.

"I thought you wouldn't have info on him until the end of the month."

"Yeah, that was the plan, but when I told my guy that Peterson and Traymen's partner was the focus of our investigation, he believed this case took precedence."

Rubbing my chin hairs, I maintain my composure. I don't want to ruin this trip for Reign. This is the most relaxed I've seen her since that awful dinner with her family. Maybe we should wait for now; let her enjoy today and tomorrow at least.

"Iight, tell me everything, but not right now," I respond,

motioning my head at the ladies.

Trent glances back, nodding. "When we get to the house, I'll tell you everything my guy found out. I also did some digging, and let's just say we need to get Skylar away from him as soon as possible. But we have to be smart. Peter has some powerful lawyers who were questioning my involvement in wanting to learn more about him."

My eyes are wide. "What did you tell them?"

Trent smirks. "What I always tell them."

"And what's that?"

"I'm a billionaire. I need to know who is in my circle," he says, pouring a glass of bourbon, the ice clinking against the glass.

Has he also looked into my past?

Nodding as if he had heard my thoughts, he takes a sip of his drink.

By three o'clock, we arrive at the cabin, and I immediately scan my surroundings, taking note of everything around me. A flight of steps leads up to the front door of the cabin, and a vast forest surrounds it, with a small, barely visible trail leading to the north. The icy breeze gently rustles the leaves, sending shivers down my spine. I hope we don't encounter any dangerous or unexpected wildlife during our stay. The ladies with smaller bags enter the cabin through a discreet side entrance that was almost completely hidden by bushes. Though Scarlette is carrying fewer bags than Reign, they all seem to be overpacked with items that I believe are unnecessary for our trip. I only brought one bag with maybe two to four outfits. Reign assured us that we would spend our entire stay at the cabin, so there was no need to bring any extra clothes. We grab the remaining bags from the bus's baggage compartment, the smell of exhaust fumes permeating the air. Meanwhile, Trent slips the driver a five-hundred-dollar tip.

"You will get the rest on Wednesday," he assures the driver, and he thanks Trent with appreciation.

As we enter through the side door, a refreshing display of royal blue, light blue, and white welcomes us. To the left is a boho-style kitchen with a brown and blue exterior and a cozy, artistically decorated interior with patterned tiles. I subtly nod at Trent, indicating that we would discuss what he had learned about Peter later. Reign gestures for me to follow her upstairs to what I assume is our bedroom, the worn wood creaking beneath our feet in the quiet house. Entering the dimly lit bedroom, a massive king-size bed dominates the space, its dark wood gleaming under the soft glow of a single lamp. A dark brown dresser with a polished finish holds a 42-inch flat-screen TV. To the right of the room, a luxurious bathroom features a jacuzzi tub and a separate shower placed in the far right corner.

The bathroom floor is covered in white tiles accented by a baby blue border and features his-and-hers sinks. After placing my toothbrush and soap on the cool ceramic countertop, I head out of the bathroom to the walk-in closet. I set my bags down on the floor. Reign pulls back the long curtains and the room is nice, bathed in sunlight streaming through the window and warming the wooden floor.

"The showerhead is detachable," Reign coos from the bathroom, her voice seductive.

"Is that an invitation or an observation?" I reply with a smirk.

"It's an observation," she says playfully, stripping off her clothes. "I'm going to take a shower."

"You're giving mixed signals," I tease.

"I'm all sweaty," she laughs.

"I bet you are from all that dancing you were doing," I reply, chuckling.

She walks over to me naked and takes hold of my forming bulge. "Perhaps I'll entertain you with a strip show later tonight," she muses.

My cock twitches under her touch, and she bites her bottom lip. I suck on the side of her neck, the taste of salt and vanilla coating my tongue. Sticking two fingers into her hole, she gasps.

"Maybe we can reenact one of those scenes you read to me from that nasty book you were so engaged in," I reply, wiggling my eyebrows.

"Oh! Gosh. I know that's where you got that damn vibrating thong idea from."

That's right, I would have never thought of that if she didn't read me that scene.

"I have some ideas on how I'm going to please you tonight," she says, slightly grinding against my fingers.

"I can't wait." Her breath catches in her throat, and I withdraw my coated fingers and bring them to my mouth, tasting her salty arousal.

Reign steps back, a smirk playing on her lips as she turns to walk towards the shower, giving me something to look at as she saunters away.

Damn, I love that woman.

After changing into shorts, I make my way downstairs to the game room, where the smell of chalk and polish mingles with the voices of Trent, Eddie, and Dante as they set up for a pool game.

Joining the banter, I grab a cue stick. "Seems like all the ladies are in the shower, huh?"

"All that damn dancing they were doing on the bus," Trent shakes his head.

"Looks like it's just us guys for now," Dante adds. "You in for a game?"

"For sure," I reply, chalking my stick.

Eddie arranges the balls in a triangle with the eight ball in the center, then sets the cue ball on the table.

Nodding at Trent as he chalks his own stick, "Let's talk about what you found out."

A serious expression crosses his face. "First and foremost, Skylar and Peter had been together for less than a year when he proposed to her. That's the first red flag, but I know some couples move fast."

I knew this already. While I found it odd that he proposed to Skylar so quickly, who am I to judge? Because of how I feel about Reign, I know I want to spend the rest of my life with her.

Trent finishes chalking his stick and continues, "Peter's mother died from an overdose some years ago. According to my sources, she was severely depressed and traumatized by the beatings from her late husband—Peter's father. She overdosed on drugs five years later after his death." A shadow of sadness briefly flickers in Trent's eyes, a ghost of a memory surfacing before he shakes his head.

"Bro, are you serious?" Eddie's eyes widen as he chalks his own pool stick. "That's heavy stuff."

Trent furrows his brow, nodding solemnly. "There's more."

Dante positions himself at the pool table, listening to the conversation and carefully aiming his shot to choose between the solid and striped balls. With a sharp crack, the striped ball sinks into the corner pocket, earning him a satisfied grin.

Eddie aims for the solid balls, sinking one after the other with precision.

Trent squints at the table. "Ten years ago, Peter's father beat his mother until she was barely recognizable, then committed suicide."

"Damn! So that would have made Peter...like what? Eighteen

years old?" Eddie croons.

Trent nods his head in confirmation and aims for the striped ball and misses, biting his lower lip.

"Charged as an adult!" Eddie and I say in unison.

"Facts," Dante adds.

"If he did murder his father that is," I say. "But according to your sources his father committed suicide afterward?" I can't seem to believe that.

My hand tightens around the pool cue, lining up my shot for the solid ball. In one swift movement, I hit the ball with such force that two solid balls go into the hole.

"Or so the reports claim," Dante says, his voice low and serious, taking his shot and missing.

I watch as the striped ball rolls to a stop, and Dante continues, "I don't think his father killed himself. I think Peter killed him and made it look like a suicide. What if Peter walked in on his father beating his mother and snapped? And they lied about it because he was eighteen when it happened."

We all exchange uneasy glances.

"I'm still digging into it. If I had access to his phone or laptop, I could hack it and find out for myself," Trent adds, his eyes narrowing in thought.

"Bro, I doubt he would store any incriminating evidence on his devices," Eddie remarks.

Trent smirks at Eddie, "You'll be surprised what I can find out from just your phone."

My eyes widen. "What do you do besides own one of the top security companies in New York?"

His lips twist into a wicked grin. "Let's just say I have my legal business and my *not-so-legal* business. But I promise I use my skills for good." He kisses his two fingers and places them over his heart.

"Scout's honor."

"Sure," I reply in a deadpan tone.

We all share a knowing laugh before Trent becomes stern again. "But in all seriousness, my guy found out that Peter beat his ex-wife about four years ago, and he paid her a hefty amount to keep quiet about it. The judge granted them a speedy divorce because he is a friend of the family."

"What type of shit?" Eddie blows out a frustrated breath.

Shaking my head in disbelief. "What kind of corrupt shit is this?"

Trent looks at us with a grim expression. "When you're rich, you can bury a lot of skeletons in your closet. It's all about who you know and how much you're willing to pay to keep things quiet. I have a few agents and detectives in my pocket, but I'm not a lowlife scumbag like this asshole Peter."

Gripping my pool stick, I fire another shot, completely missing the solid ball. I can't even focus now.

"I'm not done," Trent continues.

A crease forms between my brows. "There's more?" Why is he delivering the information with such an overly dramatic flair?

"Yeah, he also has a son."

Lost in thought, I lean against the pool table. What is good with all these dudes having secret kids? The shock must be written all over my face because Eddie claps me on the back.

"I know, bro, I know," he says, echoing my thoughts.

Chapter 13: Reign

With the "V-Day Weekend" playlist booming from Scarlette's Bluetooth speakers, the ladies and I are in the indoor pool sipping on fruity cocktails. Scarlette is known for always being the life of the party with her playlists ready to go. She plays a mix of R&B, hip-hop, reggae, and reggaeton, with some pop music thrown in. This weekend, we'll mainly be listening to R&B, my favorite genre of music. I softly chuckle as I remember Kimi and Scarlette arguing over controlling the music at one of August's brunches. It was hilarious to watch them go back and forth. Like, I just can't with them.

I briefly catch a glimpse of Dion passing by, exchanging a subtle smile filled with unspoken emotions before disappearing. We're going to have game night tomorrow which I'm sure will be a blast.

I'm glad he and Trent are getting along so well; I love this for our group of friends.

Right now, I don't want to think about work. I don't want to dwell on the three weddings coming up on the same day. I don't want to think about my treacherous mother, aunt, or cousins. And as much as it pains me to say this, I don't want to think about my sister and whatever issues she has going on. I want to enjoy my time here without thinking about any of it. Although this feeling of freedom is fleeting, tied to the inevitable return to reality, I am going to soak it all in while I can.

Tyrese's "Sweet Lady" blasts through the speakers, and my hips start swaying to the beat, creating tiny ripples in the water.

"Yes! This my shit!" I belt out.

I think my drink is starting to hit, but I don't care. I haven't heard this song in years. Sometimes, I forget how good Tyrese can sing. *90s music will always be it for me!*

The ladies look back at me and laugh, shaking their heads.

I hold up my glass. "I need a refill!"

Love made us a lovely cocktail with gin, club soda, a hint of syrup, and a garnish of mint and fresh lemon slices. She learned to make this drink from April, who learned from Richard. I usually avoid gin, but this drink is doing what it needs to do, if you know what I mean. April and Richard reignited their romance last year and have been inseparable ever since. I love that for them. Scarlette doesn't know yet, but we will be celebrating her birthday at Richard's bar in a few weeks.

Scarlette reaches for the bottle of tequila, her go-to liquor. "I'm giving you a shot instead."

Here she goes with this damn tequila again. If you ask her, she swears it's the best drink ever made. "No, Scarlette! I don't want a shot of anything from you," I playfully protest.

"*Silencio*," she chides, pouring everyone a shot of tequila before clinking glasses. *"Salud!"*

Grimacing, I throw back the shot; the harsh liquid sears my throat as it goes down.

"How are you feeling?" Scarlette asks with a mischievous grin, knowing full well that I hate the taste of tequila.

My face scrunches up in distaste.

"That bad, huh?"

"Like I just swallowed a bottle of rubbing alcohol," I gag, causing Scarlette to burst into laughter.

Scarlette tosses back another shot, as I grab a lime wedge to chase the bitter taste. How could anyone actually like the taste of tequila?

The burning sensation still lingers in my throat, and I start to feel a slight dizziness, making the room spin a little. "Love, can you pass me a bottle of water?"

Love nods and tosses me a bottle that I almost miss due to my slightly impaired coordination. *Yeah, it's definitely time for some water.* Twisting off the cap, I throw my head back and chug the entire bottle in one go.

"Damn, bitch! You was thirsty, huh?" Love laughs, prompting Scarlette and Kimi to join in.

Although the cool water soothes my throat and settles my stomach, I still feel disoriented. When I don't laugh along with them, they look at me with concern, their eyes crinkling. Their worried expressions bore into me, revealing my inner truths. I don't know what's wrong with me. I felt fine just a moment ago, but now I'm starting to feel really out of it. Emotions swirl inside me like a storm. Being a strong, independent woman, I got used to handling everything on my own without relying on others. Yet, despite my independence, I still feel lost. While my business is flourishing with tons of satisfied clients, my personal life is like a neglected garden overgrown with weeds. For years, I have endured disrespect and manipulative gaslighting from my family. They distort reality to paint me as flawed, all the while ignoring their own unresolved issues. While I may have flaws, I actively make an effort to acknowledge and address them.

"I go to therapy!" I blurt out to no one in particular under their scrutiny.

Confused looks are exchanged between my friends, and I cover my mouth, mortified that the words had slipped out without my conscious consent or control.

"No more tequila for you," Scarlette chastises me in a not-so-joking tone.

My cheeks flush with embarrassment. "Sorry, I'm fine, I promise," I mumble, hoping to shift the focus away from my outburst. "I don't want to think or talk about my own issues right now. Let's just forget about it and enjoy ourselves."

"You sure you good?" Love asks with genuine concern, placing a hand on my shoulder.

"Girl, you know I'm here for you," Scarlette reassures, looking from Love to Kimi and back to me. "*We* are here for you."

"I appreciate it, really," I respond. "Let's just have fun and not dwell on it."

Having known Scarlette for as long as I can remember, she gives me a knowing smile, understanding that sometimes distraction is the best medicine. Over the years, our bond has grown to encompass many friends. Some have remained loyal while others have drifted away, yet our steadfast friendship remains.

"Let's get this party started then," Kimi exclaims, connecting to the Bluetooth.

"Kimi, you know Scarlette has a playlist for every occasion,"

Love teases, playfully elbowing me.

"Trust me, this is one of Scarlette's faves," Kimi reassures.

The song "I Like It Like That" blasts through the speakers, and we jump out of the pool, shaking our asses and rapping along with Cardi B.

Chapter 14: Dion

Warm sunlight filters through the curtains as Reign's fingers gently move up my spine, eliciting a pleasant tingling sensation. She rolls me over onto my back, straddling my hips. She wears a seductive smile, mischief dancing in her eyes.

"Reign, what are you doing?"

"I want to do you," she croaks.

"Is that right?" I quip back, brushing my hand over her perky nipple. "Who am I to argue with that?"

She smirks, moving her hips back and forth against me, arousing my member. Her eyes grow wide as she feels my dick grow against her pussy.

"Just sit back and enjoy the ride," she purrs, leaning in to capture my lips in a heated kiss.

I taste the sweetness of her lips as my hands roam over her smooth skin, kissing, sucking, and savoring every inch of her.

As her nails dig into my back, my phone buzzes with a notification, momentarily distracting me.

"Ignore it," Reign demands breathlessly, kissing me hungrily. "I want your full attention on me."

"It could be important," I protest weakly, but her hands are already trailing down my chest.

"Nothing matters more than this," she teases seductively while pulling down my boxers.

I mention, "It might be my agent," but Reign interrupts by taking me in her mouth.

"Fuck," I groan as her talented mouth works its magic. Another notification buzzes on my phone, and I hazily glance at the screen, seeing a few texts from my agent.

"Let me see what she wants," I say reluctantly.

Reign looks up at me with a pout, her lips still glistening. "Fine," she relents, sitting up on the bed as I reach for my phone.

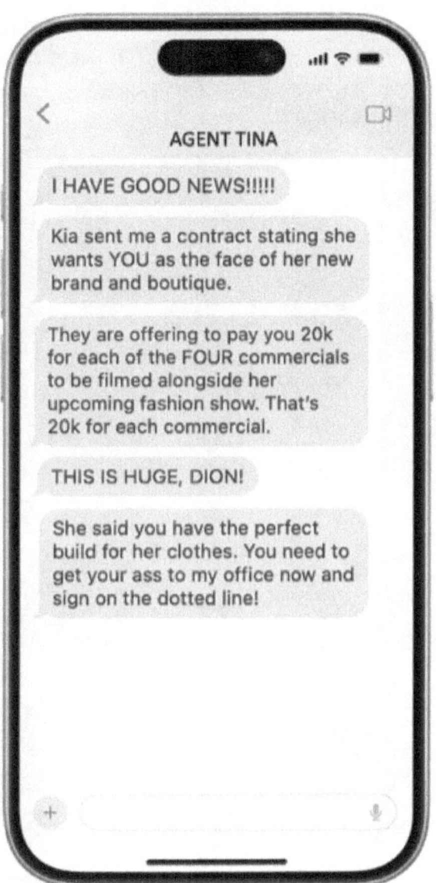

This is the big break I've been waiting for! Excitement rushes over me like a burst of sunshine.

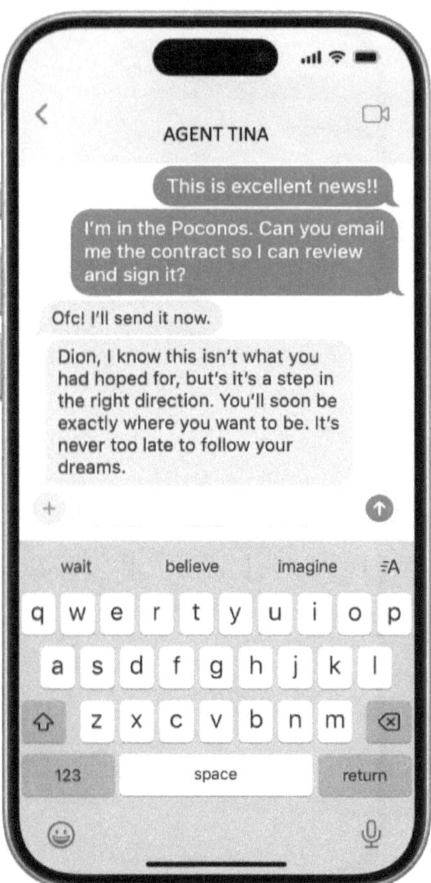

Thank you, God! Life surprises you with an unexpected gift beyond your wildest dreams when you least expect it. I can clear my debts with this kind of money in no time. While this job may not be my dream job, it lays a crucial foundation for my future. I'm incredibly thankful for this unexpected blessing, something I never imagined I would receive. *Modeling?* Walking in a fashion show has never crossed my mind before. This is crazy. And it's more than what Layla has offered me.

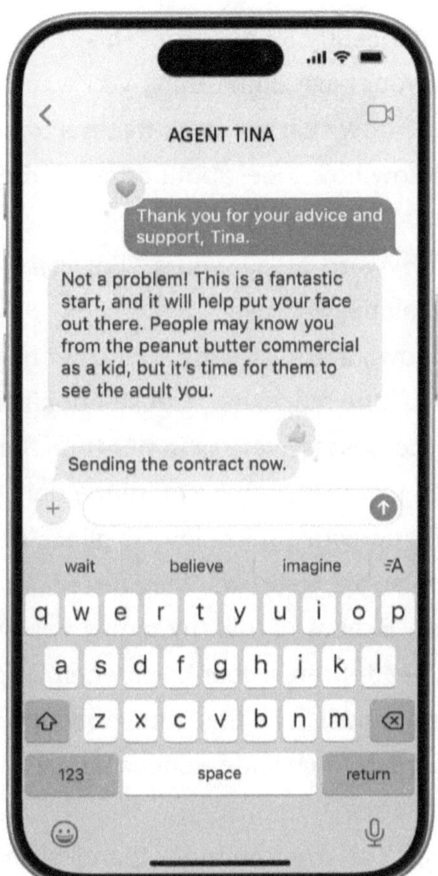

Reign's eyes are wide and unblinking, waiting for me to tell her the good news.

"Kia sent my agent a contract offering to pay me 20k for four commercials and a fashion show," I say with a grin.

Reign's jaw drops as she squeals, "You're going to be a model!" As the words sink in, a giggle threatens to escape her as she presses her lips together.

My eyes narrow, trying to decipher her reaction. "What is so funny?"

"I didn't laugh," she insists.

"But you want to," I counter, crossing my arms over my chest.

She shrugs innocently. "I'm sorry. This is amazing news, babe. I'm so proud of you. I just didn't think you wanted to be a model." Reign pushes me down on my back again and straddles me once more. "I don't know how I feel about other women lusting over my sexy man."

I chuckle. "Keyword being 'yours.' I'm *yours*. I only have eyes for you and you alone. My rose."

Reign leans down and kisses me softly, her fingers trailing down my chest. "Good," she murmurs. "Cause I don't share."

Reveling in the possessiveness in her tone, I smirk and pull her closer, "No need to worry, baby. You're the only one I want."

Her eyes light up with a mischievous glint. "I manifested this."

Intrigued, I raise an eyebrow. "Manifested what?"

Reign laughs, "Because I told my family you were a model."

Shaking my head, I remember back when Reign introduced me to her family as a model, a lie that somehow turned into reality.

"Yeah, yeah, yeah," I chuckle, squeezing her ass cheeks. "I guess I owe you for that one."

Reign teases, "You owe me more than just that," as her fingers trace patterns on my chest. "Let me celebrate you," she purrs, her eyes darkening as she lowers herself to my erect cock. "I want to pick up where we left off."

Tuesday

February 18th, 2025

Today is the day I have been dreading since Trent told me on Saturday what he found out about Peter. We're leaving tomorrow, and this much-needed quick getaway has been cool. We shared many laughs and created lasting memories. Now it's time to face the reality waiting for us back home.

We're currently sitting in the living room, and everyone knows except for Reign. The warmth of her body seeps through my clothes as she sits on my lap, completely unaware of the bombshell that is about to be dropped.

Trent clears his throat, and everyone falls silent, exchanging nervous glances. "Reign, we have something to tell you."

Her sharp eyes scan the room, taking in everyone's wary expressions.

"What is it?" She asks, her voice stern.

"My men did some digging, and we found out that Peter has an ex-wife who he used to beat and abuse."

She gasps, her hands flying up to her mouth. I pull her closer to my chest, bracing her for what comes next. "There's more."

Trent nods in my direction and continues, "Peter's brother paid off his ex-wife, and she has since disappeared. They also had a child together." He pauses, studying her expression. I can't see her face, but her body tenses on my lap. "He has a judge, and God knows who else, in his pocket. If we are to get your sister out of this situation. *If* that is something she wants, then we need a solid plan."

Trent says *if*, and it doesn't go unnoticed. He could be right about Skylar wanting to stay with him. Who knows what he has possibly been telling her all this time? He doesn't mention Peter's father. Trent suspects Peter killed him and believes it wasn't a suicide. I will ask him about that later.

Reign stands up and starts pacing the room, with everyone watching in silence.

"Reign?" Scarlette calls out. "Are you good?"

Her eyes burn into Scarlette, who looks at me.

"Reign, what do you want to do?" I ask.

With a shaky hand, she reaches for me, holding me close. She whispers, "I have to call my dad and tell him everything."

I nod, and she disappears up the stairs, heading to our room and out of sight.

"Discouragement"

The initial honeymoon period faded.
Now you are starting to understand your partner: their past, their
flaws, and some of the weight of their experiences.
It's time to decide.
Is your love strong enough to endure the trials ahead?

Chapter 15: Reign

Saturday

March 1ˢᵗ, 2025

It's been over a week since Trent delivered the unexpected news about Peter, leaving me in a state of disbelief. I have been deeply contemplating this for days, yet I find it challenging to articulate the complex emotions it evokes in me. *Ex-wife and a baby!* The news has me rolling my eyes into next week.

And when Trent said *if* she wanted to leave, it left me feeling uneasy. When I asked my sister in our secret language if Peter was hurting her, she said yes. There were no ifs, ands, or buts about it. I heard her clearly. Given the challenges women face today, I propose that a secret communication system be established exclusively for women. I know it may sound a little childish, but I think it would be beneficial and necessary.

Many women have experienced abuse but are often afraid to speak about it openly. Consider the power of a communication method that enables women to discreetly signal for help. *Unless there is already one?* However, even when women speak out about abuse, they are often not believed. While some women may lie, a larger number are too scared to speak their truth, including myself. While I have recently exposed what my aunt's husband did to me years ago to my family, I prefer not to discuss it publicly.

I'm facing a wall of unknowns. Every unanswered question leaves me adrift and without direction. I'd like to think I know my sister, but I wonder what daily conversations Peter uses to manipulate her into staying with him. People often give opinions on things they haven't experienced, suggesting what they would do differently. The reality is, you can't predict your actions in a situation you haven't faced. If Dion were abusing me, I honestly don't know what I would do. Abuse can manifest in different forms, including physical violence, emotional manipulation, and everything in between. For instance, my mother has verbally abused me my entire life. Each form of abuse has a distinct impact on the victim's mind.

After learning about Peter's ex-wife and baby, I called my father to share the news. Naturally, he was furious. The situation is burdening him as he grapples with the fact that his daughter was abused by a trusted individual over twenty years ago and the added worry of his other daughter being in a vulnerable position.

He is not okay.

I'm getting ready to head over to his place now. Dion, Trent, Love, and Darcy are going to meet me there. We need to devise a solid plan to get Peter and Skylar in the same room as us. I'm grateful to August for connecting me with Love. She's been a constant source of support throughout this journey. I'm also thankful to her boyfriend, Trent, whose kindness and resources have been a true blessing.

"My beautiful Amara," my dad greets me as I walk through the doors.

Melting into his embrace. "Hey, Dad, how are you feeling?"

He sighs and pulls away slightly, a tired look in his eyes. "As good as can be expected, sweetheart."

Withdrawing from his embrace, I notice the weariness etched into his features. Throughout my life, my father has always been strong and resolute, ready to face any challenge. Now, his defeated posture is visible as he sags with exhaustion. Dad's usual sharp appearance is replaced with a disheveled look. His hair is falling past his ears and a scruffy stubble covering his usually neatly trimmed beard.

"Dad, how are things really going?"

Meeting my gaze, I can see the fatigue behind his eyes. "Amara, there is too much going on right now. Between your mother and me, that man," he says with a cold edge in his voice, "and now Sky and Peter. I don't know."

"Dad, I understand. You don't need to beat yourself up over this," I say softly.

He lets out a heavy sigh, his shoulders slumping even more. "Your mother pushed this marriage on Sky. I can't help but feel guilty for not being there more for you girls. My goal was to provide a better life for you both so you didn't have to struggle like I did. I thought if I worked hard, I could protect you from this cruel world."

Extending my hand, I gently squeeze his. "Dad, we appreciate everything you've done for us."

He gazes at me, his eyes brimming with emotion. "I'm angry with your mother. She is my wife, but I can't even look at her now."

The pain in his eyes is palpable. "Have you started therapy?"

Dad nods. "Yes, I started seeing your therapist, but I'm not ready for couples therapy yet."

"It's okay, Dad. It takes time," I say gently as I wrap my arms around him again, breathing in his familiar scent.

He kisses my forehead when I pull away, and my phone buzzes with a notification from Dion informing me he is outside.

"Dad, everyone is here. Are you ready?"

He nods, and I head to the front door to let them in. We gather in the living room.

Trent reaches for Dad's hand. "Hi, Mr. Brown. It's nice to meet you. I'm sorry that it is under these terrible circumstances."

My dad firmly shakes Trent's outstretched hand. "Thank you, Trent."

Darcy walks over to my dad and shows him her phone. "Mr. Brown, Skylar hasn't made a post since the week of the wedding. It seems like Peter is controlling Sky and is isolating her from everyone. We haven't spoken in months."

My father stares at the screen, his expression turning grim. "What the hell is he doing to my daughter?" he asks no one in particular. "How do we help her?"

Dion suggests, "Maybe we should invite Skylar and Peter over for a family dinner." We look to him, and he shrugs, "Peter never missed a Saturday night dinner."

"Dion's right, and he was very adamant about me coming to the last dinner," I add.

My father admits, "Peter told us you paid Dion to be your boyfriend right before you came to dinner and asked us not to say anything. I wanted to speak to you privately about it, but then you revealed…"

"I know, Dad," I say softly, looking down at my hands. "I'm sorry for not telling you sooner."

"Amara, you have nothing to apologize for," my father reassures me sternly. "We need to address this situation with Peter before it escalates any further. I will not have another one of my daughters being taken advantage of."

"How about you give him a call and invite him to a family dinner?" Trent suggests.

"My wife would have to be involved if I invited him over, and I'm not ready to face her."

"Dad, I understand, but we need to speak to Sky. This is the best way to do it." Looking around the room, I continue, "Is everyone available next Saturday?"

Dion wraps me in a hug. "Of course I'll be there, babe."

"We'll move some things around," Love adds, and Trent nods in agreement.

Darcy chimes in, "Count me in too."

My father stares into space for a few heartbeats before finally relenting. "Alright, Amara. I'll give your mother a call," he says with a resigned sigh before excusing himself from the living room to make the dreaded call.

When he returns, he simply nods and says, "Saturday works for me and your mother."

"Now that everyone is on board for next Saturday, it's time to call Peter."

Dad exhales a sharp breath and dials Peter's number. He picks up on the second ring.

Dad: "Hello, Peter. How's it going?"
Dad: "Great, we are resuming family dinners next Saturday. I do hope you and Skylar can join us."

A silence stretches for a few moments before my dad replies.

Dad: "Uh, no, they won't be here. It will just be us."

My dad's gaze settles on me.

Dad: "Ah, I don't know if Reign will make it."

Another moment of silence follows.

Dad: "Excellent, we'll see you both then."

Dad hangs up the phone. "It's done."

Saturday
March 8th, 2025

A cold sweat prickles on my forehead as we arrive an hour early at my father's place. My heart aches with a heavy dread as I anticipate how tonight will unfold. Dad ordered food from our favorite Italian restaurant instead of having his chef prepare dinner. Trent hired three security guards to be on standby, just in case. They will wait upstairs with the rest of us. The plan is for Skylar and Peter to have dinner with my parents, and Dion and I will show up, followed by Darcy. My father got the impression that Peter was asking if I would be attending family dinner because he would not be if I was there. Dad relayed a message from my mother that Peter thinks I attract drama wherever I go—the nerve of him to suggest such a thing. I'm not the problem; he is, and so are the rest of my family.

Dion places a soft kiss on my forehead. "Are you mentally prepared for this dinner tonight?"

A strangled knot tightens in my throat. "I don't know. What if we're blowing things out of proportion? What if it's not as bad as we think?"

He brushes the pad of his thumb over my bottom lip. "Reign,

please stop second-guessing yourself. Even if he is not physically abusing Sky, something is definitely not right. Wouldn't you rather intervene and be sure that she is safe rather than regretting not doing anything later on?"

My gaze falling to the floor. "When you put it that way, I guess you're right," I murmur.

Dion tilts my chin up with his index finger. "Reign, he abused his ex-wife and has a kid."

"I know, I'm just—"

"I got you, Reign," Dion assures me, cutting me off and holding me close to his muscular chest. Inhaling his soothing sandalwood scent, I relax just a little bit in his arms.

The familiar aroma of my father's aftershave envelops the room as he strides in, looking like himself again in a sharp, black-tailored suit. "Your mother called from the car; she is almost here. You all should go upstairs and wait for my signal."

Dion gently releases me, and together with everyone else, we ascend the stairs.

Thirty minutes later…

"Reign, can you come downstairs, please?" My father summons me.

Sighing heavily, I look back at my friends, who all nod for me to go. Dion takes my hand in his, and we both look to Darcy to join us. I still don't like her, but I know she loves my sister. We follow my father downstairs and into the dining room. My mother and Peter are visibly surprised, nearly falling out of their seats.

"Mother," I greet through gritted teeth.

She ignores me. "Stevie, what is she doing here?" Her voice is laced with thinly veiled disdain.

"Not now, Loretta," my father's stern tone cuts her off, a look of warning in his eyes.

"I second that question," Peter interjects, standing up from his seat.

"Sit your ass back down!" My father's voice booms, silencing Peter.

His smug expression is accompanied by a smirk that makes my blood boil. He takes his seat and presses his hands together on top of the table. Skylar nervously brushes her hair behind her ears, her gaze darting between my father and me.

"Reign has something to say, and all I ask of you is the truth," Dad states firmly, his eyes looking at no one in particular.

Clearing my throat, I look directly at Skylar, who shifts uncomfortably in her seat. "Sky, is Peter hurting you?"

My mother dramatically clutches her imaginary pearls, and Skylar's eyes widen in horror. Peter slams his hands on the table, causing the dishes to clatter loudly. His smirk disappears.

"What!?" he demands, standing to his feet and ignoring my father's previous warning to stay seated.

Two large men appear in the room, and another enters from the left, his gun drawn and pointed directly at Peter's head. Skylar's face pales, tears welling up in her eyes as she looks at the three large men, ready to pounce if ordered. Trent enters with arms folded across his chest, followed by Love, Scarlette, and the rest of our friends.

Peter dryly chuckles as he surveys the unexpected reinforcements.

My mother shrieks, "Is this an ambush, Stevie?"

Dad silences her with a stern look.

Trent slams a folder on the table, causing it to open slightly and reveal images of a bruised and battered woman.

"What the hell is this?" Peter demands.

"These are pictures of your ex-wife that you used to beat!" Dion accuses with disgust. "You lowlife."

Peter's eyes narrow as he looks at the images, his jaw clenched. "This is supposed to be sealed," he mutters under his breath, sitting back down.

"Sky, did you know about any of this?" I ask, my voice nearly breaking.

Skylar robotically stands up, her face devoid of emotion. She looks over the images sprawled across the table.

"He also has a child, Sky," I add quietly, feeling sick to my stomach.

Her shaky hands pick up the black and white photo of Peter's ex-wife with two swollen eyes and a split lip.

"Please, Sky. If he's hurting you, he can't anymore. Look around! You have people who care about you and want to help," Darcy pleads.

Peter tries to take the photo from Skylar's hands, but she jerks away. "You—*you* did this?" She asks, backing away from him in horror.

Peter's face contorts in anger as he denies the accusation, and Skylar's gaze shifts between Peter and the photo.

"Has he hurt you, Skylar?" Dad asks firmly.

"I can't believe this is happening," my mother bellows, exiting the dining room in a huff like this is about her.

Dad shakes his head, letting everyone know to let her be.

Skylar continues to stare at the photo, her hands trembling. She finally looks up, a torrent of tears streams down her face, much like a river breaking its banks. She nods her head yes, and through her sobs, she weakly admits, "He only hit me once."

"Once is enough," Trent grumbles under his breath.

Dad looks between me, Trent, and Dion before charging at Peter, who rises to his feet with his hands raised in surrender. His fist swiftly and accurately strikes Peter's nose in a blur of motion, too fast for us to fully register. Trent and Dion rush forward to restrain Dad, their faces stunned.

As they pull Dad away, Peter clutches his bleeding nose, a sinister smirk spreading on his lips. "You'll be hearing from my lawyer soon."

"Go ahead hot shot," I challenge. "We have all this proof of your past to expose you for who you really are. Is this something you really want to be brought up in court?" I arch an eyebrow, subtly reminding Peter of the skeletons in his closet, even though I'm surprised by my own words. When he doesn't flinch, I continue by flipping through the sheets of paper. "I'm sure your brother wouldn't want this to get out, given how it could affect your law firm."

Trent leans in and places both of his large hands on the table, with Dion following suit. "I know men like you, and I've destroyed plenty of them. I have more resources than your small brain can comprehend. So, it's in your best interest to cooperate with us," Trent states with a menacing tone. "This is what you will do," he continues, as Dion slides documents toward Peter. Peter scans the papers quickly, a cold sweat forming on his brow. "You have two options: Sign these divorce papers and leave Skylar Brown alone, or I will go to the top news station and expose every dark secret you and your brother tried to hide. And yes, I know the truth about what happened to your father. Your call."

Peter's eyes widen like saucers as he turns his head and glares at Skylar. "Is this what you want, Sky? To divorce me?" He sounds like an arrogant prick.

She hides behind the guard pointing the gun and peeks out, meeting Peter's gaze with a steely nod. Clever girl, I smile to myself.

Peter's arrogance is quickly deflated. He shoots a venomous look at Trent before turning back to Skylar. "Your loss," he mutters, snatching the pen and signing the papers. He tosses the pen onto the floor like the pathetic waste of space he is, shooting daggers at all of us on his way out of the dining room.

Dion grabs him by the collar of his shirt to stop him. "Stay away from Skylar," he threatens.

Peter scoffs and pushes Dion away, but security steps in, ready to intervene if necessary. With a final grin, Peter storms out of the room.

Trent darts his head toward the door. "Make sure he is gone."

The three guards nod and leave the dining room. Skylar rushes to Dad, tears streaming down her face, and wraps her arms around him, clinging to him tightly. Dad holds her close, embracing her and gently stroking her hair.

"You good?" Dion asks softly, pulling me into his arms, and I nod into his chest.

After Skylar calms down in my dad's embrace, she hugs me firmly, while Darcy joins in.

"I'm sorry I lied," she whispers in my ear.

Tears welling in my eyes, I whisper back, "It's okay," as I hold her tighter.

We finished our dinner, and after my friends left, my parents engaged in a heated argument that concluded with my mother agreeing to attend couples' therapy with my father. Later, we would aim for a family session. Dad made it clear that if she failed to attend and actively work towards fixing our broken home, he would be done with her for good.

Chapter 16: Reign

Saturday

April 5th, 2025

Several weeks have passed since Peter signed the divorce papers and agreed never to contact Skylar again. Skylar bought a new phone and changed her number, and we had a long overdue heart-to-heart. As I suspected, our deranged mother forced her into the marriage. Skylar told this bitch that she did not want to marry Peter, but our mother told her, "He's rich and a handsome keeper. Nothing else matters." What mother would say such a thing to her own daughter? It's no wonder Sky felt trapped. Our mother is controlling, manipulative, and delusional. I don't know what influence my grandmother had on her to make her act this way, but there is some deep-rooted issue that needs to be addressed. There was so much emotional baggage to unpack that Sky and I spent the entire weekend catching up. Skylar's Instagram inbox was full of unread messages from men. Out of jealousy, Peter smashed her phone against the wall and prohibited her from getting a new one. What type of shit is that? Telling your wife, someone who is supposed to be your partner, that she can't have a phone? Skylar isn't a child. She's a beautiful grown woman who men find attractive; it's not like she responded to any of them. Peter's jealousy was completely unwarranted.

It's important to understand that abuse is not limited to physical violence; it can also include verbal attacks, manipulation, gaslighting, and emotional torment. I asked Skylar again if Peter had only hit her once, and she said yes, after we had left their place. He interrogated her about what we were saying. When she didn't tell him the details, he struck her across the face so hard that she fell to the floor. *That sick piece of shit!*

While I regret that our intervention might have worsened things for her, I am thankful we got her out of a dangerous situation before it escalated further. Some women end up six feet under because no one intervened. Dion advises me to give all my anger to God, but how can I do that when things like this happen in the world? It seems impossible to forgive the man who has been hurting my sister and using my accomplishments to harm her mental health. Every day, Peter's cruel words rang in her ears, a constant reminder of her supposed worthlessness. The sharp sting of his voice was more painful than any weapon as he emphasized her dependance on his and our father's wealth. He also told her she wasn't as pretty as me, his words sharp and cutting like shards of glass.

Her bottled-up confessions tore my heart apart, teaching me the importance of gathering all relevant facts before forming an opinion or passing judgment. I regret not having a private conversation with Skylar last year to thoroughly discuss what had happened. Her abandonment of our wedding planning collaboration and her failure to uphold her commitments infuriated me. My initial impression was that she was a spoiled, self-centered bitch, but the truth was far more complex and heartbreaking. The man exuded an aura of confidence and charm that drew everyone in. Contrary to appearances, he turned out to be a master manipulator who exploited Sky's vulnerability and insecurities. Her statement about feeling "peachy" makes perfect sense now. *She hates peaches.* I should have known then.

Darcy is encouraging Skylar to pursue a career in fashion because of her keen eye for design and drawing abilities. She is just as organized and skilled at planning as I am, and I'm more than happy to help her. Or, perhaps one day, Skylar can collaborate with Kia on a creative project that combines their unique styles. With that asshole in her rearview mirror, she can finally focus on her aspirations, free from our mother's expectations and Peter's constraints.

Dad called the other day, his voice lighter than it had been in weeks, to tell me that his therapy sessions with Mom had been eye-opening, and he was looking forward to our family session. He expressed his intention to never see my Aunt Shirl and her husband again but also mentioned forgiving them. Last week, I met with Carol to talk about my mother's positive traits and if there had been any progress in our relationship. The frustrating truth is that my mother is only interested in preserving her marriage to my father. Carol pointed out it's fine not to have a relationship with my mother but emphasized the need to forgive her to avoid carrying resentment. She explained that anger is detrimental to your health. It can result in severe health issues such as heart attacks, mental health issues like anxiety and depression, and a weakened immune system. I am resolute and confident in overcoming the emotional and physical pain I currently carry.

Dion provides me with incredible support and encouragement as I continue to nurture and strengthen my relationship with God. I've made it a point to attend church with him every other Sunday, and I've even started taking some of Auntie Mavis' Black History classes. Her profound wisdom captivates me. As for Dion, he's now on Kia's team and has already filmed a couple of commercials. I couldn't be prouder of his accomplishment. Although he initially planned a different career path, his transition into modeling has been surprising, providing him with valuable exposure. I am confident that this increased visibility will create future opportunities for him.

Everything went smoothly with the March weddings, and I'm currently putting the finishing touches on the preparations for my two April weddings. One will be a whimsical celebration themed around Disney's "The Princess and the Frog," complete with beignets and jazz music. Nancy and I have come up with so many great ideas for this wedding. The other bride and groom plan to wear all black for their wedding. My incredible team stepped up in a major way, shouldering the significant responsibility of guaranteeing the success of these weddings. They did an amazing job. Lost in the turmoil of my family conflict, I couldn't concentrate on anything else, so I am thankful to my team for coming through.

We're throwing a surprise party for Scarlette at Richard's bar to celebrate her 34th birthday. She knows nothing about it. Although her birthday was on the third, we chose to celebrate today to accommodate everyone's schedules. Plus, Eddie had special plans for her; I can only wonder what surprises he had in store for my girl.

As we arrive at Richard's, the neon sign of *"Ric's Lounge &*

Bar" pulses brightly, and Trent's security guard acknowledge us with a curt nod as we pass through the VIP entrance.

Richard greets us as we walk past the luxurious velvet seating and soft lighting that creates an intimate ambiance in each VIP booth.

"Wassup, Dion?" Richard fist-pounds him. "Reign, how are you?" He embraces me.

April enters from behind Richard, carrying two drinks in her hands. With a smile, she says, "Hey, hey," handing us the drinks.

"Dare I ask what this is?" I eye April and Richard warily.

"It's a pink Long Island Iced Tea," April says with a grin.

Sniffing the drink suspiciously, I inhale an intoxicating swirl of bright and sweet scents. "Oh, is that right?"

"Bottoms up, Reign," Richard chuckles at my hesitation.

I take a cautious sip, surprised by the sweet burst of citrus that explodes on my tongue. It's lovely. The almost tangy fruitiness of the drink cuts through the sweetness.

"Daammmnnn! This is good," I bellow, eliciting laughter from them.

Richard guides us through velvet ropes and past a sea of faces to the VIP section; the murmur of conversation and clinking glasses fills the air as we spot Skylar and Darcy amongst our friends. I can tolerate Darcy more now that I know how much she truly cares for Sky; she is still a bitch, though.

Dion fist-pounds the guys, and I hug my girls. We enjoy ourselves, dancing and laughing until Richard has the DJ shout out Scarlette as she and Eddie make their grand entrance.

"Yo, yo, yo! Let's give it up for the birthday girl," the DJ sings/shouts into the microphone, followed by a string of alarms. He mixes Stevie Wonder's "Happy Birthday" with "Say Aah" by Trey Songz and a popular viral TikTok mix as Scarlette and Eddie walk in. She's swaying her hips and clapping her hands to the beat as they make their way to our VIP booth. We surround Scarlette with cheers and, foolishly, dance and sing to the songs. All eyes are on us as we drop it low and barely bring it back up. *My knees aren't what they used to be.* Blame it on *"Pop, Lock, and Drop it."*

"Mi amores, gracias, gracias," Scarlette shouts, blowing us kisses. She throws her arms around my neck, pulling me into a tight hug. "I love you, girl!"

"I love you too!" I hold up a shot glass of her favorite tequila. "Here's to Scarlette for being the incredible and phenomenal person she is," I shout. We all clink our glasses together in a toast to Scarlette, the life of the party, hooting and hollering in celebration of her.

August raises her glass high and proclaims, "Let's toast to our success and dreams coming true."

"Hear, hear," Dion shouts over the crowd, clinking his glass with Trent, Eddie, and the rest of the guys. We all have so much to celebrate that we take turns toasting each other.

As the night goes on, the music gets louder and the dancing gets wilder. We were having a great time until something at the far left end of the bar unexpectedly caught my attention. Dion's intense stare was also fixed on it, and it immediately disrupted our carefree mood. A commotion ensues as a man loudly argues with the bouncers.

"I'll be right back," Richard shouts, rushing to the scene.
CRASH!

A brick smashes through the window, and the DJ abruptly cuts the music, followed by the deafening crack of a gunshot. We all hit the floor, hearts pounding, and remain still, not daring to breathe. A hush fell over the bar, so quiet you could hear a pin drop. Not even the clinking of glasses broke the stillness.

"You shot me!" cries out a familiar voice.

Chapter 17: Dion

My heart hammers against my ribs, a frantic drumbeat, while sweat drips down my temples, stinging my eyes. We are on the floor, dust and grit clinging to our clothes, waiting for the police to arrive. *Was that Peter?*

"Was that Peter's voice?" Reign echoes my thoughts, her eyes wide with fear.

My throat tight with dread, I nod. *What is he doing here?*

With flashlights cutting through the dimness of the bar, the officers carefully walk through the scene, assessing the damage. As soon as we can stand with our hands raised, the paramedics start walking around, carefully inspecting everyone for any visible injuries. My attention is drawn to the front of the room, where a paramedic has just patched up Peter and a cop is now handcuffing him.

"Sir, are you hurt?" A tall, dark-brown skinned paramedic asks me.

I brush his hand away and say, "I'm fine." Then, I take hold of Reign's hand in mine as we walk to the front of the room. "We are with the owner," I say, walking through the crowd.

"You have the right to remain silent," the police officer reads out Peter's Miranda rights as we approach. "Anything you say can and will be used against you in the court of—"

Peter interrupts the police officer, demanding, "Where is she?"

"Law," the officer continues, ignoring Peter's outburst. "You have the right to an attorney. If you cannot afford an attorney, one will be provided for you."

"Where is Skylar?" Peter roars again above the officer.

"Do you understand these rights as they have been read to you?"

"Where is she? Tell me where she is!" Peter is slobbering at the mouth as they push his head down and insert him to the back seat of the car.

"Where is *who*?" Richard's eyes narrow, watching Peter being put into the police car.

"Sir, do you know this man?" An officer asks Richard, who shakes his head in response.

"No, I have no idea who that man is. He wasn't served at my establishment. He showed up enraged like this and then threw a brick right through this window," Richard explains, pointing at the shattered glass on the ground.

"That's my sister's almost ex-husband," Reign says, stepping forward. "How did he know we were here?" She covers her mouth with her hand in shock.

Skylar was aware that the divorce process could take up to six weeks, even though she hoped for a quicker resolution. Including the physical abuse incident would prolong the divorce process. There's another one to two weeks left before the divorce is finalized.

Skylar hesitantly approaches us with Darcy in tow. The sight of her sends Peter into a frenzy, his head violently slamming against the glass. What the hell is wrong with him?

The officers cautiously reach for their holsters. "Sir, I'm going to need you to stop what you are doing, and please remain calm."

"Skylar!" Peter yells at the top of his lungs. "How could you do this to me?"

Skylar's eyes well up with tears. Reign anxiously gestures for Darcy to take her away from the scene. Darcy quickly embraces Skylar, holding her arm firmly and leading her away from Peter.

"Sky, no! Please!" Peter continues to shout, his voice growing more desperate, and Skylar's face twists in anguish as Darcy drags her away.

Richard glares at the broken glass of his bar, seething at the sight of the destruction. "I want him to pay for the damages! Take him out of here!"

One of the officers circles his pointer finger in the air, and the rest of them load up, while another police officer walks over to us, notepad in hand, his tone curt but professional. "We'll need statements from everyone who witnessed what happened for the official report and investigation."

Reign rubs her temples wearily and takes a deep breath. The rest of our friends appear unharmed, thank God, though worry is etched on their faces. April walks over with a concerned expression, asking if we're okay. Still reeling from the unexpected turn of events, I nod and clench my jaw.

Reign murmurs, "I'm fine."

"Where is Sky?" Scarlette asks, scanning the area with a frantic look in her eyes.

"Darcy took her away," I answer.

After the remaining officers finished questioning everyone, we returned to my place, unable to sleep properly because of what had transpired.

Wednesday

April 16th, 2025

Over a week and a half has passed since the incident at Richard's bar. Skylar has been walking on eggshells ever since that night. She told Reign about their mother's forced apology, which felt hollow and unconvincing. That woman was adamant about Skylar marrying Peter, and she is the epitome of toxic. I'm sorry that Reign and Skylar have a mother like that; the emotional distress they must have endured under her care is unimaginable. For as long as I can remember, my mom has stressed the significance of choosing the right partner to start a family with, warning me against making a poor choice. Now she wonders when I will give her grandchildren, fantasizing about their tiny feet and chubby cheeks. I thought about it. I love the idea of leaving my mark on the world, but this isn't the right time.

Tina, called to ask if I'd somehow offended anyone in the industry. When I expressed my confusion, she revealed that several film producers had considered me for a role worth around $80,000. A powerful source informed the producers that I had a reputation for being difficult to work with, so they declined to offer me the role. I'm not sure who would do something like that, but Trent is looking into it for me. But God has the last word and what is meant for me *will* be for me. I have been offered a chemistry read with an actress named Rose. If everything goes well, she'll play my new wife in Seventeen: Magic is Real Part I. and Earth: Magic is Real Part II. By the end of the project, I should have at least $48,000 more in my bank account. Filming will start in August, which means I won't be able to continue coaching the Little League team indefinitely. I had intended to stay involved, but with Kia's fashion show approaching, it is too much for me to do. Eddie and I met with them last week to discuss it, and although they were happy for me, they were disappointed.

Eddie, Trent, Dante, and I just finished up a game of ball. Now we're just shooting around talking about that night at the bar and everything else that's been going on.

I ask, while dribbling the ball, "The divorce is finalized now, right?"

"Yeah, it is," Trent responds. "Due to the bar incident, he lost his job."

Eddie takes the ball from me and says, "Damn, really?"

"Yeah, man," Trent adds. "Richard doesn't play when it comes to his business."

"But all he did was break the glass. How did that result in him losing his job?" I ask.

"Do you know Richard's background?" Trent responds.

"Nah, I don't really know him."

"His father was a well-known and respected detective," Trent reveals.

"Bro, what don't you know about people?" Eddie jokes.

Dante grins. "This guy knows everything about everyone."

"He ran background checks on all of us," I say, slapping Trent on the back.

Eddie's eyes widen. "No way," he croons, and we all share a laugh until it dies down.

My expression turns serious, and Eddie and I share a silent understanding.

Trent shrugs his shoulders. "I also told Peter's brother that I knew it was Peter that killed their father. That further persuaded the decision to let Peter go."

We nod. "I thought so, when you said you knew the truth about his father. But damn, if you weren't such a cool dude, I would feel a type of way," I say half-jokingly, stealing the ball from Eddie and shooting a three-pointer.

"Show off," Eddie mumbles, shaking his head as the ball swishes through the net.

Trent chuckles, his eyes crinkling at the corners, and Dante claps Eddie on the back.

We play another game of ball before heading to our respective homes. Reign and I are having dinner with my parents tonight. She was hoping for Auntie Mavis to join us, but she won't be there. Reign has become a cherished member of our family; Mom and Auntie Mavis adore her, and Dad and Uncle Bernie are also very fond of her. They've been curious and asked if I see a long-term future with her. Auntie Mavis is texting me more and more, asking when I plan to marry Reign. I had to tell her to calm down. They've really hit it off since Reign started attending her Black history classes on Saturdays. I don't even attend those classes.

Reign walks into my bedroom, dripping wet with her crochet braids wrapped into a tight bun. Standing on her tiptoes, she gently kisses my lips before getting ready. I watch her attentively as she combines baby oil and Japanese cherry blossom lotion, applying it to her sexy legs.

She looks up at me as my dick hardens under my boxers. "Not now, Dion."

"Why not?" My voice whines, and I fold my arms across my chest like a toddler seconds away from a full-blown tantrum.

Reign shakes her head no, pulling up her stockings over her legs.

Knowing that she's playing hard to get but secretly enjoying the chase, I lick my lips. "But baby, you look so damn good."

She rolls her eyes to the back of her head. "No, Dion. I already know what you want, and we don't have time for that right now. Stop distracting me."

"Just a quickie," I tease, inching my finger along her thigh. "We can make it fast."

"Boy! Get dressed. I don't want to be late for dinner," Reign scolds, trying to sound stern but failing as a small grin form on her lips.

I seductively sway my hips around in a circle. "You know you want it too."

She grasps my erect cock firmly. "I will handle this later, but right now we need to go." She licks the side of my neck and whispers, "I suggest you get rid of it."

"Urgh," I groan aloud.

We are met with nothing but warm smiles, the moment we arrive at my parents' apartment. They greet Reign before they greet me, guiding her into the dining room. At this point, my parents see Reign more like their own child than they see me. My mom prepared a simple meal tonight with smothered chicken, string beans, corn bread, and mashed potatoes.

"Mom, dinner is so good," Reign compliments.

Mom responds with a smile, "Thank you, baby. How are things going with your sister and that, um, situation?"

I specifically told my mother not to inquire about the whole situation, and here she goes. One thing about her is that she is going to be all up in your business. Since she now sees Reign as a daughter, nothing is holding her back.

Reign clears her throat and responds, "Well, the divorce is

final now, and Skylar has a restraining order against him, so he is not permitted to be near her, or he will be arrested."

Mom scrunches up her nose as she picks at her corn bread. "I don't trust those pieces of paper."

I open my mouth to interject but then my dad pauses mid-bite to rub his forehead. "Dad, are you okay?"

He sighs and looks up. "I'm fine, Dion, just a headache. Y'all finish up. Imma go rest my eyes for a bit."

Worry clouds Mom's face. Her voice barely a whisper, she asks, "Honey, do you want me to bring you some aspirin?"

Dad shakes his head and stands up. "Uh, no, I just need to lie down." He excuses himself from the table and disappears down the hallway.

Mom straightens up, her back cracking slightly. She looks at Reign and me with a small smile. "So, Dion, have you found a real job yet?"

Reign coughs, nearly spitting out her food. Mom glances at her and offers her a lukewarm glass of water, which she quickly accepts. Then she returns her attention to me, her brows pinch together. "Well, have you?"

Shifting uncomfortably in my seat. "Mom, I'm a model now."

A look of skepticism crosses her face. "Modeling, huh? So, are you saying you're a stripper now?"

Reign bursts out laughing beside me, and I give her a pointed look. She covers her mouth with her hand, still chuckling softly to herself.

Shaking my head. "No, Mom, I'm not a stripper. I'm a model."

"What's the difference?" She poses.

With a lopsided grin, "Do you think my lady would be okay with me stripping?"

She looks to Reign. "Maybe you can convince him to get a *real* job," she says, picking up the empty plates and taking them to the kitchen.

Reign looks at me with amusement in her eyes. "I love your mom."

Groaning, "I love her too, and she means well. I just wish she supported my career choice a little more."

"I do support you," Mom reassures as she returns to the table. "I just don't know how I feel about this modeling thing."

"I understand, Mom. I do have a chemistry reading coming up for a part in a movie, so hopefully that will show you how serious I am about pursuing acting as a career."

She throws her arms around my neck. "Don't let them ruin you," she whispers, squeezing me tight. "Remember, you're a child of God."

The industry ruins people, if you let it.

After enjoying my mom's homemade cheesecake and switching to lighter topics, we then return home for my favorite dessert: *Reign.*

Chapter 18: Reign

Monday
April 21st, 2025

Before Scarlette arrives for lunch, I'm at work putting the finishing touches on the Princess and the Frog-themed wedding for Ms. Kyle and Mr. Medina. The wedding is scheduled for Thursday, April 24th, and I intend to ensure that everything runs smoothly without a hitch. I bought a stunning, dark purple dress. It's low-cut with a T-strap, a long side slit, and best of all, it has pockets. *Yay for pockets!* It's the little things! I plan to pair it with elegant silver stiletto heels.

Dion will be wearing grey slacks paired with a matching silk purple button-up, long-sleeve shirt. He is going to look so damn fine in it. Nancy has been handling most of the planning for this wedding due to my ongoing family conflicts being a distraction. Speaking of family, my stomach is in knots because I have a session with them and Carol right after I leave here. Skylar hasn't spoken with my mother in two weeks, and that woman is devastated by it. My mother doesn't care if I talk to her or not. But oh God, Skylar, her baby, isn't speaking to her, and she feels like the world is ending.

My door creaks open, and Scarlette pokes her head in. *"Hola, mi amor."*

"Come on in," I say, clicking out of my checklist and shutting my laptop.

Scarlette closes the door behind her and places a big brown bag on the table.

My eyes light up instantly, and a smile spreads across my lips. "Did you get sushi?"

"Of course I did," she replies with a grin, pulling out the containers from the bag.

I love my California rolls. The combination of creamy avocado, the mild sweetness of the imitation crab, and the tanginess of the seasoned rice does something to my taste buds. The flavors on my tongue dance to the beat in my head, creating a party in my mouth.

"So, what's up?" I ask in between bites.

Scarlette gives me a pointed look, raising an eyebrow inquisitively. "I should be asking *you* that. How is everything? How are you feeling, Reign?"

Reeling in nothingness, I slowly chew on my California roll. Scarlette gazes at me, and I swallow the vortex of emotions threatening to spill out.

"Good," I finally reply, mustering a smile.

Her brows furrow. *"Mentiras!"*

Knowing she can see right through me, I chuckle. "Okay, maybe not good," I admit. Scarlette is my girl, and she knows me inside and out; I couldn't lie to her even if I wanted to. "I have therapy after this, so we'll see how that goes."

"Okay, girl, I'm not going to push." She reaches for my hand across the table, squeezing it gently. "Just know that I'm here for you, no matter what."

A small tear glistens in the corner of my eye. "I love you."

Scarlette is someone who won't force a conversation when I'm not in the mood.

She winks at me. "I love you too, girl."

I wipe away the single tear and change the topic to something lighter. "Well, what's going on with you?"

"I'm good," she says, leaning back in her chair. "Work has been busy, but nothing I can't handle. I've just been worried about you and Sky. Peter is straight *loco.*"

I agree. Showing up uninvited at Richard's bar and shouting for Skylar was alarming. I don't understand why my mother ever pressed such a man on my sister.

"I know you don't want to talk about it, but damn, girl. I want to talk about it. You might want to consider getting a restraining order. Hell, all of us should."

Usually, Scarlette doesn't push, at least not with me, but I guess we are being annoying today. Feeling a dull ache behind my eyes, I instinctively massage my temples to relieve the throbbing pain.

Through gritted teeth, I address Scarlette by her full name, "Escarletta Lucia Rodriguez, please stop."

She throws up her hands in surrender. "Okay, okay. I'm done."

Rolling my eyes to the back of my head, I shove another bite of my sushi into my mouth.

We're both mute for a moment, finishing our meals in silence. Finally, Scarlette breaks the quiet by saying, "I'm thinking about moving in with Eddie."

Considering Dion claims that she already lives there, I nearly choke from laughing so hard at the irony.

Of course, she wants to break the silence by saying that.

She laughs along with me. "What? I think we should make it

official."

"Scarlette, I hate to break it to you, but you already live with him."

"No, I mean like officially official. I still have my own place, so it's not official-official," she quips back.

Amused by her logic, I shake my head. "You practically already live together. You might as well get rid of your place and make it official-official."

She sighs dramatically, her eyes shifting to the side.

"What is it now?" Now, I'm pushing because there is something she isn't saying.

"What if Eddie and I break up? Then what?"

"Is that why you're still holding onto your place? Because you're worried about what will happen if things don't work out with Eddie?"

"I mean yes and no. It's just that... do you think it's too soon? With... umm... uh... never mind. You don't want to talk about it."

Leaning back in my chair, I sigh. "Scarlette, say what you need to say."

She exhales sharply and finally admits, "The whole Peter thing has me questioning my relationship."

My brows furrow in confusion. "Why? You and Eddie are solid. He is a sweetie and treats you like a queen."

"You think so?" she asks, smiling slightly.

"Well, duh, Scarlette, you practically moved into his apartment, and he didn't even say anything about it. The man is definitely whipped."

Scarlette laughs and twirls a strand of her hair around her finger playfully. "He is, isn't he?"

Rolling my eyes. "It's kind of sickening."

She giggles and shrugs, "I can't help but feel like we might be moving too fast. It hasn't even been a year yet."

"Not every man is like Peter, and not every relationship is like Skylar and him," I say softly.

She straightens up, a look of realization crossing her face. "You're right. The same could be said for you and Dion."

"Yeah…"

Scarlette narrows her eyes. "Out with it, Reign."

"I don't want to move to Long Island. I don't want to leave the city," I confess.

"Does Dion know that?"

I sigh. "He will soon enough."

The remainder of our lunch was filled with chatting, laughing, and catching up. This was a brief but welcomed distraction from the stress of my upcoming therapy appointment.

The closer I get to Carol's waiting room, the more frantically my pulse beats in my ears. My mother has been awful to me for as long as I can remember, and after Skylar was born, she became nonexistent in my life. Skylar is our mother's most loved and cherished child, holding a special place in her heart unlike me. During my childhood, I was a tomboy, spending my time playing basketball, while my sister preferred a more princess-like lifestyle, participating in beauty pageants and similar activities. Instead of accepting me, my mother subjected me to a bitter tirade of criticism and comparison. It seemed as though she had exhausted all her love, leaving none for me.

"Hi, Reign, come on in," Carol greets me from the waiting room.

I fall in step behind her as I make my way to her office.

My parents are already seated, holding hands, as I enter the room. Carol offers me a chair to sit across from them and places another chair in the middle.

She begins the session. "Hello, Mrs. and Mr. Brown. I'm so glad to have you here today. Reign, I'm happy to see you as well. Skylar is not with us today, and she has given me permission to inform you that she will not be attending today's session because she needs some more time."

My mother sighs heavily. "How much more time does she need? I have apologized over and over again," she says, her voice sounding broken.

It's almost impossible for me to hide the annoyance that flickers across my face. I have longed for the same affection or any emotion from her that she gives to Skylar.

Carol responds calmly, "Everyone heals at their own pace, Mrs. Brown. It's important to respect Skylar's need for space and time." My father nods in agreement. "Let's get started," Carol says, steering the conversation back to the purpose of the session. "Who would like to go first?" she asks, looking between my parents and me. She has her notepad and pen poised, ready to take notes.

I slightly raise my hand, feeling embarrassed as I do it. "Why do you hate me?" I ask point-blank. There is no time to sugarcoat anything.

My mother coughs awkwardly, clearly taken aback by my directness. She scratches the back of her neck with her free hand and looks around the room for a few seconds too long.

"Mom! I'm talking to you," I say, pointing at her. "Why do you hate me? Because you sure as hell don't love me."

"Mrs. Brown, Reign asked you a question. Please answer honestly. No one will pass judgment on your response," Carol interjects gently.

I will.

My mother's brows pinch together, and she clutches her imaginary pearls as she finally meets my gaze. "Reign, I don't hate you. I envy you."

"Me?" I point to myself, and suddenly, I'm laughing hysterically. All eyes are on me as I continue to laugh because, umm… what? Okay, sure, I'll play along.

"And why do you envy me?" I ask deadpan.

She looks at Carol, who encourages her to keep going. How can Carol be so understanding of this bitch?

This is why you aren't a therapist, Reign. You lack empathy!

"I envy you for growing into the woman you are and living the life you choose, even though it wasn't what I wanted for you." She trails off, her gaze shifting to the side. "My mother taught me to be a housewife. She said, *'Black women like us don't dream big.'* It took me talking to Carol to realize how toxic that comment was. It was as if she didn't want us to succeed in life, and I passed that belief on to you."

Her words are like a physical blow, and the sour taste of bile stings my tongue.

"I also didn't see myself having children," she continues, her voice heavy with regret. "You were a mistake."

A burning rage boils beneath my skin, threatening to erupt like a volcano. Fury rises in my chest, a hot, suffocating pressure that makes me feel like I'm about to break.

"Reign? Are you okay?" Carol asks, concern etched on her face.

"Amara?" my father calls out. "Are you okay?"

"I'm sorry," I snort. "I'm doing my best not to pass judgment and, more importantly, not to lose myself in anger, but what does this have to do with the question I asked you? You had made me feel less than nothing my entire life, and it was even worse when Skylar was born."

"That's not true!" she protests, letting go of my father's hand. "I *did* love you."

Did? So, past tense?

What happened?

What did I do to her that caused her to stop loving me?

"Did?" My father repeats, posing the question that's burning in my mind. His eyes are wide, his brows are pressed together, and his lips are twisted in a frown. "Lo, what do you mean, *did?*"

Tears fall from my mother's eyes as she stands to her feet.

Carol hands her a box of tissues, and she takes one, wiping her eyes. "I—I want to sit somewhere else."

"Oh, oh, of course. Reign, would you mind sitting next to your father? Mrs. Brown, you can take Reign's seat," Carol suggests.

When I sit next to my dad, I can't even look at him. How could he love such a human?

My mother wipes her eyes again and takes a deep breath. She straightens her posture and shakes her head, blinking her eyes two or three times as if she were a robot rebooting herself. "Look," she starts, her tone now sharp like a double-edged sword. "It's time I told you the truth."

Carol notices the change in her demeanor and quickly records it in her notepad, and my father becomes stiff in his seat.

My mother looks at him and says, "Stevie, I'm sorry, but it's time your precious Amara knows how I truly feel."

"Loretta, please," his voice warns, almost pleading. "We talked about this already."

Ignoring my father's warning tone, she retorts, "No, Stevie. I can't keep pretending everything is fine when it's not. I'm done."

I finally look at my dad and see the sadness in his eyes. "Dad, what is she talking about?"

"Mr. Brown, I think it's time Reign learns the truth about her mother's feelings," Carol interjects gently. "This is the only way we can move forward with the healing process."

My father throws his arms up in defeat and then folds them across his chest. "Fine, Loretta. Talk."

My mother takes a deep breath before explaining, "I didn't want children, but when you were born, I loved you. *So much*. I was happy to be a mother. *Your* mother. It was the two of us against the world. I wanted to protect you from everything, even from myself." My eyes widen as I listen to her confession. "Your father worked long hours, and I was left alone with you most of the time. I suffered from postpartum depression. I didn't know or even realize that could happen to me," she says in a condescending tone and chastising herself. "Not Loretta Brown. No, no." She adjusts the small amount of hair that has fallen out of her well-put-together bun and continues, "You would cry and cry, and I was tired. You were so needy, always wanting attention and care, while I longed for some rest. I was exhausted and overstimulated, so I would drop you off at my sister's to have some alone time, which made being a mother a little less stressful. But then I got pregnant again."

I say in mock disgust, "With your golden child."

My mother glares at me, her eyes narrowing. "No," she replies sharply.

My mouth snaps shut. *No?*

"I was pregnant before I got pregnant with Skylar," she admits, pausing for a dramatic effect. "I lost my baby because of you."

A searing pain tears through my heart, like a white-hot knife twisting in my chest. My mind swirls with chaos, and a strange internal pressure builds within me in tumultuous waves.

Standing up, I stumble back a step. "What do you mean it was my fault? Are you delusional!?"

My father stands up from his chair, placing his hands on my shoulders to steady me. "Reign, please calm down."

I know my dad means business by using my government name.

Tears well up in my eyes, "Dad, h-how i-is i-it m-my f-fault?"

His grip tightens on my shoulders, and he sits me back down gently. "Reign, I need you to listen to me. It's important that you hear me out," he says firmly. "You were two and a half years old and playing in your playpen in the living room. Your mother went upstairs to get more diapers because I forgot to fill them, but then you started screaming loudly. In a panic, your mother slipped and fell down the stairs. There was a decrease in fetal movement, and your mother was bleeding and in pain. Later, we discovered that there had been a placental abruption. She was fifteen weeks."

"And I blame you!" My mother shouts. "I blame you for everything that happened that day!"

Tears flood my eyes and spill down my cheeks at her accusations. My father pulls me into his arms, and I bury my face in his chest. "It's not my fault," I muffle into his shirt.

He holds me tighter, and Carol steps in. "Mrs. Brown, I can only imagine how much pain and trauma you felt when you lost your baby. It's okay to feel angry and hurt, but do you understand that Reign is not to blame for what happened? It wasn't your fault either. It was an unfortunate and terrible accident that no one could have predicted or prevented."

My mother looks at Carol. "I hear you, but it doesn't negate the fact that I have blamed Reign this entire time."

"Do you still blame her now?" Carol asks softly.

My mother looks at me, then at my father, before looking me directly in the eye. "Yes."

More tears fall down my cheeks, blurring my vision. Grief and anger stir within me as I grapple with the loss of my parents' baby.

How is it my fault?

How can she blame me? I was only two.

Carol nods understandingly, acknowledging the complexity of my mother's emotions. "Okay, we'll stop there for now. Thank you for your time, Mr. and Mrs. Brown. If you don't mind, I'd like to spend the remaining fifteen minutes speaking with Reign."

"Amara, I will call you," my father promises, and I shoot daggers at my mother's retreating back as she walks out of the room without a backward glance.

Carol clears her throat. "Reign, would you like to talk about how you're feeling right now?"

Tears stream down my face like a waterfall. "H-how was it my fault?"

"It wasn't. You were just a child," Carol reassures me softly. "Unfortunately, that's what your mother believes, no matter the facts. This is how she feels, and she has the right to her own emotions, as do you. Today's session was intended to help you understand why she treated you the way she did."

"I still don't understand," I huff.

Carol softly rests her hand on mine. "I know, Reign, and I'm sorry. But this isn't *your* problem. This is *her* problem. This is something that *she* needs to work on." She lets me ponder her words for a moment before continuing, "Try to put yourself in her shoes."

"I would never blame my child for an accident."

"It's easy to say what you would or wouldn't do if you haven't been in a particular situation," she points out. "This was her experience. Did I say it was right? No. Is it your fault? Of course not. However, this is how she feels, and her feelings are just as valid as your own. Both of you are entitled to your own perspectives and emotions."

Folding my arms across my chest, I blurt out, "Not all women who call themselves mothers are true mothers."

Her eyes widen, almost as if she agrees with me. However, she remains silent, her lips pressed together tightly. We schedule our next appointment, and I leave feeling worse than I had in a long time.

How do I forgive her? How can I put myself in her shoes and empathize with her feelings?

Returning home drained from my therapy session, I find Dion already there, waiting for me with dinner ready.

"You good?" he asks as I walk into the kitchen.

He takes a pan of cornbread from the oven and places it on the counter next to the fried chicken, mac and cheese, yams, and collard greens to cool.

"No, I'm not," I admit, placing my keys and purse on the island.

Dion approaches me with his arms extended, inviting me into a warm embrace. I collapse into his strong arms, overwhelmed by the soothing scent that envelops me. He consoles me tightly, allowing me to release the pent-up emotions from my therapy session.

"Do you want to talk about it?"

Burying my face into his chest, I scream, "My mother doesn't love me!" My body collapses to the cold, unforgiving floor. Tears blur my vision, and my sobs echo through the empty kitchen.

Dion kneels down beside me, wrapping his arms around me as I cry, and gently rocks me back and forth. I cling to him desperately, feeling vulnerable and exposed. "Please don't hurt me," I plead, my voice barely audible over the sound of my own crying.

His brows furrow deeply, forming a crease between his eyes. "Reign, I don't know what happened in therapy, but I want you to know that I would never intentionally hurt you."

"A m-mother's role is to nurture and protect, not to cause pain, but here I am, an adult woman with emotional and physical scars inflicted by the one person who should have been my protector and guardian of my heart," I barely manage to choke out, snot running down my face.

Dion gently lifts my chin with his finger, forcing me to meet his gaze. He wipes away my tears with his thumb, his eyes filled with compassion and understanding. "Reign, my rose, your heart will always be safe with me."

His words wrap around me like a warm blanket, soothing the ache in my chest. I rest my head on his, and we stay on the floor until the weight of my grief begins to lift.

Chapter 19: Reign

Thursday
April 24th, 2025

Dressed in our finest, Dion and I are on our way to the Kyle-Medina's Princess and the Frog-themed wedding. Although it's strictly business, I'm treating this event as a date night given my current emotional state. I don't see the relationship between that woman and me getting any better. While I understand the need to forgive her—not for her sake, but for mine—I do not want a bond with her. Nancy and her date, both looking stunning in matching rose-gold outfits, step out of an Uber ten minutes after us. Stephanie, Kandace, and Skylar arrive shortly after them. Skylar is also helping with the wedding, and it was good for her to be out and about with us. Since the incident at the bar, she has stayed at home and evaded public events to avoid running into Peter. He shouldn't be a problem tonight; it's not like he knows the couple getting married or has any reason to be at the wedding.

"You two look amazing," Skylar compliments me and Dion, approaching us outside the venue.

"Thank you, Sky. You don't look half bad yourself," I reply with a smile, motioning for her to give us a little twirl.

She obliges, twirling around in her pink mermaid-style dress that hugs her curves, the fabric shimmering as she spins.

"You look beautiful," Dion adds.

"Why, thank you, kind sir," Skylar responds with a playful curtsy. "You look okay, too."

The three of us share a laugh. The conversations between Dion and Skylar are much more than they were last year. We compliment the rest of the group before heading inside with our game faces on. Ultimately, this is a work event, and it's time to get down to business. Nancy, Skylar, and Kandace head to the ceremony area, while Stephanie, Dion, and I make our way to the reception hall. I love it when clients choose a venue that hosts both the ceremony and reception. It makes my job a little easier and minimizes my travel time.

We enter the brightly lit reception hall, the staff's quiet chatter and movements creating a ballet of efficiency. They bring gleaming white plates with delicate gold trim to the tables. Why are plates being brought in when some tables still do not have centerpieces?

Stephanie hands me my clipboard, and we walk around, discussing what has been done and what still needs to be. The guests will arrive for the cocktail hour just before the reception, giving us a two-hour window to get the room ready. There are twenty-two tables in the room. Ten tables are arranged in a circle on the left side, while another ten tables in a similar layout are placed on the right side of the room. One is a small circular table fit for the bride and groom. To the left of it, there is a long rectangular table for the bridal party and their plus ones. All twenty-two tables have ivory tablecloths.

"Tablecloths. Check," I say, marking it off the list.

"Ten tables are missing the centerpieces," Stephanie points out.

I address a passing worker who avoids eye contact with me, "Excuse me, where can I find the missing centerpieces?"

"They're on the cart back there," she says, pointing behind me before rushing off.

Turning around, I see a cart loaded with centerpieces. "Stephanie," I call out.

"On it," she responds, walking over to the cart.

"Is there anything else you need help with?" Dion asks, his sexy left dimple making an appearance. He loves watching me in my element.

Smiling at him. "Can you please make sure that each table has the fairy lights wrapped around the lily pad with a lotus flower?"

"Of course," he grins, placing a soft kiss on my forehead and heading off.

Upon scanning the room, the only missing items are the gold rose petals and white lotus flowers. Where are those lotus flowers?

Stephanie voices my thought, appearing beside me with furrowed brows. "I have no idea where the lotus flowers are."

My eyebrows furrow in a tight knot. "What!?" I quickly scan the room again, pressing my forehead against my palm and feeling the dull throb of a headache starting to form.

I spot another worker in the back of the room and make a beeline towards him. "Excuse me, sir."

He looks me up and down, deepening the lines on his forehead. "Do you know where I can find the white lotus flowers?"

The man scratches his head, wasting time we don't have.

"My name is Reign Brown, and I'm the wedding planner for the Kyle-Medina wedding. I need to find those flowers ASAP."

His eyes widen with recognition, and he apologizes profusely before leading me to the storage room.

One hour later, the wedding venue is beautifully decorated in emerald green and gold, and cocktail hour is in full swing. Each table has an ivory tablecloth with gold rose petals scattered across it. The lily pads are wrapped in fairy lights, with a white lotus flower on top of each one. The chairs are gold, and there is a train that runs from the front of the room to the back, stopping at the bride and groom's table.

The bride wears an ivory princess gown with green trim and a Kia-designed green rhinestone hairpin. There are four bridesmaids and groomsmen. The bridesmaids have on emerald-green mermaid-style gowns with gold heels, while the maid of honor wears a similar gown with a halter neckline. The groomsmen are in fitted tuxedos in rich green, complemented by shimmering gold ties, with the best man's gold bow tie adding the perfect accent. Because of my input, the groom's ivory slim-fitted tuxedo with green trimmings perfectly complements his bride's dress. The beauty of my work, brimming with vibrant colors, intricate details, and satisfying results, overwhelms me with joy.

As the MC begins to announce the bridal party, a familiar face catches my attention from the far left of the room. A wave of nausea washes over me as my heart thumps against my ribs. His eyes meet mine, and blood rushes to my cheeks.

Peter?

Nudging Dion's elbow, the sharp tip of my fingers digging into his flesh, but his eyes are fixed on his phone, his brow furrowed and tight with concentration.

"What's wrong?" I whisper, my gaze still locked on Peter.

Dion finally looks up. "It's my father. He had a heart attack. I have to go," he whispers, hastening out of the reception without another word.

My heart is hammering so hard in my chest that I can hear the thudding in my ears.

Dion's father had a heart attack.

I don't know any more details, but I'm worried sick.

And why is Peter here?

How is he here?

Skylar can't know.

What do I do?

Think. Think. Think.

I take my phone from my clutch and text Love.

I scroll to Scarlette's name in my contacts and text her too.

Three dots immediately pop up on my screen.

What did she hear?

She couldn't have heard about Peter, could she?

My phone rings, but I hit ignore; I can't answer Scarlette right now. Panic sets in, and Nancy notices my distress.

"Reign, are you okay?"

Shaking my head, I quickly reply, "Uh, no, but I don't want to cause a scene."

I need to avoid doing anything that might turn into a public spectacle. This is my job, and my livelihood is at stake; I cannot have a commotion.

"What do you need?" Nancy springs into action.

I look around and try to find Peter, but I don't see him. Where did he go? *Shit!*

"Where is Sky?" I ask Nancy, trying to keep my voice steady.

She looks around and points towards the dance floor; Skylar is dancing with Stephanie. But where the hell is Peter? I don't see him anywhere now. Calling the police might cause a scene, and he knows I don't want to do that. *Is that why he is here?* I am completely spiraling right now, and Dion isn't here. Oh, my God! His father. Is he okay? URGH!

"Nancy, please listen to me. Skylar's ex-husband is here, and I don't know where he went," I say urgently, my phone buzzing incessantly with text messages from Love and Scarlette.

Nancy's eyes widen in alarm.

"Please keep an eye on Sky while I make a call."

Nancy nods, her expression tense. She whispers something into her date's ear, and he looks at me and nods. I leave the reception room and walk down the hall toward the bridal suite. My hands are shaking so violently that I can barely punch in the four-digit code.

Calm down, Reign! Focus!

2-3-6-6.

The door beeps, indicating that I have punched in the incorrect numbers. My heart is racing as my phone rings again; this time, it's Love calling.

What is the damn code again?

2-3-6-9.

The door turns green, and it unlocks.

Thank God! Swiftly closing the door, I cautiously scan the room for any other bridal party members. Relieved to find the room empty, I initiate a three-way call with Scarlette and Love.

Love: "Reign, what the hell?"
Me: "Add August to the call."

Love: "Hold up, let me call her."
Scarlette: "What is going on?"
Me: "Hold on, Scarlette. Love is merging August into the call."

"Is that Reign?" I hear Eddie ask in the background.

"*Si*, we are waiting for August to get on the line. Apparently, Peter is at Reign's wedding venue," Scarlette informs him.

"Oh, shit!" Eddie shouts.

August: "Can someone explain why we're all on this call right now?"

My friends all start speaking simultaneously, making it difficult to understand what anyone is saying.

Me: "Shh, please, I don't have long."
August: "What is it? Are you okay?"
Me: "No. Peter is at the wedding I'm at."
August: "What do you mean Peter is at the same wedding as you?"
Me: "He's here, at my client's wedding venue. Sky is here too."
August: "Wait, what? Call the po-po!"
Love: "Nah, she's at a work event. She can't call the police."

Exactly, I don't want to get the police involved.
Not here, not now.

August: "Then what else is she supposed to do? Sky has a restraining order against Peter, so the man shouldn't even be anywhere near her."
Scarlette: "What do you need from us, Reign?"

Me: "I need back—"

The knock at the door cuts me off.

Scarlette: "Reign?"
Love: "Reign, is someone there?"
August: "Reign, press a button if you can't talk."

I quickly hit the mute button and press my ear to the door. Another knock booms against the door, louder this time. Holding my breath, I don't move a muscle. Whoever it is, if they knew the code, they would have used it instead of knocking.

Love: "Y'all give me a second. Let me get Trent."
Scarlette: "Reign, if someone is in the room with you, press a button twice."

Scarlette and August breathe a sigh of relief as they hear silence from my end.

Scarlette: "Okay, Reign. Press a button once if you're alone in a room."

I hit a button.

August: "You're alone but can't talk?"

Slowly backing away from the door, I hit a button once again.

Scarlette: "Is there someone outside the room?"

Another knock startles me and can be heard through the phone. I quickly hit a button once.

August: "Text us the damn address!"

Fumbling with my phone and nearly dropping it, I send them my location.

August: "I'm on my way. I'll be there in twenty. Scarlette?"
Scarlette: "Yes?"
August: "Stay on the line with her until Love comes back."
Scarlette: "Got it."

When August hangs up, Eddie's voice crackles in the background seconds later, "We have to go to the hospital!"

Scarlette muffles her response, clearly worried and causing panic to rise in my chest.

Dion's father. I want to know what's going on and be there for Dion, but Peter is here, and he is a threat to Skylar.

I send Nancy a text message asking if Skylar is still on the dance floor. She informs me that there is no sign of Peter and that Skylar is having the time of her life. *Good!*

Love: "Reign, Trent is sending three of his bodyguards to the venue. Stay put, okay?"

I hit a button once.

Love: "Do you need me to stay on the line with you?"

I hit a button once again.

Scarlette: "Reign, we have to head to the hospital. Eddie just got off the phone with Dion, and his father's condition is critical."

Love: "What the hell is going on tonight? Is it a full moon or some shit?"

Scarlette: "Girl, I don't know. Keep me posted."

Scarlette disconnects from the call.

Love: "I'm here, Reign. Just let me know when you're able to talk."

Pressing my ear against the door again, I strain to hear any sound coming from the other side. The silence is deafening, so I lower myself to the floor, attempting to peek under the crack beneath the door. All I can see is darkness. I press my phone so close to my lips that I can practically taste the metal as I whisper.

Me: "I don't know where he is."

Love: "Okay, okay. Where is Sky?"

Me: "She's on the dance floor around a lot of people."

Love: "Good! He won't do anything while she is in public. At least, I hope not."

Me: "She doesn't know."

Love: "Damn. Are you going to tell her?"

The lights on the lock suddenly flash green, and I hear it click open. I clutch my phone tightly, my knuckles turning white and my breath catching in my throat. When Nancy walks in with Skylar, it's as if she has seen a ghost.

Skylar rushes to me, throwing her arms around my neck. "He's here, Reign, he's here."

Love: "Is that Skylar? Where are you?"
Me: "Yes, Sky and Nancy are with me in the bridal suite."
Love: "Okay! Stay in there until Trent's men arrive. There are three of them, dressed in black suits with Trent's logo on the front."
Me: "Thanks, Love! I'll call you back."
Love: "Be safe, Reign."
Me: "I will."

After hanging up the phone, I console Skylar, who is visibly shaken by Peter's presence. "I know, Sky, I saw him too."

She clutches onto me tighter.

"Nancy? Can you please do me a huge favor?" I ask, as Nancy nods in response. "Can you watch over the wedding party for me? I'm going to wait in here with Sky until security shows up."

Nancy gives me a reassuring smile and agrees to keep an eye on things, hurrying out of the suite.

I pace back and forth. My heart is beating so fast that my brain can't catch up with everything happening at once. Dion's dad had a heart attack. I need to get to the hospital. I need to be by Dion's side. Peter is here. I need to protect my sister. I'm at a work event. I'm not supposed to leave until it's over. *What do I do!?* I rest my forehead in the palm of my hand and focus on breathing.

"What security?" Skylar asks after a few silent beats, pulling me out of my spiral.

"Love told Trent, and he hired security to come get you and protect me. That's what I'm assuming because I can't leave yet, but you can."

"Reign, what if he follows me?" Skylar's eyes widen.

I place my hands on either side of her shoulders. "Listen, they'll protect you, and he won't follow you. I'll confront him and distract his crazy ass."

Skylar shakes her head violently. "No, Reign, I can't ask you to do that."

I pull her into a tight hug. "You're not asking me to do anything. I'm choosing to protect you because that's what older sisters do. I got you, Sky!"

Skylar's eyes glisten with gratitude, and we wait in tense silence for the inevitable confrontation. Twenty minutes later, Nancy returns to the suite accompanied by August and three sizeable men in black suits. The men have Trent's large gold logo on the left side of their jackets.

"Hello, which one of you is Reign?" The tanned and typical tall, dark, and extremely handsome man asks.

"That would be me," I reply, stepping forward.

August brushes past the large men and throws her arms around Skylar, pulling her into a tight hug.

"These two will escort your sister off of the premises, and I will stay back to protect you," he informs me.

The other man steps forward, his eyes deep and crystal blue. "We understand that this is your place of work, and Mr. Collins told us to move discreetly."

"Yes, that is correct. I'm going back to the reception to find Peter and keep him busy."

"Are you sure that is what you want to do?" The strong man asks.

"Yes, you're here to protect me, right?"

"Yes, but the manager has restricted access to the reception hall without permission from the bride or groom."

I don't want them to know about this.

"Peter is crazy, but he's not *that* crazy to hurt me in front of all those people in there."

"I will be by her side as well as Stephanie," Nancy says, inserting herself into the conversation.

"Okay," the strong man agrees, spinning his pointer finger in a circular motion. "Let's move."

Skylar sends a message to Darcy to meet ASAP. Meanwhile, August stays in the hall with the security guard to call Calvin and update him on what's going on. She was at Kimi's house when she got the call and was able to rush here in no time. I love my friends! Scarlette and Eddie are at the hospital, awaiting updates on Dion's dad's condition. I wish I were at the hospital with him.

As we head back to the reception hall, I spot Peter immediately on the dance floor with a woman. Before I gather my bearings, I shoot Dion a text message letting him know I'm here for him. Ten minutes later, I check for his response, but there is none. Exhaling a sharp breath, I make my way to Peter, throwing on the fakest smile and tone.

"Peter? Is that you?" I ask in a high-pitched voice as if I'm excited to see his psycho ass.

Peter immediately breaks away from his date, or whoever she is, his stone face softening into a slight delight. The woman's eyes skate over me as Peter's deep, hearty laugh sends shivers down my spine, and not in a good way.

"I'll be back, baby," she says, giving me a once-over again before gliding away.

I place my hand on Peter's arm, trying to maintain the facade of being thrilled to see him. "You've moved on already, I see."

He leans in close so that only I can hear. "Cut the shit, bitch. What do you want?" His words tumble out like venom.

Anger bubbles up inside me, but I force a smile. "Bitch? Well, seeing as I am beautiful, intelligent, talented, creative, and a hottie, I'll take that as a compliment, Mr. Peter Peterson."

He snorts. "You're quite good at putting on an act. Did your fake boyfriend teach you that?"

I smile sweetly. "Actually, he did. But I'm sure you're familiar with acting, considering how well you pretended to be a kind gentleman but in reality, you're an arrogant jerk."

His jaw tightens, and I know I've hit a nerve.

"The better question is, what are you doing here?" I ask, squinting at him.

"What does it look like? I'm here for a wedding," he gestures around the room, swaying awkwardly to the music playing. I observe him flinch as he moves his injured leg that was shot by a rubber bullet. *It should have been a real bullet instead.* The security guard at Richard's bar doesn't carry a loaded gun. *Is it bad that I wish it were a real gun?*

"How do you know the couple?"

His piercing green eyes bore into me so intensely that I almost pass out. "My date is a friend of the bride," he finally answers, followed by a deep-throated laugh as he looks around the room. "Where is Sky? I know she's here."

And there it is, the real reason for his presence at the wedding. Releasing his arm, I check my phone for a message from Sky, who informs me that she and Darcy are temporarily staying at a hotel because Peter is clearly batshit crazy.

I purse my lips. "She has a restraining order against you. Why are you here?"

He leans in close to my ear, the woodsy scent of his aftershave tickling my nose. "How could I know she was here? It's not like I keep tabs on her. We're divorced."

Trent hired a lawyer named Siobhan and spoke with her about expediting the divorce for NYC. In an uncontested divorce, both parties must agree to the terms. However, if there are any claims of abuse, it can make the process more complex and lengthier. Skylar didn't want any delays, so they went through with the paperwork.

"You always seem to conveniently show up wherever she is," I retort as his date reappears.

"Nice seeing you, Reign. I hope to see you again," Peter says cryptically, taking his date's hand and spinning on his heels, slightly limping away.

Chapter 20: Dion

One hour ago…

Now…

Heart pounding, I burst through the hospital doors, the staff's hushed tones and hurried footsteps swirling around me as I rush to the front desk. "Hello, can you please give me any information on Timothy James?"

The woman wags a finger in front of me as she places a call on hold. "Hello, sir, please give me a moment to look him up."

With each tap of my fingers on the cool, hard counter, time

stretches until she finally points me in the right direction. I stride with purpose into the sterile, brightly lit waiting area, surrounded by the soft buzz of fluorescent lights. My mother is hunched in a chair with her head buried in her hands, while Auntie Mavis' gentle touch soothes her back.

"Mom, w-what happened?" I rasp, trying to hold my composure.

When she looks up from her hands, more tears fall, replacing the dried ones.

"Auntie Mavis?" My aunt shakes her head back and forth, not saying anything.

"Can someone please tell me something?" I shout, my voice coming out more aggressively than intended.

"H-his heart stopped!" My mother chokes out between sobs, her eyes red and swollen.

My heart feels like it's been ripped out of my chest as tears well up in my own eyes. I sit beside Mom and wrap my arms around her, the scent of her perfume mixing with the saltiness of her tears.

"I'll see if I can get any updates," Auntie Mavis says, patting my leg and standing up.

"What do you mean?" I ask, wiping the pesky tear from my betraying eyes.

I need to be strong for myself and my mother.

"He was taken in for emergency surgery after his heart stopped," Auntie Mavis explains, and my mother starts crying all over again.

A lump is forming in my throat, but I swallow it down and text Eddie, telling him to get to the hospital as soon as possible.

He arrives in record time, with sweat beading on his forehead, and Scarlette's face is pale, both of them wide-eyed with worry. Uncle Bernie arrives ten minutes later, clutching onto Auntie Mavis's hand.

The doctors haven't gotten back to us about my father's

condition. I only know that his heart stopped for three minutes before they were able to revive him and rush him to surgery. It's been a few hours now, and the lack of updates from the doctors is making me increasingly uncertain.

God don't let my father die. Please help my father get through this. I pray silently. God never said we wouldn't go through it, he said to look to him and he will help us along the way.

Auntie Mavis, holding Uncle Bernie's hand, offers a prayer for my father's recovery. "Y'all bow yo heads as we take this moment to pray." Somehow, she knew how much my mother and I desperately needed this. "God, we thank you for all the blessings you have bestowed on this family."

Thinking about all the good times I had with my father, a warmth spread through my chest. I couldn't have wished for a better dad. Shaking my head, I return my focus back on my aunt.

"Lord, Let, your will be done!" With a final "amen," we settle back into our seats, each of us anxiously waiting for an update.

Scarlette and Eddie are whispering to each other, which I can't hear from where I'm sitting or want to hear. My only focus is my father. I left Reign at the wedding and can't bear to speak with her right now. I just need my father to be okay. I'm not ready for him not to be here.

How likely is it that my father will be saved, as my mother was?

I don't want to have any doubts in my heart, but the longer it takes the doctors to update us, the more impatient and anxious I become. *Please let my dad be okay.*

"Mrs. James?" I look up to see a man with a salt-and-pepper beard. He introduces himself as Dr. Thompson, the head surgeon working on my father's case.

I help my mother stand up, and she leans on me for support as we speak to Dr. Thompson. Everyone else listens intently as he explains.

"Mr. James suffered a severe heart attack, also known as STEMI."

"W-what does that mean?" Mom asks, her voice shaky.

"ST-segment elevation myocardial infarction. It occurs when a major artery supplying the heart becomes completely blocked, preventing blood flow and causing significant damage to the heart muscle."

Clearing my throat, I ask, "Is my dad going to be okay?"

"Your father did well in surgery and is now in the ICU."

"Can we see him?"

Dr. Thompson nods, "Yes, but only for a few minutes, and only immediate family members are allowed in the ICU at this time."

I reassuringly squeeze my mother's hand, and we fall in step behind Dr. Thompson as we head towards the ICU. As we approach my father's room, he is hooked up to various machines and monitors, but he rests soundly.

"Baby, I'm here," Mom's voice croaks over the beeping machines, kissing his forehead gently. "We both are here."

Seeing him lying there so vulnerable tugs at my heartstrings because I don't know the full extent of his agony and distress. I place my hand on his arm and close my eyes, silently thanking God for sparing him.

We walk out of the room, and my mother wipes away her tears. "I should've known something was up with him."

"What do you mean, Mom?"

"The shortness of breath, his recent insomnia, and waking up in the middle of the night. I should've paid more attention." She covers her mouth with her hand as more tears spill from her eyes.

She leans into my embrace, as I wrap my arms around her. "I should have known."

IS LOVE ENOUGH?

Monday

May 12th, 2025

A few weeks have passed since my father suffered a heart attack. As a result, I check in with my family more frequently to offer support and ensure their well-being. It's sometimes difficult to realize that as you reach your thirties, your parents are also getting older. It's like one day my dad was in his forties, and now he is seventy-one years old. Because my parents are aging, I need to pay them more visits. My father was in the ICU for two nights and then under observation for five more nights. He is scheduled to see a cardiologist next week.

The steady flow of paychecks is gradually helping me pay off my mountain of debt I've accumulated. I've paid off two major credit cards and have one fashion show scheduled in June for Kia's new line. I'm not only thrilled about the money but also about the exposure this opportunity will bring.

Reign told me that crazy fool Peter attended her client's wedding and how Trent and his men handled it. I'm not sure how I feel about this man and his problems or how they might be causing a strain in my relationship with Reign. There is something she isn't saying, and I haven't been in the mood to push for an explanation. Scarlette's insistence on filing a complaint against Peter has me questioning whether taking legal action is a battle worth fighting. She suggests we get a restraining order against him, but I'm not sure how all that works. Peter only showed up at the bar when Skylar was with us and then again at the wedding Reign had planned. *The common denominator is Skylar.*

Reign's thirty-fourth birthday was on the eighth, and we had a low-key celebration with our friends at Eddie and Scarlette's place. Her energy was a little off, but I didn't press. Skylar and Darcy are also thinking about moving to Long Island instead of staying in the city, and I don't blame them. I've never understood how a piece of paper could make anyone feel safe.

I recently finished a taxing audition for the role of a head chef in a new movie set to release in late 2026. As for auditions, Trent is still looking into the vampire movie role that was initially on the table for me but later retracted due to a false rumor about my complex personality. I don't know whose toes I may have unknowingly stepped on, but perhaps that role wasn't meant for me in the first place. My agent informed me that someone in the industry opposed me having the part, but I have no idea who— *I hope this doesn't jeopardize my chances for the head chef role.* Then again, nothing can stop what God has planned for you.

With a sharp exhale, I turn the key in the ignition, starting my car with a familiar hum. My tire light blinks on the dashboard. Stepping out of the car, I check my front tires and notice they are both flat. *What the hell?* I check the back tires, and they are also flat. This must be some kind of sabotage because all four of my tires are slashed. I look around, as if someone is watching me, and run my hand through my hair. How did I not notice this before getting in the car? My mind is so preoccupied with someone in the industry conspiring against me, my bills, my father's illness, Reign, and our relationship that I fail to notice the condition of my car. Now I'm stuck here with four flat tires. I call Eddie to come pick me up from my audition—luckily, he is off this week.

Forty-five minutes later, Eddie arrives.

"Thanks, man, for helping me out," I say, giving him a fist pound.

"It's all good, bro. Have you called for a tow truck?"

"Nah, I'm going to call now that you're here."

Eddie nods and waits with me while I make the call for a tow truck. I sit in his car weighing my options. It's late now, and I won't get my car back until tomorrow. I have another audition and a chemistry reading tomorrow. Maybe I can borrow my dad's car in the meantime, but I don't want him to have to come get me.

"Bro, who do you think would slash your tires?" Eddie accuses.

I shift my gaze to him, confused by his question or, more importantly, his tone. "What you mean by that?"

Eddie leans back in his seat. "I mean, do you have any kids you don't know about or exes who would do some shit like this?"

"Man, what!? You know damn well I don't have any kids out there. And my exes? They're all cool, I think."

He surrenders by waving his hands back and forth. "My bad, my bad, bro. Bad joke."

"Dude, you know I haven't been in the mood lately," I scoff.

"Nah, I know. That's my fault, bro. But real talk, though. What if someone is after you? What if it's that fool?"

"Who? Peter?"

He nods.

Why would Peter slash my tires? That's a bitch move. How could he have known about my audition?

In response to my silence, Eddie pushes further. "I mean, dude is crazy, and he keeps showing up."

"He didn't show up at your and Scarlette's place for Reign's birthday."

"Yeah, but it's probably because none of us posted about it on social media."

I sift through my memories. Nancy created an Instagram page to promote Reign's business and posted about the upcoming Princess and the Frog-themed wedding. However, Scarlette's birthday celebration at Richard's bar was a surprise. Then again, I think the girls posted about it when she arrived. But what does that have to do with me?

"Nah, man ain't no way he knew that I have an audition. I didn't even tell Reign."

"All four of your tires were slashed, bro. Someone definitely knew where you were going to be. You need to let the police know and file a report."

"I think you're letting Scarlette get in your head, man," I murmur.

"And I think *you're* being too laid-back about this. Clearly, someone is after you."

"You know I don't like dealing with the police."

"Bro, I get it. I don't know what it's like to be a Black man in this world, but I do know what it's like to not be white and have people assume I'm an illegal immigrant or criminal. Shit is wild!"

"Yeah, I hear you."

"But not all police are bad. I'm sure if you file a report, they would look into it."

"Nah, I know, but when I'm in danger, they're not the first people I think to call. I've had more bad experiences than good ones, and that's just what it is. And with everything going on right now, nah, I'm good. If anything, I'll let Trent know."

"Iight, bro, that's better than nothing. I'm glad he's on our side," Eddie agrees, pulling off the curb.

"Facts."

We talk about the audition, how I think I did, and whether Reign is okay with me kissing other females. Reign did express her feelings about possible sex scenes, but I'm not looking for such roles. Although I understand that intimate scenes can be negotiated, especially when working on a new project, I want to be clear that I am not interested in roles that are sexually explicit or resemble pornography. Many actors do not take on roles like that, and I plan to be one of them. The conversation shifted to the financial realities of modeling versus the artistic fulfillment of acting, and I admitted that, while modeling pays the bills, acting is my true passion.

Trent gives me a ride to my audition for the role of a detective investigating a murder who falls in love with one of the victim's daughters. I had to dig deep and really relax my mind to portray such a convoluted character. I would be honored to bring this character to life, as he possesses a rich inner world and a compelling backstory. After the audition, Trent dropped me off to pick up my car so I could drive to my chemistry reading. If the reading goes well, the part will be mine, and Tina will send me the contract to review and sign.

"Mr. James, please follow me," a woman's crisp voice cuts through the quiet casting room.

Trepidation coils in my stomach as I fall into step behind her. Have you ever watched a movie or show where you could sense the tension between the actors, leaving you with a sour taste in your mouth? That's the purpose of chemistry readings—to assess if the actors have the right on-screen dynamic.

The director cast Rose, a new and up-and-coming actress, as my on-screen wife, and we need to have natural chemistry to succeed. She has been in two hit movies that collectively grossed over $1 billion. This film casts her in a minor role, but it would still be an incredible opportunity for me to be a part of it.

Rose walks in with a radiant smile blooming on her face, extending an inviting hand. "Nice to meet you, Mr. James."

I shake her hand, returning her smile. "Nice to meet you, too.

You can call me Dion."

"Let's get started," the director announces, handing us the script. "I want to see that chemistry right away," he adds.

Rose and I exchange a quick glance. Upon reviewing the script, the scene depicts a past conversation between the couple that took place a few months earlier. Although not part of the book, which I will read soon, this scene has been incorporated into the script.

Script:

INT. Main Bedroom—Night
Gabriella (exhausted and on edge) sits on the bed with a book open in her lap, her gaze unfocused despite scanning the pages. The room door opens, and Chance (exhausted) enters.

Chance
(Sighs.)
We have to move back to Mashalville. It's important to me that my daughter learns about her heritage and makes her own decisions based on it.

Gabriella
(Slams the book shut.)
Babe, I understand why you want to move back, but I can't. They will be after me if I return.

Chance
(Exhales a deep breath, a look of concern in his eyes.)
I understand, honey.
(Looks away and then back again.)
Perhaps we can go on our own and then come back after she has

made her decision?

Gabriella
You know they won't allow that. Besides, you don't know what she will choose. And what about my daughters?

Chance
I know. We can figure this out as a family.

Gabriella
(Sighing.)
I don't think you took the time to think this through.

Chance
I have Gabriella, and I think this is best for our family.

Gabriella
(Sighing and sucking her teeth.)
Fine. Let's move back to Mashalville.

Chance
(Sighing with relief.)
And face the consequences together.

Gabriella
(A tear forms in her eyes, and she wipes it away.)

Chance
(Nodding his head and opening his arms for an embrace.)
Together.

End scene.

"Great job! How did that feel?" The director asks as we separate from our embrace.

"I think we nailed it," Rose responds with a smile, and I nod in agreement.

We act out the scene a few more times, with the same intensity and dedication to delivering the lines, until the director and crew congratulate me on landing the role. It was as if Rose and I had known each other for years, and we were portraying the characters as in love but in a tight situation. We hit it off almost instantly, and after, Rose hands me her card. The cast and crew plan to spend some time together before filming starts in August.

I go back to Reign's place after my chemistry reading and wait for her to return home. Eddie has been pestering me about our relationship, asking if we plan to officially move in together. The problem is that I don't think Reign, being a city girl, would want to move to Long Island. I don't want to push it; she stayed at my place for a week before going back to hers. However, with the money I'm currently earning and will earn after this movie, I might be able to afford a place in the city, even though I hate it. I only visited the city on special occasions, but now I'm here to see Reign.

My attention shifts from the flickering images on the screen to the sound of the door opening, and I notice Reign's troubled expression.

"Hey," she mumbles, walking over to me and snuggling into

my side.

"Hey, yourself," I reply, wrapping my arm around her. "You good?"

"Not really," she shakes her head. "I had another session with my mother and Dion… I just hate her," she sobs, burying her face in my chest. "I've been trying to understand her perspective and upbringing, but I don't know what I want from her or how to figure her out. I'm praying to God; does he hear me? I feel like he's not listening to me. Dion, I don't want this woman in my life."

I stroke her hair gently. "Reign, it's not easy forgiving someone who has hurt you. Trust me, I know, but I didn't forgive those people for them. I forgave them for me. You owe every human being in the world love, but you do not owe them access to *you*." I lightly tap my finger on her chest. "You can forgive your mom without granting her access back into your life."

Reign continues to sob softly, her tears soaking my shirt. A thousand words get stuck in my throat as I hold her close, consumed by worries about our future, doubts, and fears, yet all I can do is hold her tightly while she cries.

Chapter 21: Reign

Thursday
June 19th, 2025

Following Dion's advice, I've been trying to pray and surrender for forgiveness. Confronting the past can be incredibly difficult, but letting go of the pain is surprisingly liberating. My mother's constant criticism and belittling remarks created a hostile and emotionally draining environment. Despite knowing what my uncle had done, she kept sending me to my aunt's house. You might be wondering why I referred to the sick bastard who stole my innocence as *my uncle*. I forgave for myself, not for him. It felt as if a heavy weight had been lifted off my shoulders, granting me a sense of freedom that I had not realized I needed. Shonda was the only one of my three cousins to reach out to me last week and apologize for how she and her sisters had treated me. However, I don't see myself being close with them, *ever*.

I forgave her and the other two, even though they haven't spoken to me. I'm not sure how anyone else would react in this situation, but this is how I choose to handle it. I've forgiven everyone who's ever hurt me, yet I struggle to forgive the woman who gave birth to me.

I'm on my way to Dion's family church in Long Island to celebrate Juneteenth. Attending Auntie Mavis's Black History classes has been eye-opening, as I learned about the injustices suffered by people who look like me. It's heartbreaking realizing that such discrimination and racism still exists in some ways. She also has a list of books that she recommends we read. I can't imagine the suffering, fear, and uncertainty my ancestors endured. For all these years, I celebrated Independence Day believing that everyone was free, which was not the case. Juneteenth is a holiday that commemorates freedom for all. Learning that the enslaved individuals in Texas were unaware of their freedom for an additional two years after the Emancipation Proclamation was disheartening.

"Hi, Reign," Auntie Mavis greets, wrapping her arms around me. "Happy Juneteenth!" she bellows, and the folks in the greenspace behind the church return the greeting with smiles.

Dion joins us, wrapping his arms around both of us, and his mom, Eddie, and Scarlette greet us with warm hugs and smiles. I feel terrible for admitting this, but it bothers me how close Dion is to his mother. I wish I had the same connection with my mother. There is a minor strain in my relationship with Dion, which stems from my slight resentment of him for his close relationship with his mother and aunt. I know that it's a bit childish, but I can't help how I feel. Also, I'm a little upset that he left me at the wedding back in April. Yes, I know his father had a heart attack, but for some reason I still feel a type of way. Since his father stayed home, I'm sure his mom won't be staying long. Besides, most of the people in attendance have work tomorrow.

We gather around one another; meanwhile, Auntie Mavis goes to the front of the yard and grabs the mic for an announcement.

"Hey, y'all. Thank ya for coming here today to celebrate a holiday that many of us were unaware of," she begins, her voice booming across the yard. "On January 1st, 1863, the president issued the Emancipation Proclamation, freeing our enslaved brothers and sisters. However, the news of this change was not communicated to them in Galveston, Texas. It took two years…" Auntie Mavis pauses with tears in her eyes, looking up at the sky. Taking a deep breath, she continues, "It wasn't until two years later, on June 19th, 1865, that those women and men learned of their freedom. And it took the 13th Amendment to abolish slavery nationwide. Why did it take all this for Black people to be recognized as humans? I will never know, but this is our history. Never forget."

The crowd chants, "Never forget," as the rest of the festivities begin. A large rectangular table, laden with a plethora of food, sits in the middle of the space. The table has BBQ chicken, smothered chicken and turkey wings, collard and turnip greens, hamburgers, turkey burgers, mac and cheese, baked beans, black-eye peas, cornbread, corn on the cob, potato, macaroni, and egg salad. My mouth is watering as I take in the sight before me.

"My mama doesn't cook food with soul like this!" Scarlette shrieks, licking her lips.

"Baby, I thought yo momma was Black?" Auntie Mavis asks.

"She is half Black, and she grew up mainly on Hispanic food." Scarlette shrugs as she animatedly scoops up another spoonful of mac and cheese, causing the rest of us at the table to laugh.

Auntie Mavis tells us stories about her good and bad experiences in this country, each more revealing than the last. She spoke about the marches she had participated in and how fighting had become second nature to her. I love this woman; she's so strong and embodies qualities I wish my mother had. Even though I've forgiven my Aunt Shirl, the bond between Dion and his aunt moves me to tears because I've never had a connection like that with my own aunt.

Sunday

June 22nd, 2025

The church bells chime eleven as we arrive for the second and later service. There are two services to cater to the diverse needs of its congregation. Dion's parents usually attend the 9 AM service. Dion's dad said, "It's better to go early so I can relax for the rest of the day." I don't blame him for wanting to be in and out and back home, especially after his heart attack. I love and envy the relationship Dion has with his parents. I know I've said it before, but have you ever looked at the bond someone has with their blood relatives and thought, "Wow, I wish I had something like that?" It's ironic because I thought having dinner with my toxic family every week made us close, when in fact we weren't. Dion has shared many stories about his family and childhood. While he isn't close to some cousins, he's cool with others when he sees them. They live in North Carolina and Georgia, and some also reside in Florida. They only visit for special occasions. Dion told his parents we were coming to church today, so they decided to attend this service instead. His parents, Auntie Mavis, and Uncle Bernie are the only ones who live in New York.

"Good morning, Reign," Mom greets me, throwing her arms around me.

"Good morning, Mom," I reply with a smile.

"Happy Sunday," Dad says, lowering slightly to kiss me on the cheek.

"Happy Sunday to you, too, Dad," I reply, returning his radiant grin.

"Good morning, my beautiful Reign," Auntie Mavis chirps loud enough for everyone in the row ahead of us to turn around.

"Good morning, Auntie."

"Reign, it's nice to see you again," Uncle Bernie greets.

Nodding my head, I embrace Uncle Bernie before taking my seat.

Dion is dressed in navy blue slacks with a white and blue button-up shirt. I'm wearing a light blue dress to match him. We sit in our usual seat toward the back of the church. I don't like being too close to the front, where I feel like there are a bunch of eyes staring at me from behind. I usually attend the earlier service with Dion and his parents a few Sundays a month. However, after continuing our Juneteenth celebration with our friends last night, we opted for the later service to catch up on some sleep. His dad is feeling okay after suffering a major heart attack, and you'd never know it from the way he jokes around. Auntie Mavis mentioned we would have food after church, and I'm looking forward to it.

As everyone enters and greets one another, filling the pews, Dion hands me a Bible and takes my hand in his as the chorus sings praise and worship. I listen to the women, men, and children sing their hearts out, hitting each note perfectly, and I scan my memories, thinking about all the times I've ever felt at peace or this free. When I played basketball in school, on the court, I felt free, but then I thought about the lack of support. I understood that my father had to work, but my mom wasn't doing anything and still wasn't there for me. Pulling away from Dion, I clench my fist. How will I ever be able to forgive her if the memory of her pisses me off? After the morning announcements, songs, and prayer, it is finally time for the pastor to preach his sermon.

"Good morning, church! I said, good morning!" His voice is smooth yet gruff. "It's a beautiful Sunday morning, and I am glad to be here." He uses a handkerchief and swipes the beads of sweat off his forehead. "Today I will be reading from *Ephesians 4:31-32, Matthew 6:14,* and *Proverbs 4:23.*"

I thumb through the Bible, searching for the verses the pastor will be preaching on, and I purse my lips.

Dion leans over and asks, "Why the face?"

"Of course, this sermon would be about forgiveness," I whisper back.

Dion gives me a knowing look and replies, "God works in mysterious ways and knows when his children need to hear something."

I give him a playful nudge before returning my attention to the preacher.

"Have you ever found yourself in a situation where a friend or colleague receives more recognition than you for something you both did?"

Some people in the audience say, "Mhmm and yeah!"

The pastor flips to the next page and says, "And then this bitterness starts eating you up."

Another person in the audience shouts, "Preach!"

The pastor waves his hand back and forth. "That bitterness can quickly turn to anger. And the next thing you know, you're wishing them harm."

My heart drops, and the audience starts shouting, "Oh no. We don't do that."

The pastor smirks knowingly. "I just wanted to make sure y'all were paying attention. We don't do that, right? Because that's not godly. Yet, some of us let our bitterness toward others eat us up, but we know what the good word says in *Ephesians 4:31-32*."

While listening to the pastor speak, I reflect on my memories, searching for moments when I harbored bitterness towards others. I remember feeling sour toward Skylar and wishing our mother would pay more attention to me rather than her or show that she cared. Now, I find myself envious of my boyfriend's close relationship with his family. But how can I release these thoughts, as the scripture suggests?

"We are all human, and we are all sinners," the pastor reminds us. "None of us are perfect, and if we can't forgive those who have hurt us, how can we expect forgiveness from the Lord? See *Matthew 6:14.*"

People in the audience shout "Mhmm" and "Yes, Pastor!"

That has been a burning question in my mind: how can I expect forgiveness if I can't find it in my heart to forgive? And when you factor in the effects of rage and anger on your mental and physical health, it's too much.

"All that anger you feel, let it go. All that rage that you feel, let it go. All the hate you feel towards God's children. Let. It. Go. Stop holding onto it. Stop letting it bring you down. You weren't meant to carry this load. Give it to God!"

My feelings are valid, but I must let go of my bitter, consuming anger toward my mother; it is poisoning me. While this suffocating anxiety and harsh resentment are my reality, I can no longer endure this emotional turmoil. Every cruel word that cut me like a knife, every belittling glance that made me feel worthless, every instance her love seemed absent, and the pain of being an outsider in my own family—*let it go.*

Suddenly, I find myself on my feet, hands clapping in response to the preacher's booming voice that captivates me and fills the room with beautiful energy.

As the applause dies down and the audience hangs on every word, he concludes with the following statement: "You have to protect your heart and your mind. Your body is a vessel, and you need to treat it right. Your anger affects your body, mind, and soul. *Proverbs 4:23.*"

Following the service, those who stayed went downstairs to the dining area, where Auntie Mavis and some other church members provided a meal. Fried catfish, green beans, mashed potatoes, sweet corn, eggplant, potato salad, and salad are among the tasty dishes on the table. Hunger stirs in my stomach as I fill my plate with food.

"I'll take my plate to go, Mavis," Dad announces, sitting beside me on the bench.

"Alright now, what do you want on yo plate?" Auntie Mavis asks.

Dion plants a gentle kiss on my cheek, causing me to blush.

"Hmm, young love," Mom teases us, nudging Dad.

"I love seeing you two together," Dad adds, as Auntie Mavis beams from ear to ear while handing him his plate wrapped in aluminum foil.

Uncle Bernie nods in agreement, his mouth already full of sweet corn.

Taking in my surroundings, I see Dion's church family joyfully engaging in fellowship, sharing a meal, and celebrating life.

"You good?" Dion asks, his left dimple deepening as he smiles at me.

A sense of warmth and gratitude fills me as I cherish being a part of this special moment. "I've never felt better," I reply, returning his smile.

Dion's parents embrace us warmly before leaving, their hugs infused with love. We savor our meal while being drawn to Auntie Mavis' lively stories and gentle teachings. When that woman speaks, her voice commands attention, and her words resonate with deep experience and knowledge.

The creamy potato salad is so good that I go for another spoonful. However, my enjoyment is interrupted as my phone rings and my mother's name flashes on the screen.

The calm before the storm.

Me: "Hello?"

Mother: "Reign! Sky and Darcy have been in a terrible car accident!"

Her cries are so loud that I have to hold the phone away from my ear. Hot tears stream down my cheeks as she recounts the gruesome details, each word delivering a fresh stab of pain. My mind races, my emotions are in turmoil, and reality is slipping from my grip. After we hang up, my phone rings again. Scarlette calls this time, followed by August, Love, and Kimi when I don't answer. It was like having an out-of-body experience. I feel disconnected, as if I'm a ghost watching my own life play out, while my senses are muted and the world appears distant and unreal. One moment, you're at peace, and the next, your world crumbles, as if unseen hands are pulling the strings of your life. It's like a puppeteer deliberately orchestrating obstacles to knock you off balance, reveling in the drama of your downfall and escalating chaos.

"Reign? You good?" Dion asks, waving his hand in front of my face.

My mouth is dry, and my body is rigid. Skylar and Darcy were in a car accident, and it's bad. That was all my mind could handle before a mental break drove my legs into a panicked flight, the pounding of my feet echoing like a frantic drumbeat in my ears. It took a few moments before I noticed my body's strange movements and heard Dion's frantic shouts from behind. I request an Uber. Dion, Auntie Mavis, Uncle Bernie, and a woman whose face I can't place yelled over each other, their voices a blur, desperate to get my attention before I slid into the backseat and was whisked away to the hospital.

Chapter 22: Dion

"What happened?" My aunt and uncle shout in unison.

"I—I don't know," I reply, dialing Reign's number. When she doesn't answer, I call Eddie.

"Wassup, bro?" he answers on the first ring.

"Hey, bro. Reign just left church without saying anything. I think something happened," I explain, trying my best to keep my voice steady.

"Oh, shit! Hold that thought," he says before the line goes mute.

Auntie Mavis asks again if everything is okay. I raise my finger, and she looks offended for a moment, but Uncle Bernie rubs her back while we anxiously wait for Eddie to return to the line. I pace back and forth on the sidewalk; my aunt and uncle, and Sister Moore, watch me with worried expressions on their faces.

After what feels like an eternity, Eddie returns to the line, with Scarlette's frantic screams audible in the background. "Sky and Darcy were in a major car accident!"

"What?"

"It was a hit and run! They crashed into a tree, and Dion, it's not looking too good," Eddie shouts.

"What hospital?" I ask urgently.

I hang up, inform my aunt and uncle about the accident, and rush to the hospital.

My heart hammers against my ribs, the air thick with the smell of antiseptics and the sounds of beeping machines, triggering the same gut-wrenching panic I felt when my father was in this place. When I walk into the waiting room, Reign's pale and distant gaze meets mine at the entrance. I approach her cautiously, but her red-rimmed eyes create an invisible barrier, as if she's already shut me out completely. Her mother is slumped against her, quietly sobbing. Meanwhile, Darcy's parents are lost in their own sadness. Reign's cousins Shonda, Raquel, and Robyn, along with their husbands, pace nervously back and forth in hushed conversations. Eddie and Scarlette hold each other, while Reign's aunt, with her husband absent, leans against the cool wall, shaking her head. Mr. Brown firmly stated he never wanted to be near that man again, leaving no room for discussion. Rubbing his beard with tears brimming in his eyes, he seemed oblivious to my attempts to get his attention. I don't know what to do. Fortunately, August, Love, and Kimi arrive fifteen minutes later, with their men following close behind. They embrace Reign's parents and her, but Reign remains emotionally removed, exhibiting a coldness.

"Any word?" Love whispers so only I can hear.

"They aren't speaking to me," I murmur back, feeling helpless.

Love nods understandingly and squeezes my hand in support before turning her attention back to the family. August and Scarlette are consoling Mr. Brown while Kimi sits quietly next to Reign, offering her silent support.

Following an agonizing wait, the doctors eventually exited the operating room. Reign, along with her family, waited with bated breath, hoping to receive good news. Skylar sustained a broken leg and arm, three cracked ribs, and a concussion. Unfortunately, Darcy is in worse condition. With both legs fractured and a traumatic brain injury, she is currently in an induced coma, her breathing shallow and monitored. Darcy's mother collapses to the floor in a flood of tears, while her husband tries to console her, his own eyes filled with worry and fear.

"Who did this!?" She cries out to no one in particular.

Suddenly, the doors swing open, and Peter rushes in disheveled, with sweat pouring from his temples. He shouts, "What happened!? Where is Skylar!?"

Mr. Brown charges at him. "You sick son of a bitch! You did this!"

Trent, Eddie, and Raquel's husband quickly intervene to restrain Mr. Brown off Peter, and the front desk calls for security.

Peter stumbles back, finding Mr. Brown's accusations amusing.

"Get your hands off of me! I know he did it!" Mr. Brown struggles against Eddie and Raquel's husband's grip. Trent shoves Peter towards the exit, and nods for me to follow him.

"How could you do this to our daughter?" Mrs. Brown wails

at Peter's retreating figure, clutching onto Reign's hand.

With a clenched jaw, Trent slams Peter against the wall, the impact causing a loud thud. Peter's sickly grin stretches wide as he surrenders, his hands raised in a futile gesture.

Trent loosens his grip a bit and asks through gritted teeth, "Why are you here?"

A passing employee looks cautiously at the altercation but decides to walk away, choosing not to intervene.

"My wife was in a car accident, and I came to see if she was okay," Peter says simply.

"She's not your wife," I scoff.

His icy green eyes meet mine. "She is *still* my wife." He points to his heart. "In here."

"Not anymore," I retort. "Get out of here, Peter."

He looks from me to Trent and then back to me and taunts, "Or what?"

"Or you will be the next one lying in a hospital bed," I warn.

"Or six feet under," Trent adds, nudging him back against the wall.

Peter lets out a loud, booming laugh that echoes throughout the room, as if we were joking with him. He pretends to shiver in mock fear. "I'm so terrified of a billionaire and a washed-up actor who can't get a role." He wiggles his brow suggestively, as if he knows something I don't.

Trent and I exchange a knowing glance. This sick asshole is why I didn't get the role. He had something to do with it, and he probably had something to do with my tires. As the realization hits me, Peter winks at me. My blood boils with anger, and I punch him square in the nose. Crimson liquid gushes from his nostrils as he laughs manically, wiping the blood away.

Security rushes in, forcibly separating me from Peter, who

laughs uncontrollably. "Can I get a doctor, please?"

He needs a psychiatrist!

Trent's calm and measured voice cut through the tension as he explains the misunderstanding to the guards, while I scramble to piece together the events of the past hour. If I wasn't involved with Reign, I wouldn't be entangled in this mess.

What did I get myself into?

Monday

July 7ᵗʰ, 2025

Another day, another string of unanswered texts from Reign. This time, though, I find a strange peace in it. My life is full of good news that I want to share. However, Reign is so consumed by Skylar's recovery that she can't focus on anything else. It's not like I don't understand how she feels. I was in the same situation a few months ago when my father had a heart attack, but this is different. My involvement with her led me to lose more than one job.

No, I didn't get the part of a chef. Tina called to tell me that they wanted to hire me but were advised not to by their law firm. Guess what law firm advised them against it? *Peter's.* Even though he is no longer employed there due to the agreement with Trent, he is still pulling strings. I was able to keep my role in the two-part fantasy series I did that chemistry reading for because the director and screenwriter operate independently and have enough funds to support the cast and crew.

Skylar's condition has improved; she is still in the hospital, and they expect to discharge her at the end of the week. I spoke with her, and she appears to be in good spirits. However, Darcy remains in a coma. The police haven't found any leads in the hit-

and-run. It's as if the jeep materialized out of nowhere, hitting them and causing a collision with a tree before vanishing into thin air. Peter was at the top of the list due to Mr. Brown's outburst at the hospital, but he had an airtight alibi. Despite the police ruling out Peter's involvement in the accident, we all seem to think otherwise. I'm not sure how Reign or Skylar feels about it. I think they are numb to the possibility and don't want to talk about it.

Eddie is on his way to pick me up for a trip upstate with the cast and crew of my new movie. We are set to start filming on August 15th. They've been saying for some weeks now that filming would start in August. I assumed that meant the beginning of August, but that's fine. Eddie is coming with me since Reign won't. I know she wants to be here for her sister. However, I wanted her to accompany me on this trip to meet the crew I will be filming with for three to four months. I also wanted to introduce her to my co-stars. Scarlette promised to talk sense into Reign, but Reign has also been distant with her and the others. Love suggested giving her some time because this is a traumatic experience for her. She almost lost her sister; she needs time to cope. I don't want to compare, but I almost lost my father and *did* for three minutes.

A knock on my door takes me out of my thoughts; it's Eddie. I grab my bags and head to the door.

"Wassup, bro," Eddie greets, giving me a fist pound. "How you feeling?"

I frown in response.

"Ah, man, that bad, huh?"

Closing the door behind me as we walk to Eddie's car, I give a curt nod.

"Look, bro. You need to perk up. You've landed a role in a film; this is what you've worked so hard for, and you are getting paaiidd," he grins, rubbing his hands together.

"Nah, I know, man, and I'm excited about it, but I can't get my mind off Reign and this distance between us."

Eddie claps me on the shoulder. "Listen, she's dealing with some shit most of us couldn't imagine. Her mother hates her, her uncle did the unspeakable, she was cheated on, her sister was abused, and now—"

"Man, I didn't need a recap," I cut him off, getting into the passenger seat of his car.

"My fault, bro, I'm just saying. Give her some grace?" He shrugs, starting the engine and pulling into traffic.

"What about me and my feelings? Are they invalid, or am I not allowed to have any because I am a man? I love Reign, but all of this drama and toxicity has made me wonder if love is enough."

Eddie stares into the distance, his expression a void that somehow spoke volumes. We share an unspoken understanding as we ride in silence the rest of the way.

"Bro, would you look at this view?" Eddie whistles, stepping out of the passenger's seat to survey the row of trailers reserved for the cast, crew, and company. "We made it!"

"We?" I smirk, following him out of the car. We switched places at a rest stop on the way here.

"Ahh, there he goes," Eddie grins, throwing an arm around my shoulder.

We approach the front trailer, and a staff member hands us both badges. I receive one that reads "actor," and Eddie receives one that reads "guest." Heading to my trailer, we take turns showering and getting ready for tonight's events. Later, the director is hosting a get-together in a larger building where some of the magical stunts will be performed. But first, Quincy takes us on a tour of the place.

"This is your home when the movie starts, and then down the street is where you will move to," Quincy points out.

Eddie chuckles, his eyes widening in shock as he takes in the scope of the set.

"What is the joke?" I ask, smirking at him.

He gestures around at the different buildings with his hands. "This is awesome, man. Everything is on one strip."

Clapping him on the back, I take it all in. The attention to detail is impressive, from the magical high school to the storefronts to the street signs. Following the tour, we go to the director's building and hang out with the rest of the cast and crew. As we get to know one another and some of their companions, I find myself wishing Reign was here to share the experience with me. Rose, who plays my wife, introduces me and Eddie to her fiancé, a professional wedding photographer. We exchange contact information. After a night of networking, we return to my trailer, and I text Reign good night. This time, she responds with a goodnight text.

By the end of the week, I have learned and grown to respect the people I will be working with for the next three to four months. Now I understand why some people become close to their castmates because they spend so much time together.

Today, we will be taking pictures for the promo.

"Dion, you're up next," the photographer calls out, drawing my attention away from my phone.

Reign just texted me to say she loved me. Hmm… she hasn't sent a "I love you," text in a while. *Maybe she is coming around.* I quickly reply before taking my place in front of the camera. I start with about ten solo shots, followed by some with Rose, a wardrobe change for family photos, and finally pictures with the entire cast.

After three and a half hours of posing, camera clicking, and bright studio lights, I'm exhausted. We wrap up the photoshoot, and I head back to my trailer, scrolling through my phone. I see Reign's earlier message and smile. When I return to my trailer, I see Eddie's face contorted with sheer terror, sweat beading on his forehead.

"You good, man?"

"I—I think you should take a seat," he says, instead of answering my question.

"Not until you tell me what's going on," I reply, a sense of unease creeping in.

"Bro, I'm being serious."

A knot of worry forms in my stomach as I watch Eddie's expression grow even more grave. What does he have to tell me? Is it about Reign? I slowly sit down, my mind racing with possibilities, each one more alarming than the last.

"What happened?"

Eddie takes a sharp breath. "Reign... she's missing."

My heart plummets to my stomach, my worst fears coming to life in an instant.

Chapter 23: Reign

Three days earlier…

When I arrive at the hospital to pick up Skylar, I check on Darcy first. Despite our less-than-harmonious relationship, I wouldn't wish her current ordeal on anyone. Her parents visit her every day, showing unwavering hope for her recovery, occasionally throwing pointed glares towards me and my family. After my father attacked Peter, the prevailing belief shared by the majority was that Peter bore some responsibility for the accident. A *thorough* police investigation exonerated Peter from any involvement, rebutting this theory. Unfortunately, Darcy's condition remains unchanged with no improvement in her symptoms. Skylar will be discharged from the hospital today rather than Friday, as originally planned, due to her steady improvement.

"Hi, Sky. How are you feeling?" I chirp, entering her hospital room.

Her face grimaces slightly, but she offers a weak smile. "Great," she says, deadpan.

"I know, I know. You're all banged up, but at least you get to go home early, right?" I try to lighten the mood, but Skylar's smile fades as she looks down at her hands.

"Home? I'm not going back to my place. I share it with Darcy."

Pinching my brows together, I pause. "So where will you stay then?"

"I'm going to stay with our parents. At least until Darcy gets better." She lowers her voice, "*If* she gets better."

"I'm sure she will," I reassure her. "Now come on, let's get going. We can grab some food on the way. Hospital food sucks," I say, trying to change the subject.

Skylar nods, swinging her legs to the side of the bed, as I collect the rest of her things and place them in the duffle bags she has on the chair. Her leg is in a cast covered with our signatures and notes.

"Have you spoken to my brother?"

Her question interrupts my routine of gathering her things. "Your brother?"

Her lips curve into a teasing smile. "Yes, my brother. You know that man loves you, but instead of spending time with him, you've been moping around like a depressed kitten."

Feigning offense, I pretend to throw something at her. "Really? I've been busy taking care of you, remember?"

"Well, you better make time for him soon, Reign! I know that one-track mind of yours tends to shut down when you're dealing with something."

"I'm sorry, who is this woman speaking to me with such wisdom? I'm older than you."

"Yeah, but my experiences have made me wiser," she retorts with a smirk.

"Yeah, yeah, okay," I reply, rolling my eyes. "Let me find the nurse."

I go to the nurse's station to inquire about Skylar's discharge instructions and a wheelchair. Returning to her room, there are four men in suits, each of large stature.

"We were hired to escort you and your sister off the premises," the tall and slender man says, stepping forward.

"And *who* hired you?" I ask, reaching for my phone. If these are Trent's men, why aren't they wearing his logo?

Another man appears from behind me and snatches my phone out of my hand. "You won't be needing that." He points to a pistol with a silencer on it, tucked into his waistband. "You scream, and I'll shoot this bitch in the head before you can blink twice."

My blood runs cold, a chill settling in my bones. We are in a hospital. If he shoots, he will be arrested and detained. But it would be after he shot us.

This can't be happening!

This isn't real!

Skylar sat frozen on the bed, her face pale as a sheet, her body stiff and unmoving. Unaware of the danger in the room, the nurse walks in with Skylar's discharge papers and a wheelchair. The man to the left of her offers to retrieve the wheelchair from her, and she gives him an awkward smile. Her face was initially confused, but she quickly regained her professional composure and informed us that Skylar was cleared to leave. I tried to catch her eye, silently pleading for help, but she was still unaware of the imminent danger and turned to leave the room. The men escort us out of the building, and one demands that I hand over my keys. He takes my car, while the other three men load us into a white van. Tears well up in our eyes as the harsh reality sinks in that we are being kidnapped, and there is nothing we can do about it. After about five minutes, we pull into a garage, and the man places a bag over Skylar's head first, then mine, cuffing my hands together. Encircled by complete darkness, I'm blind to my surroundings, with only the frantic thumping of my heart against my chest as fear grips me tightly. The muffled sounds of Skylar's sobs echo in the enclosed space. My brain tells me to scream, but who will hear me?

"Use her phone to text the last person who texted her, so no one is concerned," a gruff voice instructs. "Here, send a text on her phone as well."

It felt like hours and hours before the van came to a halt, and then some men roughly dragged me out and shoved me forward. My sister has a broken leg and is unable to walk; I have no idea where she is or what they are doing with her.

I have to pee.

I'm hungry.

Where is Skylar?

God, please don't let us die.

"Push her in there," a man barks, and I stumble into a room with a foul smell.

"Get the other bitch," another man orders.

"She can't walk. Her damn leg is broke."

"Well, carry her in then," the man replies gruffly. "She's the one the boss cares about."

Peter. I try to listen for any sign of Skylar's voice, but all I hear is the sound of my own heartbeat pounding in my ears.

A man pushes me forward, and I fall onto a hard stone floor. Someone is removing the bag from my face while my hands are cuffed to something else.

My eyes adjust to the dim light, and I scan the room; it looks like an unfinished basement.

"Hello, Reign," Peter's familiar voice greets me, and I whip my head around to look at him.

"Peter," I spit through gritted teeth, straining and struggling against the unforgiving cuffs with all my might, to no avail.

His cold eyes meet mine, a sadistic grin spreading across his face as he takes a step closer. "You've been such a bitch, Reign, taking my wife away from me."

She's not your wife anymore.

"Where is my sister?" I shout.

"Where she belongs!" He spits back.

Tears threaten to spill from my eyes, but I won't let them. I will not give him the satisfaction.

"I—I thought you loved her?"

"I do, which is why we're leaving."

We? She is still alive.

"What do you want with me?"

"Out of my way!" he bellows, shoving me aside as he storms out of the room.

One of his men approaches me and unlocks my handcuffs, replacing them with chains before leaving the basement. Although the chains offer limited mobility, they are a better alternative to the restrictive nature of handcuffs. I meticulously survey my surroundings. I'm in an unfinished basement with no windows, and the only way out is through the entrance the men used to come in.

I have no phone—nothing on me that can help get me out of this situation. There's just a bucket next to me. I have no idea where I am or if I'm still in New York. I'm tired, hungry, and thirsty, and I have to pee. I'm wearing a skirt. *Oh God! Please don't let these men hurt me or my sister.* I try to make a plan, but the only thing that occupies my mind and dominates all other thoughts and feelings is a desperate need to use the bathroom. I carefully slide off my skirt and underwear before positioning above the bucket to relieve myself.

This is extremely humiliating.

I redress and curl up into a ball. Dion's face flashes in my mind. I think about the wonderful times we've had and regret how I should have responded to his messages.

Why do I have such a one-track mind?

I miss and love Dion so much.

Will I ever see him again?

Time stretches endlessly, each day a torment of deprivation caused by the lack of food and water that becomes increasingly unbearable. I know that without water soon, my body will shut down from dehydration, and I will die.

Is this really my end?

Never in my wildest dreams did I imagine this would be my final farewell. I always imagined something more spectacular, more fitting, like dying peacefully in my sleep. Kidnapped by my sister's crazy ex-husband was not on the list.

This is it.

I can feel my life slipping away as I close my eyes. I want to stay awake and fight, but there is no way out of this. I think of my friends Scarlette and August; I love them. My thoughts drift to my growing friendships with Love, Kimi, April, and Jieun. My successful business. Soon, all of them—my dad, my sister, and my family—will be distant memories.

Whispering a final goodbye, "I love you, Dion Atom James, and I'm so sorry. Scarlette, you've been my girl ever since I can remember. I love you. August, girl, you haven't changed since I met you. Love, I love our growing friendship. I will miss you. Kimi, I'll never forget your bubbly energy and swag. April and Jieun, thank you for being you. Eddie, Trent, Calvin, Edwin, and Dante, I love the way you love my friends. Dad, I will miss you. Skylar, I'm so sorry."

If I weren't so dehydrated, tears would be streaming down my face as I bid my farewells. I extend my heartfelt thanks to my bonus family. "Mom, Dad, Auntie Mavis, and Uncle Bernie, thank you for treating me as one of your own." With a final blink, darkness descends, signaling the end as the world fades to black.

Scarlette materializes before me. Her presence feels so vivid, so tangible, but I know it's not real.

It can't be.

My mind must be playing tricks on me in my final moments.

"*Mi amor,* you have a boyfriend, bonus family, a dad, a sister, and friends who love you. You need to fight."

She isn't here with me. She is back in New York, living her life without me.

"I'm hallucinating. This isn't real," I croak.

"How dare you say I'm not real!"

"Stop yelling, Scarlette. You're not really here," I weakly mutter.

"Listen to my voice, Reign!"

"I'm so tired," I whisper, feeling the weight of exhaustion pulling me under.

"You need to fight!"

A soft, warm light shines at the end of the tunnel, promising peace and no pain. The gentle glow beckons me toward it, and I don't have the energy or the urge to fight it. The captivating light drains my strength, making it impossible to resist.

Turning to Scarlette, I whisper with exhaustion, "I can't. I'm too tired."

"Reign, your earrings!"

"M-my e-earrings?"

"Despertar! Wake up!"

Abruptly, the light floods back, and I fumble for my earrings, a birthday present from Love and Trent. Reaching for my ears, I feel the metal's familiar weight before pressing the side-tracking button, which sends a silent signal.

Three sharp red blinks fill my vision before everything fades to black.

"Fight"

Cling to those you love and never surrender!
No matter how difficult the struggle.

Chapter 24: Reign

*I*n the transition from life to death, a calm stillness descends, gently lifting the burdens of the physical world. You feel a sense of weightlessness as the sounds of the realm fade into a peaceful silence.

Reaching for the light, you find that all the stress, anger, and pain that weighed you down for years vanish, replaced by a warmth spreading through your body as you accept it.

With peace so near, worries, sickness, and pain fading, why would anyone want to come back?

What is the point?

On Earth, stress weighs you down, pain stabs you with agonizing force, illnesses spread like a slithering darkness, conflict erupts with a deafening roar and hate festers like a menacing wound.

There are times when the weight of the world becomes unbearable, and the prospect of escaping it all may seem appealing.

Colors drain away, and the sounds of the world soften to a whisper, leaving only a sense of calm.

This is it.

Your time is up.

Suddenly, you hear a voice calling you, pleading for your return.

What do you do?

Do you follow the light, feeling the warmth on your face as you find peace, or do you listen to the familiar, comforting voice that calls out your name?

The decision is yours.

"Please wake up! Can you hear me?" *A familiar voice calls to me.* "Reign? Please come back to me!" *the gruff male voice pleads.* "She's not waking up. Why isn't she waking up?"

My heavy eyelids are sealed against his intense gaze, feeling the warmth of his eyes on my skin, yet I find it difficult to open them.

"Reign! You have to come back to me."

Memories of laughter, shared meals, and inside jokes flood into my mind, each intertwined with the distinct sound of a voice calling my name. Then the bad memories, vivid and painful, assault my brain, and I yearn to escape this torment, this endless suffering, and move on to the next world.

"Come back to me, my rose!"

But where there is good, there is always darkness, and I must fight to overcome it.

Both my triumphs and heartbreaks, each with its own imprint, have molded me into the person I am today. I wouldn't trade those experiences for anything, because they helped shape who I am.

So, I will fight.

My eyes snap open, disoriented, to a blurry scene; I can't tell where I am or who might be near. The sterile smell of antiseptic fills my nostrils, and the beeping of machines in the background slowly comes into focus. *I'm in a hospital room.* My gaze moves to my arm, where a needle is embedded, connected to a clear IV bag.

"She's awake!" A voice shouts from behind me, and a nurse rushes to check my vitals.

"Reign, my rose!" Dion exclaims, kissing my forehead, cheek, and nose.

"W-what happened?" My voice is hoarse and weak.

As Dion recounts the events, a tidal wave of memories crashes over me, connecting the fragments of the kidnapping. My earrings flashed a subtle signal that alerted Trent, who then called the police and gathered his security team. The authorities tracked us down at Peter's secluded property in New Jersey. The police stormed in with weapons drawn, thwarting Peter's schemes and rescuing my sister from his clutches. Two of his four security guards were killed with him. The remaining two were charged with kidnapping and attempted murder.

"Thank God you're okay, Reign," Dion sighs, tears welling up in his eyes. "I love you so much."

"I—I love you too. I'm so, so sorry for everything."

He gently kisses my forehead. "Shh, it's okay, baby. You need to rest. I'll be here when you wake up."

Nodding, I close my eyes, and the machine's rhythmic beeping lulls me to sleep.

"Commitment"

The conscious decision to stay together despite the flaws and disagreements.
You commit to one another, promising yourselves a lifetime of love, trust, and understanding, building a bond stronger than any other.

Epilogue

Acloud of hairspray and perfume fills the air as I sit in the makeup chair, surrounded by the joyful chaos of my friends, all buzzing with excitement for my wedding. I can't believe I'm marrying the love of my life. Dion and I purchased a penthouse two blocks away from my boutique. I was willing to move to Long Island, but Dion said that it would be better to live closer to my business. I love that man more than words can describe.

Our colors are lavender and black. The ladies exuded their individual styles in one-of-a-kind lavender gowns by Kia, while the men wore tailored black suits.

"*¡Ándale! ¡Ándale!*" Scarlette, my maid of honor, glides by in a strapless lavender mermaid-style dress, her laughter echoing as the fabric shimmers.

My other maid of honor, Skylar, walks in behind her in a halter-top lavender maxi dress with delicate silk that rustles softly as she moves. "Will you stop yelling at us!"

Love and Kimi wear nearly identical dresses, but Love's dress features a daring slit that reaches up to her thigh, unlike Kimi's more modest hemline.

Scarlette urgently informs, "We only have ten minutes to get ready before we need to start dressing Reign!" She then hollers a string of Spanish words to someone on the other end of her phone.

August excitedly waddles over, her bright eyes shining, as she carefully presents me with a small, worn box containing something old, new, borrowed, and blue. Her princess-style dress fits her pregnant belly perfectly, accentuating her radiant glow.

"Are you good?" I ask, rubbing her round stomach.

She sits in the chair in front of me, swinging her legs from side to side. "Girl, I'm good, but I'm so ready to drop this load."

I laugh. "I can only imagine!"

"What do you think, Reign?" My makeup artist spins me around to the brightly lit mirror, showcasing the beautiful job she has done.

"I love it!" I admire my reflection.

She claps her hands together with a smile, her eyes sparkling with pride. "Excellent."

"Time for the dress!" Skylar shouts with Scarlette trailing behind.

The ladies close in, a symphony of whispers and rustling fabric as they carefully guide my dress onto my body.

"You got a little thick!" Skylar teases, tugging on the back of my dress.

"That's what you call happy weight," Love giggles, adjusting the fabric.

"Sure is," I laugh. "I had no intention of losing weight for this dress. It was made to fit me, not the other way around."

"You know we have three phases of the month," Scarlette adds, winking.

"What does that mean?" Kimi questions.

"First part of the month, you're a skinny mini," I start.

"Second part, you might be a little bloated," Scarlette explains.

"And then the third part, you just super bloated, girl!" August chimes in, and we all start laughing, agreeing with one another.

"Not *super* bloated," Love giggles.

"Being a woman is so annoying," Skylar concludes, rolling her eyes.

"And let's not even talk about those annoying period pimples," August adds, taking a sip of her water.

"Seriously, you only look good, like, one week of the month," I comment, causing everyone to nod in agreement.

Standing in front of the mirror, I'm wearing a stunning ivory mermaid dress. It's a halter-style dress with a low-cut neckline that accentuates my figure beautifully, adorned with lovely lavender details, and pockets! *Yay!* I have on my signature gold bracelet with the single black rose. My silk-pressed hair gleams under the light as it is styled into a high bun.

We reach the reception hall fifteen minutes before the men are scheduled to arrive for the reveal. A reveal is the moment when the groom sees his bride for the first time in front of the bridal party. The bridal attendant directs me to my spot, where I will wait for my soon-to-be husband and the groomsmen to take their places across from my bridesmaids. My heart is racing as I wait to be called in.

"Please follow me this way," the bridal attendant directs.

Falling in step behind her, I carefully walk toward the

greenspace. The air is filled with freshly cut grass, and the background is ringing with the murmur of excited chatter. Walking through the double doors, my bridesmaids are on the right and the groomsmen are on the left. My father stands beside Dion's father, mother, Auntie Mavis, and Uncle Bernie, tears glistening in their eyes. If you're wondering, my mother is here as my father's plus one. However, this moment is reserved for those who hold a special place in my heart. While I forgive her for how she has treated me, I don't owe her full access to me.

"Reign, you may step forward," the bridal attendant announces.

Striding down the long runway toward Dion, who stands with his back to me, his broad shoulders and sexy build is highlighted by the sleek, tailored ivory tux he is wearing.

The photographer snaps a few pictures, the flash momentarily blinding, as I gently place my hand on Dion's shoulder. He turns around and his gaze meets mine, and his beautiful light brown eyes are glossy with unshed tears. He takes my hand and spins me around before placing his lips on mine. Our friends and family clap and cheer as August shouts, "Alright now, save some of that for the honeymoon!"

Dion pulls away, his smile wide and infectious. "I love you so much."

"I love you too, babe," I smile back, falling into his broad arms.

The videographer walks around us, angling the camera just right, as the photographer snaps photos. After we've taken our pictures, we walk inside and down the hall to the wedding ceremony. Everyone lines up with their partners, and Skylar and my father walk me down the aisle to my man.

"We are gathered here today to celebrate the union between Dion James and Reign Brown," the wedding officiant announces. "The bride and groom have decided to recite their own vows to each other. Dion, you may proceed."

Dion takes my hands in his; his gaze is so intense and full of love that it sends shivers down my spine. "Reign Amara Brown," his deep voice announces, "I never thought in a million years I would fall so hard for someone like you. We are too different and come from opposite worlds, but you consumed me. I felt in my heart that you were everything I wanted in a woman. When we played ball together, the chemistry was so real that I knew I needed to spend the rest of my life with you. And on that awful day when I almost lost you, the pain of the possibility of never seeing you open your eyes again was unbearable. I knew then, if you were to return to me, I would marry you without hesitation. I want to love and cherish you every day for the rest of my life. I want to focus all my energy on you and me. Reign, baby, my rose, I'm ready to take this ride through life with you."

My eyes well up with tears, and the audience sniffles as Dion finishes his heartfelt vows. I can see the sincerity in his eyes, and I know that he truly means every word he says.

"That's my brother right there!" Scarlette sniffles.

"Mine too," Skylar adds, wiping away a tear.

Our guests laugh through their tears, then the attention settles on me.

The officiant gestures for me to go.

Clearing my throat, "Dion Atom James," I begin, my voice shaking slightly. Dion smiles at me, his left dimple deepening as he listens intently. "I love you with my entire soul. I never knew what it meant to be loved by a man until you came into my life. When we first met, I was attracted to you, and I was terrified of how you made me feel. When we kissed for the first time, I knew in my heart that we were meant for each other. And thinking about the day in the hospital, it was your voice that brought me back. It was our shared memories that gave me the strength to fight for my life. It felt as though..."

"God made you for me," we say in unison.

"Rings?" The officiant announces.

Scarlette and Eddie step forward to present the rings, which we then slip onto each other's fingers.

"I now pronounce you husband and wife. Dion, you may kiss your bride."

Dion's lips meet mine in a kiss overflowing with joy that sends my heart soaring.

The crowd bursts into applause and cheers as we embrace each other as husband and wife for the first time. Walking back down the aisle, hand in hand, I scan the faces of our loved ones. Scarlette's parents and cousin Edwin, Jieun, my friends April and Richard, Nancy, and even Darcy were all smiling and teary-eyed, congratulating us on our union.

My heart swells with such intense happiness that it feels like it will burst.

Two weeks later…

Sunlight streams through our hotel room's sheer, light blue curtains, casting a soft glow.

"Good morning, wife," Dion says, a grin spreading across his face as he leans in to kiss me on the lips.

"Good morning, husband," I brush my lips against his.

"You already know what I want," he groans.

"Breakfast in bed?" I tease, settling back onto the pillows with a seductive smile. I open my legs invitingly, feeling the cool air tickling my exposed skin.

Dion hovers over me and inhales my sweet scent. "Breakfast is the most important meal of the day." He spreads my legs wider and inserts three fingers, hitting my sweet spot just right.

I gasp, my body instinctively arching towards his touch.

"You're so wet," he murmurs, withdrawing his fingers to suck off all the juices before shoving them back into my wet folds.

"Come for me, my rose," he says, using his other hand to draw circles on my clit.

My breath becomes more erratic with each thrust of his fingers, pleasure building with each stroke. "I'm close," I whimper, feeling the heat pooling in my core.

With each lick, suck, nibble, and gentle blow on my pussy, Dion skillfully guides me to an orgasm.

"Yes, yes, yes," I cry out.

He swiftly lowers his head to my sex and devours me. His fingers curl inside me, hitting all the right spots. He eagerly licks and sucks on my swollen nub, intensifying my pleasure.

"Ahh! Yes!" I shout, back-to-back orgasms crashing over me as I grip the sheets tightly.

I have two minutes to catch my breath before he positions me on all fours, his hard dick lined up with my entrance. He cups my breast and plays with my nipple with his pointer finger before pushing in with a hard thrust that causes me to yelp.

My moans mix with his grunts, the sound of skin slapping against skin as he pounds into me relentlessly.

"Reign, you're soaking wet," he growls in my ear.

I arch my back, meeting his thrusts with equal fervor. The pleasure builds and builds until I can't hold back any longer, my body shaking with the intensity of my release. He flips me onto my back and continues to thrust deeply; his eyes locked with mine. "I love you."

Pulling him closer, I wrap my legs around him. "I love you too."

Dion pulls me in for a bruising kiss, the taste of my arousal lingering on his tongue. His hands grip my hips possessively, and with one final deep thrust, he releases inside me, sending me over the edge once again. My body feels weightless, as if it's being transported to another realm.

He collapses on top of me, breathless and satisfied, our heavy breathing slowly returning to normal. Staring into his eyes, I'm so in love with this man. He is everything I've ever wanted and needed.

So, is love enough?

No, it's not. Love is the foundation, but it requires more for it to last.

It takes respect for one another, honesty, appreciation, commitment, communication, and compromise to make love last a lifetime.

And I have found that with Dion Atom James.

Retrieving my handcuffs from the side table, I swing them back and forth in front of Dion.

His eyes widened with interest. "This time, I want to use them on you," I purr seductively into his ear.

"Anything for you, my rose," he says, surrendering control to me.

The End.

If you have enjoyed reading this story, please consider leaving a review on Amazon, Bookbub, Goodreads, Fable, StoryGraph or anywhere you can. It is extremely important for Indie Authors, even if it's just a rating.

Please help spread the word.

Keep reading for the sneak peek at *"Tainted Past"* Prologue part I.

Sneak Peek: Tainted Past

Prologue (Part 1.)

College Senior Year

Five months—five *agonizing* months—have passed since the hit-and-run accident that killed my parents. A beat-up, unmarked truck collided with their car, causing my father to lose control and crash into a large oak tree. The driver of the jeep fled the scene, and when emergency responders arrived, they pronounced my parents dead on scene.

It was a normal Tuesday afternoon. Sunlight streamed into my dorm room, and the air smelled of stale pizza. My roommates and I were studying when the jarring headlines from the 5 o'clock news interrupted the stillness, shattering my world into a million pieces.

BREAKING NEWS
WE JUST RECEIVED WORD THAT LONG ISLAND
DETECTIVE BRIAN WILLIAMS AND PROSECUTOR
RACHAEL WILLIAMS WERE BOTH KILLED IN A FATAL CAR
ACCIDENT.
THERE IS STILL MUCH TO LEARN ABOUT THIS
DEVASTATING TRAGEDY, AND WE WILL PROVIDE
UPDATES AS THEY ARE AVAILABLE.
THE COUPLE LEAVES BEHIND A TEENAGE DAUGHTER.

A day before the hit-and-run accident that took my parents' lives, I was in my room packing to move into my dorm when my mother walked in.

She brushed aside my goddess box braids, gently cupping my chin, her green eyes boring into mine. "I'm so proud of you."

I smiled back at her, and she went on, "I always hoped you'd follow in my footsteps and become a lawyer."

"Mom, you know…" I playfully swatted her hand away.

"But seeing you pursue your passion in owning an indie bookstore makes me even prouder," she said with a smile.

I hugged her, not knowing it would be one of the last times. "Thanks, Mom. You and Dad are my biggest supporters."

"Your father and I always joked that your head was always in some fantasy or romance story."

We both laughed. "What can I say? Reading is my escape from all things I don't have control of."

She smiled sympathetically. "I know, baby. I will never fully understand the horror you must have experienced in that home, but please know that I am here to talk about it whenever you want."

"Earth to Love," Kendall calls out, snapping her fingers across my watering eyes.

I quickly wipe away the tears, and Kendall asks, "Honey, where was your mind just now?"

Choosing not to recount one of my painful memories with her, I shake my head, pretending nothing is wrong, and continue to get ready for this party I do not want to go to.

My other roommate, Jordyn, should be back soon; we are heading to the party together when she returns. Kendall doesn't push further; instead, she turns back to her own preparations.

My parents adopted me when I was ten years old. They changed my life by providing me with exceptional care and unconditional love. I felt accepted for the first time, fostering a new understanding and appreciation for the wonderful and kind people in the world.

They saved me from my troubled past and gave me a second chance at happiness.

I avoid talking about my time at the orphanage like the plague, or about the demon's spawn, also known as Mrs. Jaymore, who was in charge. She was a cruel woman who made my time there a living nightmare; my existence was enough to bother her. At times, I felt singled out and treated worse than others; she seemed to have something against me without reason. She ultimately died in the fire that destroyed Jaymore's Orphanage. I'll admit, I felt more relieved than saddened; however, the stench of ashes, burnt flesh, and the screams of children trapped inside still haunt me to this day. I survived the ordeal, and was transferred to another orphanage. Children not adopted by a certain age were assumed to never be, and once they turned eighteen, they were on their own. I don't know much about my biological parents except that they were teenagers and gave me up for a chance at a better life. Instead, I spent ten years tortured and beaten. Mr. and Mrs. Williams saved me.

Imagine losing two sets of parents.

For months, I was too terrified to speak; my parents tried several therapists to get me to talk about what I had gone through. They tried everything, from spiritual awakenings to religious retreats. Nothing worked; I never wanted to talk about what I had been through, even now. When I walk around campus, students always give me weird looks, as if I'll never recover from losing not one but both of my parents. *I'm an orphan all over again.*

"Hey, hey! Are you two ready yet?" Jordyn walks into the room, swaying her hips back and forth.

"Yes, honey!" Kendall answers for both of us, clasping my hand in hers.

I smile weakly and send a quick text to my other friend Kimi, asking if she wants to join us at the party. After ten minutes of dots appearing and disappearing, Kimi finally responds with a cryptic message.

I'll take that as a no.

Unspoken issues loom over Kimi and my roommates. Whatever transpired between them—whether a screaming match or fight—was so awful that Kimi requested a solo room. Details have been lost to time, and they all instinctively avoid discussing it, making me want to know even more about what happened.

Jordyn hails a yellow cab, and without fully grasping Kimi's text, we head to Julian Cambridge's condo. I've secretly admired him for months, even though he's two years older than me. But since my parents' death, the thought of talking to him feels emotionally burdensome. When we arrive at the condo, two football players from our school greet us at the front door, acting as bouncers.

"Wassup, Kendall. When you going to let me hit that?" One of them says, smirking at her and then winking at me.

I turn up my nose in response as Jordyn smirks and Kendall giggles. Kendall is so naïve and willing; I grab her hand and briskly shove past him. That fool doesn't have an ounce of respect for women.

"Jerk," I mutter under my breath as we walk past him.

"Stuck-up bitch," he retorts.

I can't stand little boys who pretend to be men. *I knew I shouldn't have come!*

Looking around the nearly deserted square, I notice the emptiness and check my watch: it's 8:00 PM. *Maybe the rest of the guests will show up by 9 or 10.*

Jordyn hands us a cup of E&J brandy. I've never been a big drinker, but my harsh reality makes me want to forget it all, and dark liquor promises an escape. Shrugging my shoulders, I toss back the cup, grimacing at the fiery sensation of the amber liquid cascading down my throat. I know I shouldn't be drinking. I can't imagine what my parents would think, but they're not here to judge. *They're dead.*

The music blasting from the speakers drowns out my thoughts, while the dark liquid courses through my bloodstream, numbing the pain temporarily. I loosen up, closing my eyes and swaying my hips while letting the beat pulse through my veins. The room spins as strangers surround me, offering more drinks and compliments.

Feeling wobbly, I decline and push them away, looking around for Kendall and Jordyn. *Weren't they just here a minute ago?* I stumble into a nearby hallway, trying to steady myself against the wall, and I catch a glimpse of them surrounded by a group of guys. My stomach churns with panic—we were the only three girls at this party. Kendall whispers something into Keith's ear. No wait, I think that is Kevin; he nods his head and looks in my direction, ushering more and more dudes my way. *What did she say to him?* He hands her two cups of something dark and rich, licking his lips expectantly as she downs it in one gulp.

A deep, unfamiliar voice behind me asks, "Do you want to get out of here?"

Alarmed, I quickly shake my head no. I don't know this dude. Why would I want to get away with him?

I look over at my friends, who are laughing and joking with the other guys who are staring at us like we're snacks. A nauseating feeling creeps up my spine. Feeling like I'm about to vomit, I turn on my heel and try to find a bathroom. Something is off. I have been drunk before, but this feels different. My thoughts are muddled, my mouth is dry, and my heart is racing. I make my way to the bathroom and quickly lock the door, attempting to gather my bearings. Except it's not happening. I splash cold water on my face and look at my reflection in the mirror, but the dizziness only worsens. Pulling out my phone, I struggle to make out the screen through my blurred vision. Knocks at the door startle me, and my heart pounds even faster. I don't know what to do.

"Love, are you in there?" A familiar gruff voice calls to me.

Julian?

"Uh, yeah?" I reply shakily.

"Open the door, Love. I want to make sure you're okay," Julian's soothing voice seeps through the door.

Although every instinct screams for me to stay in the bathroom, I hesitantly unlock the door against my better judgment.

The door creaks open, and Julian's handsome face comes into view. He steers me out of the bathroom, but my blood runs cold at the scene unfolding in the living room. Kendall and Jordyn are making out with four of the guys while half-naked on the sofa. A sickening realization washes over me—this wasn't just a regular party; it was a setup. Julian's grip tightens on my arm, and I fumble with my phone, but Julian has already taken it from me.

"Everything will be okay," he says, his voice laced with false reassurance, and everything goes black.

End of Part I.

Please note: This is a sneak peek and will not be the final version. "Tainted Past" will be out in 2026/27. We will see. Stay tuned as the narrative continues, unveiling more secrets and surprises. Follow Love Williams and Trent Collins as they navigate their unexpected relationship and are haunted by ghostly whispers of past mistakes.

A note from the author

I'm not sure who actually reads this, but here we go!

Thank you so much for taking a chance on this book; it means the world to me. My hope for this story was to portray two people working toward different personal goals: Reign towards forgiveness and peace, and Dion towards his dream.

I was also working on similar goals of forgiveness and pursuing my dream. Still am when it comes to this writing dream, lol.

Writing is therapeutic for me, and I draw inspiration from my own experiences for most of my stories.

I did have someone call me the N-word when I was in 7th grade. That never left my memory, and I also had someone in management insult my intelligence when I was just asking for help. I've lived through things my family is unaware of, and while this story is fictional, it's rooted in the very real pain I've conquered.

I forgive those who have hurt me deeply. I forgive those who subjected me to racism and colorism, and I forgive those toxic family members who bullied me.

The betrayals from those who were supposed to protect me and the constant belittling remarks from coworkers had unknowingly internalized experiences that manifested as anger when I began writing this story.

How do I create a character who forgives those who have hurt her when I struggle to forgive those who have hurt me?

I forgive those who hurt me for my own peace and healing, not for them. However, that does not grant you access to me.

A dear friend of mine said, and I quote, "I owe you love. But I don't owe you access."

Please remember, you have the power to release anger, hurt, or toxic family members' influence over you; you are in control.

Always shine brightly; never let anyone dim your light!

And when it came to Dion following his dreams, no matter what, he kept going. Regardless of all the no's he received, his dream never faltered.

This is my dream, and no matter how much I want to give up, especially with everything that is going on in the world and life, I will continue.

It breaks my heart to say goodbye to Reign and Dion—I love them both dearly.

The two of them have taught me so much!

Farewell you two!

Please note: The history of Central Park, Juneteenth, and Segregation/Desegregation can be researched online. It was important to me, including this in my story, as Black History is actively being erased.

I would love to connect with you, let's be friends!

Please find me on any of the social media platforms below and join my newsletter.

My website: https://kcmcmillian.mailchimpsites.com/

Newsletter: https://eepurl.com/iJtSzA

Instagram: www.instagram.com/kcminspired_author

My Broadcasting Channel on Instagram:

https://ig.me/j/AbbtqGM3rQEE4wwD/

Facebook: www.facebook.com/kcmcmillianauthor

TikTok: www.tiktok.com/@kcminspired_author

GR:

www.goodreads.com/author/show/22481124.K_C_McMillian

Acknowledgments

First and foremost, I would like to thank God. Thank you for loving me unconditionally. I have survived so much through my belief in Him, and I will forever be grateful.

To my mom and aunt Lucille, who inspired auntie Mavis's and Mary's characters, I love you two. First thank you for supporting me with my books and sharing my posts on social media. Second, I love that you have shared so much of your history—our family history—with me, and I will never forget any of the stories you two have told me. I will continue to teach and spread the word—with all those who are willing to listen.

To my dad, thank you for sharing so much of your childhood growing up in Mississippi it has been eye-opening learning more about you and what you've been through.

To Troy, my husband and the father of my two boys, I thank you, babe. I love you so much! Thank you for teaching me about Seneca Village!

To Shalinie and Amy—thank you for supporting my dream. Thank you for listening to my ideas and including me in your busy schedules. I love you two.

To Alicia, thank you for your support and catching the "in" & "on" mistake, lol! Love you girl!

To my author friends, EC, Zowie, LC, Caron, Mirna, Mary, HB, and Louise your support and guidance have meant the world to me throughout this writing journey. Thank you.

To my launch team members who posted for me, I extend my gratitude for your support. Thank you for taking a chance on me!

I extend my love and respect to all who have supported me,

whether or not I have met you all in person. Please know that I adore each and every one of you.

Thank you!

Books by K.C. McMillian

Young Adult Fantasy:

- <u>Bright A Forbidden Love Story</u> (second edition), available now.
- <u>Seventeen Magic is Real Part I.</u>, available now.
- <u>Earth Magic is Real Part II.</u>, available now.
- <u>Magic is Real: Seventeen & Earth Hardcover Special Edition</u>, available now.
- Fire & Ice: The Toussaint Sisters (TBA)

Adult Romance:
Intended for readers 18+ & older.

- <u>Loving Reign: A Fake Dating Romance Story</u> (Book One) available now.
- <u>Is Love Enough? (Book Two of Love & Reign series)</u> available now.
- Tainted Past (TBA)

Adult Fantasy:
Intended for readers 18+ & older

- The Forbidden Fruit: Tales of the Remi Clan (The Nosis Series) (TBA)

About the Author

When Kiana "K.C." McMillian was a child, she would make up stories in her head and write them down. While attending high school, her favorite play was Romeo and Juliette, and she enjoyed reading it, but she sometimes fumbled over her words while reading in front of her classmates. And, of course, children can be cruel. Kiana didn't like being made fun of and lacked confidence in herself, and she felt that if she couldn't read in front of a crowd, then perhaps she wasn't good enough to write. She didn't think her stories would be well received and feared failing at something she loved. Kiana knew back then that she would one day want to share her imagination with others, but she wasn't sure about putting herself out there.

Fast forward twenty years later, after the death of her husband's grandmother on January 13th, 2022, she decided she wouldn't let the fear of failure hinder her from following her dreams. Before "Gran," as she and her husband called her, left this earth, she said, "I have lived my life, and I've done everything I wanted to do; I'm ready."

K.C. knew that if her life suddenly came to a tragic end, she wouldn't be satisfied. That statement inspired her, and she decided to follow her dream of becoming an author.